AN IN

HUNTING NIGHTMARES

LIV MACY

Also by Liv Macy

INFINITES UNIVERSE

RECOMMENDED READING ORDER

Becoming Justice

Resetting Destiny

Hunting Nightmares

Tempting Curses (2024)

CONTENT/TRIGGER WARNINGS: DEATH,
VIOLENCE, SEX, STRONG LANGUAGE,
TORTURE.

ISBN: 979-8-9872661-5-1

Printed in the United States of America

"In all my dark places there had never been light. I had thought its existence was meant for others. And I was okay with that, for without dark you can't see the light. So, I played my role and did it well. But what if the dark was hiding the light? Concealing it, protecting it? What if the dark wasn't broken, but forged? Well, that would be a different kind of hell."

Contents

Chapter One

A scream rips the colors to shreds, and they dissipate, as fleeting as my rest had been.

I jump out of bed, simultaneously grasping the twin blades by my side and thrusting them into their holsters on my back. Ten steps and I'm pulling a black leather jacket off its hook and shoving my arms in. I clear the door and yell over my shoulder.

"Lock up."

The automated series of clicks behind me turns my home into a fortress, but I'm already running down the street. The screaming sounds louder and the sick panic in it surges adrenaline through me. *Move, Arnica.* My internal GPS homes in, thrusting urgency into my legs and stretching them to their capacity. At a hard run, it takes me one minute and forty-five seconds to the house a couple blocks from my own. Dammit. I should've been faster.

I'm approaching a brick townhouse at full speed and already calculating the mathematical equation I need to gain entrance. There's no one on the streets this early on a Saturday morning, and the solid door stands like a single sentry, but I'm my own damn army.

Phantom rough textures layer themselves on my tongue. *Wood.* My eyes close milliseconds before I leap, and I pass through the door, landing silently in a crouch in the foyer on the other side, a palm on the carpet to brace myself. My internal radar, sonar-like and just as accurate, senses only one person on this level and another upstairs, verified by heat signature. The clink of glass, pots and pans being used in a back room, filters through the silent air.

But the screaming continues in my head, and I swivel—following the pull—taking a set of steps three at a time, my hands reaching for my blades.

I'm always ready for battle. I live for it.

The door's slightly ajar, and there's the barest wisp of white lace on a bassinet. The innocence and goodness pour over and out like molten gold, a beacon in the dark, for the dark.

The thing hovers over it, almost a shadow, solidifying into an inky shape, fingers stretching out and attempting to harness the light.

Not today, asshole.

Standing in the doorway, booted feet planted, arms steady and holding my blades out at my side, my black energy vibrates through the room and the pull tugs at me—like attracted to like.

The screaming of the baby's soul screeches to a halt as the Nightmare changes its focus from good to dark and the silence echoes uncomfortably in my brain.

I smirk at the smear on Earth. Its existence fucking annoys me, and it will pay for it with its life.

"Hi there."

My voice comes out rusty, but it doesn't matter. It probably can't understand a word I'm saying—only that its energy matches mine and most likely thinks it's got backup. Dumbass.

It moves fast, as all Nightmares do, coming to join forces. With arms wide open, I stand firm and take the hit. The Smudge enters my body, swirling around, searching for the dark energy. I'd like to think it's whirling around asking itself where I'm at.

It's not going to find anything. I'm empty and hungry for it.

My internal cage slams shut, separating soul from Nightmare, and it comes out of me, a ghostly shade of itself. The Smudge's soul is mine now, and I have every intention of keeping it. The moment it realizes it's no longer in possession of it, it attacks.

With a few swipes and feints, I end its tenure of preying on pure goodness. Its corpse, if they have one, disappears. It must have just been created because the new ones aren't very large, and they don't know what to do in a battle. And though desperation can never be discounted, they will never be a match against me.

The loss of a soul drives every living creature to its death. Even something so simple-minded as this thing understands the end of its existence and will fight for it. Too bad it met me tonight.

I'm the best Nightmare Killer there is.

I sheath my swords and peek at the face of the chunky cherub lying in the bassinet. The baby kicks its legs and the tight-squeezed fists flail. The tears, like crystals on their lashes, shimmer, reminding me of the rainbows I see during my rejuvenation periods.

I dare not touch it.

The innocence, that beautiful gold, pulls at the dark soul rattling in my ribcage, a natural prison. It needs to stay there.

I back away, my voice almost raw, whispering, "Go forth and do good shit, little one."

Dammit. Someone's coming up the stairs. I peer out the windows. Thank the Fates for the fire escape ladder. There's no blurring through the wall out into thin air.

Even I don't fly.

Stepping over and out, I barely shut the glass before a very human shadow reaches the doorway. I duck, scuttling over to the steps, and quickly and silently run down them.

My head aches a split second before the screaming begins again, and I'm already pivoting and searching. My body homes in and I run full out, jumping over fallen trash cans and one snarling chihuahua intent on tripping me like a damn cat. Its owner, holding the leash, yells obscenities at me.

Clearly, that's someone I won't ever need to save, and I lift a middle finger over my shoulder. The shards of the soul in me lunge in an attempt to escape. Pleading with me for release. I know better.

Every once in a while, I wonder if the screams ripping through my brain cause any damage. No one else can hear it, but it's all I can focus on, and that can't be good.

I shrug as a metallic zing slides over my tongue. This time the door is solid steel. My legs pump faster, picking up impossible speed, and I blur through it. Landing on the other side, I run down a set of stairs to yet another kid's room. The dark soul slams into me with a sick sense of joy in what it finds.

Like the earlier one, it too will be disappointed. My cage tightens.

This time, the shadow—looking like a soul-less lion—exits my body and turns to me with red-rimmed eyes, promising a much harder fight. I whip my swords out and immediately duck back, a large paw swiping at me.

Shit.

I duck and roll under a massive limb. Anger rushes

through me at the sting on my back when its nails catch my skin. I grit my teeth and catapult my body over and onto its back. With a swiping motion, both blades slide across the shadow's neck, and it disappears. Dropping to the floor, the balls of my feet easily absorb the impact, and I sheath my swords and look up.

With a halo of gold, a little boy watches me with wide, green eyes. A dimple flashes in his cheek...and then he waves.

It never ceases to amaze me how they are petrified of the thing haunting their dreams but are totally okay with waking up and seeing me fighting it. I shrug and wave back. With a finger to my lips, I back out. The coast is clear, and, like a normal human, I exit the house, softly shutting the door behind me.

The sun is higher in the sky and the streets are busy. I need a new jacket. One of the benefits of living in a city, and why I chose it, of course, is the anonymity. Most people just can't be bothered with others, and that suits me just fine. But when your clothes are shredded even they tend to side-eye you. Next time, I'm taking a car.

Chapter Two

The pump of the bass slams to a stop. My sneakers hit the treadmill and echo through the room in the gap of music. *Slap-Slap-Slap.*

Suddenly, an electric screech peals through the air, the sound more at home in a rave than in a basement, but it suits my pace. Choosing this life may have been the biggest pain-in-the-ass decision I've ever made, but I wouldn't have it any other way. I admire the woman in the mirror. The muscles in my thighs bunching with ease as each leg lifts, as the heel strikes, as my arms pump in time to the blood in my veins. Nothing weak here. Once, there were people who were stronger than me.

Now I ask for the pain. I invite it in, kick its ass, and spit it back out.

Like the legal bullshit no one ever reads in contracts, I hadn't paid attention to the words that were uttered that night. I had only grasped the ones that conveyed saving me from the crushing pain of having my soul ripped out.

I mean, fuck. Who wouldn't?

But damn if it wouldn't be nice to sleep through the night, every night, like I know damn well other people do. The machine beeps, and I sigh. I want to keep stretching my legs on the never-ending rubber.

The woman in the mirror wipes sweat off her brow, looking for all the world like an average person walking on the treadmill. The mirror doesn't show the sweat that works its way down my spine, the ends of my ponytail dipping into the rivulets. Or the smidgeon of a black soul still trapped inside my sculpted body.

Running is my guilty pleasure. But there're squats and leg curls to get in before I beat on the heavyweight bag and then food...and possibly a shower. I need calories more than I need to smell clean.

I turn the machine off and wipe it down. If there's a bit of mechanical methodology to my movements, I can't blame myself. Years of training will do that. Muscle memory in all its glory. It's not all action and sweat. I smirk at my reflection. The ropey muscles in my arms, back, and legs look good. Defined. I twist my torso back and forth. Do my abs look smaller?

Shit.

I'll have to add more core work into my routine. My life depends on my physicality. The screaming of an electric violin rips through the speakers on the wall. The frantic pace of the melody contradicts the slow, measured movements of my squats.

A lesson learned long ago—controlling the sinew and bone that wants to move in time to the beat. Mind over matter. I control my muscles.

And nobody controls me.

The euphoric burn sizzles in my glutes and quads. I've lost count of my sets, but there isn't anyone here to tell me I fucked up.

I snort. I out-learned and out-trained everyone else a long time ago with my natural inclination toward violence.

And it serves me well.

Laying on the bench, the music slows, and I straighten my legs and bend them back in a tight movement, the leg curls strengthening my hamstrings and calves. This is my least favorite of exercises. Because each one is important, I power through, count each rep, each set, intent on getting it done quickly.

I groan, then force out an extra set, the muscles quivering. There's nothing to be gained by taking shortcuts. Disgusted with myself, I swipe at the bench with the disinfectant-saturated cloth.

Have I learned nothing? Have years of pain not taught me to do what it takes?

A bin overflows with other used cleaning cloths, and I groan again.

Fucking shit.

The contents should be in the laundry room. Right. Cause I have so much free time. I yank down my boxing gloves and glare at the pile. I should just give in and get laundry service, but the thought of someone in my house destroying my peace makes...something...twist inside me.

I pivot on my heel and slam a glove-strapped fist into a heavyweight bag, swinging it wildly from the ceiling. The gulls' screeches disappear and a hot, slick beat pounds out from behind the delicate covering of the speakers.

A smile lifts my lips, and the faster the beat, the faster my fists fly. The sweat no longer drips down, but pours, soaking my tank top and capris. One tempo melts into the other, and I use the bass rumbling down the walls to move faster, harder. If I let my mind take over, I could stay here for hours.

Until I can no longer stand from sheer exhaustion and empty on calories and hydration. Like a feral animal, my body will keep going. Wearing itself out past the point of no return. But the body is nothing without the mind telling it to stop. To get a grip on reality.

The incessant beeping of the timer finally penetrates the haze of endorphins. I'm smart enough to know my limitations...and to remember to set the damn thing.

Panting, I rip the gloves off, spray them, and get an electrolyte drink. One last glance at my workout room and I smile. It's my happy place, but...food. Maybe later I'll come back down.

The lies I tell myself cause me to run up the stairs to the kitchen faster than normal. One day, maybe, it can be truth.

The yards of gleaming silver are any chef's paradise. My realtor assured me I needed it. All I know is how to fuel my machine. If it tastes good, bonus. Grabbing a pan, I slap it on the grate and turn the knob until the flame erupts on low beneath it.

While the butter melts in the pan, I snip dill and parsley from the pots on the counter. The fragrance of cut herbs simmer on the air. The entire top shelf of my subzero has dozens of eggs, each carton cut in half. Pre-portioning my food saves me time.

Because Nightmares wait for no one.

And when I can't do it myself, well, there are a *few* places where I'm nearly positive I won't get poisoned. Cracking the eggs, I drop them onto the sizzling butter, adding the herbs and cheddar. A few quick stirs and I slide them onto a plate.

I barely taste the food I'm shoving into my mouth. My body needs the fuel, even though it's seven ten in the morning and I'm ahead of schedule.

I place my plate in the dishwasher along with the others stacked in a row. I swipe a towel across the counter and nod, making sure everything is as it should be before rushing into the shower.

Standing under the needlelike spray after washing off sweat and disappointment is a luxury I don't get often. I allow myself two extra minutes because, after this morning, I fucking deserve it. And who's gonna tell me no?

I towel dry in record time, the cotton wicking away moisture still clinging to my skin, and slather myself in unscented, hypoallergenic cream. Not because I have sensitivities, but because I don't want the dark to know I'm coming. Or other people who might live in the house of the one I'm saving. People tend to wonder why a stranger is inside their home.

I slip into soft, black leggings that hug every muscle, accentuating every curve. It's not for ego. The fabric, loose enough to not tear when I'm spinning or kicking, needs to be tight and slick enough to not give my opponents the ability to grab me, should they manage to get that close. And if they do, I've got bigger problems than modesty.

Skintight black shirt, socks, and boots complete my outfit. I'm not even into black. I stare into the mirror. My dark hair makes my pale skin even paler. The dark eyebrows, slightly upturned, become angry slashes over dark eyes. I nod at the image. "But it sure as hell hides stuff. Better to get judgmental stares from people on the streets than horrified calls to the cops. It's difficult to explain away blood splatter patterns."

My voice sounds rustier than earlier, and I clear my throat as I slide a black leather holster onto my back, cinching the straps till they creak. "There's no room for comfort. You can be comfortable when you're dead."

My eyes look huge in my face. There's no one here to judge my rough voice. Why the fuck do I bother speaking out loud at all? Talking to myself is probably a sign of something.

Damn.

Maybe I should get that laundry service after all. I shudder at the thought of someone in my home and stalk to the bed where I gently lay my butterfly swords on the nightstand. The minute my head touches the pillow, I close my eyes and the rejuvenation begins.

Chapter Three

The rainbow colors behind my eyelids flit and flutter, the dragonflies of dreams. They are my salvation. The light to all the dark. Without the color sparkling around my brain, I'd be pulled in. Like a drain sucking the dirty water out of the tub, swirling into an abyss that I can never return from.

My subconscious dances in the light. It revels in the colors drifting like visible air currents full of glowing greens and bursting blues. The blushing pinks and happy oranges blend into ice cream cone twists circling one another with delight.

The purples and yellows chase one another, idyllic children playing tag. The reds and violets, the robin egg blues, the pastels of all the hues come together. They flow through and around, pulling the dark wisps that remain in me, absorbing them. The charcoals and grays disappear to who knows where. All that matters is that they are no longer within me. A smile moves the muscles of my lips as my subconscious is overjoyed, unburdened, and swathed in the colors of light, happiness, love. All the emotions that bring pleasure to the innocents, until I could burst from it.

A long, guttural scream scuttles the colors, and my swords are back in my hands before the sound ends. I check myself and alter course from the front door to the garage. Definitely the Ferrari. I need speed.

The screams begin growing fainter.

Faster. Faster.

Panic fuels my limbs. I never miss a Nightmare. I shift into drive and yell for the security system to lock up, flooring the gas pedal.

The engine whines, the speedometer ticks up. Streets flash past me as I dodge in and out of traffic. There's a final, faint scream, and I lose the sense of direction. Silence echoes painfully in my head before the sound of people around me fills up the space.

Fuck. Fuck. Fuck.

I slam my palm into the steering wheel. Too late. This is the first time in years that I haven't made it to the soul's owner.

I pull over into the nearest empty space and lean my head against the leather-wrapped wheel, inhaling the peculiar scent of sleek sophistication on wheels and listening to the normal, everyday sounds of the world.

My leg muscles quiver uselessly, my eyes fill with tears that I don't allow to spill over. My pounding heart accompanies the guilt eating me until I think I'm going to get sick. Dammit. I will not lose control. *I will not lose control.*

I know I can't save them all, no matter how much I want to. It's one of the first hard lessons I learned at the Weaponry. It doesn't change the blow of disappointment which doesn't sting—it hammers me—and my shoulders hunch in. Sadness seeps through my pores. My failure. My lack of good. If only I were better.

I slam back against the seat. This is no time for pity parties.

I just gotta study methods of travel and make sure I prepare better so I won't ever miss another one. No more mistakes.

On cue, a scream reverberates through my head, and I bare my teeth in a feral grin. I pull out into thick traffic, and the throaty growl echoes my own, the Ferrari as frustrated with slow drivers as I am. Don't they know how much is at stake? I dodge cars like mosquitoes in the summer air. Each small stretch that opens up, I rev the engine.

The stock car can go from zero to sixty in less than three seconds and to one hundred and twenty-four miles per hour in less than eight—and will buy me precious time. But mine's special, even faster, and I love her. Rounding the corner, I slam on the brakes, and the tires lock and puff smoke from the rubber grazing the asphalt.

I jump out, climbing the nearest fire escape ladder of the apartment building, hand over hand, hauling myself up faster than a human could. The screaming in my head gives me a headache. I battle with it, forcing it to the side so I can focus. The rocky aftertaste on my tongue is dry. Brick is a little harder to force myself through. I crouch and take the leap, landing on the other side.

Right into a bedroom.

The sight of the fully naked man wrapped in a sheer, golden sheet and fast asleep on a bed a mile wide intensifies the dryness of my tongue.

The shadow charges me, and I let it. My eyes continue to feast on the body sprawled in front of me in all its glory.

I can look but never casually touch.

Confusion. Panic. An internal tremble. The shadow's... feelings?...almost overwhelm me. Oops. I know better anytime I share a soul with them. *Focus*.

Inhaling, my ribs expand, the cage around my core reining it in, and the soul is trapped. Siphoned from the dark entity.

Like the others, its panic turns to all-out desperation. It slips out with fingers that solidify faster than it should, wrapping a hand around my neck and lifting me off my feet.

What the fuck?

Too late. This isn't a simple shadow, but another Nightmare creature too lazy to completely reveal itself. Fuck. A Terror. That's what I get for ogling.

Throwing my legs up, I wrap them around its arm, and the move forces the thing to loosen its grip on my neck. Prying myself out of its hold, I throw myself backward, legs still holding on, swinging downward like a child on a jungle gym. I yank the blades out and slash where the knees would be. Howling in pain, it grabs me with its other hand and rips me off with an incredible amount of force and drops me.

Instead of falling flat on my face, I land on all fours, palms and feet, much like a cat. And like any feline, I hiss at it.

Un-fucking-acceptable.

Spinning out a combination of kicks and twists, I force it back against a wall. One blade barely skims its neck when a tail manifests out of nowhere and whips the skin on my already raw back. Wrapping around my torso, the tail yanks me backward, and I crash into a bookcase.

I push the pain down until I feel nothing. Blowing air out of my lungs in gasps, my eyes widen as the shadow solidifies into a full-blown, seven-foot dragon.

Oh, fuck me.

And the man's still asleep! How is that possible?

Oof.

The dragon uses its fully formed barbed tail and smacks me to the side. Needle-like pain lances through my arm. Black fire erupts from its mouth and leaves a smoldering mass wreckage of a chair.

My eyes narrow. What are the chances of getting on its back and slashing the throat like I did the lion?

The powerful dark wings beat the air and I nix that. The way today is going, it will fucking fly me somewhere and drop me into a nest of them.

Hell no.

My eyes pinpoint the soft underbelly. Ducking and rolling, I distract it, forcing it to think I'm going for its back. I barely miss a stream of fire on my arm and then grit my teeth when heat hits my spine. A few feints to my left and I back it into a corner. I retreat quickly, causing confusion. It shakes it off and advances, black fire spewing, lumbering at me as quickly as it can in a bedroom of a penthouse apartment.

With a running start and a massive surge of energy, I throw myself onto my back and slide, biting my lip hard when grains of wood and carpet fibers shove themselves into the split skin. The momentum glides me under the dragon, and I pierce and drag my swords side-by-side down the entire underbelly, pushing the metal in as far as I can, forcing the hilt and part of my hand into its black warmth.

I yank against the paltry resistance of guts and bowels, until it disappears and all I'm left with is oozing liquid down my arms.

Gross.

I choke down the gasp that wants to erupt out of my mouth, the searing pain blazing a trail in my back now that I'm not actively fighting.

No weakness.

The black shit drips from my arms, and I swipe them futilely on my leggings and pick up my swords. My harness has long given up, and I'm left with one strap around my shoulder. I wiggle it off and take in the destruction. My jaw drops.

The man's *still* passed out and oblivious to the fight happening steps away from his gloriously golden and inert form. How the fuck is that possible?

A shadow slams into me from behind, and like any

seasoned warrior, the knowledge has already processed in my brain. Kill it quick and wake the unknown man the fuck up so the Nightmares can stop coming.

The second the shadow ghosts out, I'm ready, and I behead it faster than it can register options. It's already disappearing behind me when I stalk to the bed.

"Hey. Sleeping Beauty. Get your ass up."

He doesn't stir. He must be on something. I quickly glance around. There's got to be something I can use to wake him up. I can't afford to leave him. And I sure as shit can't touch him. Not with one black soul, let alone two in various stages of death in me.

Damn—incoming.

The next one barely inches out of me when I slice its throat. Five more take a hit on their lives before I dump a small trashcan in the adjoining bathroom and fill it with water. Each step takes an eternity. The dark grows in me. I can handle it. That's not the problem.

It's getting harder and harder to be in the same room as golden boy.

The dark always wants the light, and the pull wraps itself around me, an unseen rope tugging me to him. I slip on the overflowing water on the bathroom floor and stumble as yet another shadow slams into me.

Lobbing the bucket at the man on the bed, water pours out mostly on him and lands perfectly on his head.

I've about had enough of these fuckers today.

I spin and take the—hopefully—last shadow diving into me. It exits out the back, and with lightning speed, I pivot and slash the head right off. Panting, I grip my sword tight, blood and black liquid on the hilt dripping on the rug. Wisps of hair, escaping the tight bun low on my head, are plastered to my forehead and neck.

As the shadow disappears, I look through it straight down the barrel of a silencer. I follow the steel line up and into stormy, dark-blue eyes of the finally wide-awake, naked man.

"You've got to be fucking kidding me! Do you know how many times I've saved your ass today?"

Chapter Four

The gun never wavers. With an exasperated sigh, I throw my hands up in the universal sign of surrender.

The gravelly voice sounds disoriented. "Why shouldn't I kill you? I can sense you're dark."

"Oh, I don't know. Because I saved you? Multiple times?"

He sensed me? How? I fucking hate it when things surprise me. The amount of Nightmares should've clued me in that this wasn't going to be a normal save.

The blond brows draw together in confusion, and he blinks rapidly.

"Multiple times? How long was I out?"

"How the hell should I know? I don't come till your soul starts screaming."

He moves to stand and quickly covers his groin with one hand. The other still holds the gun. But it's wavering. He better lower the damn thing before he shoots me by accident.

I smirk. "That ship has sailed."

"Can you get me my clothes?"

"Do I look like your maid?"

His gaze bores into mine until I roll my eyes.

"Fine. Where are they?"

His gaze shoots past me and he yelps. "What the hell happened to my furniture?"

He must've spotted the chair that's been demolished by fire and smoke. Wait till he sees the rest of the room. I shrug and don't bother to answer, instead keeping my face blank.

He motions with the gun toward the bathroom. "I have a robe in there."

I step carefully on the sopping tiles. No way can I end up with my back on the floor. I'm already shaky with pain. Show no weakness, own no weakness.

I raise my eyebrows and pick up the robe hanging on the back of the door with my finger and thumb. My lip curls. There's a delicate monogram in gold thread on the lapel.

BCD.

I turn the corner, holding the white silk in my hand, my eyebrows winging up. BCD's cheeks flush pink, and I can't stop the sharp bark of laughter. He finally lowers his hand and places the gun on the bed.

"My mother gave me that robe for my birthday."

"Mm-hm."

I toss the robe and back away. The pull slowly diminishes as my body learns to handle the weight of the souls trapped in me, but I still need to be farther away. There's never a safe level of tugging. At least my eyesight's just fine.

Like a starving person, I feast my eyes on his physique. The cut abs, the lean, muscled chest, the V plunging past hips and disappearing from view behind the robe he now holds at the apex of his legs. Can't really go wrong with that can I? At the dramatic, over-enthusiastic clearing of his throat, my attention wanders back to his face and the slight pink of his cheeks. That interesting combo has my mouth drying, and I close my parted lips.

"Can you turn around?"

With a grin, I comply. "You do realize that you were on display the entire time I was here?"

And he'd been clearly dreaming some spicy dreams, the way that marvelous appendage had been standing at attention —I'd briefly wished I wasn't there to fight. There's the whisper of his hands sliding into the robe, his body getting out of bed, then nearly silent footsteps on the lush carpet, and finally the pads of his feet on the wood before the slide of hangers echoes from farther away. I continue to stare at the wall in front of me, giving him the privacy he obviously desires to get dressed.

I'm not sure what keeps me here. I don't have conversations with those whose golden innocence I save. I can't afford to build friendships with people I can't touch. It's not even a sexual thing. It's an everyday thing.

A brushing of skin, a smoothing of hair. All innocuous to most people but deadly to the goodness I can easily siphon like any of the dark things I dispatch. I refuse to be a part of that. Better to just maintain my distance where they can't touch me.

Besides, most of them are babies. Infants, toddlers, the occasional kid. Rarely do I encounter adults with so much gold. Adults with true goodness in them that the dark craves are few and far between. Not that other people can't be good. But the golden essence flowing out of them is far more than simple goodness.

It's pure. It's fix-humanity, save-the-world shit. Far beyond my scope. And damned if I'll save them just to take them.

The souls left in me strain backward toward my spine when he gets nearer, warning me, even if I couldn't hear him a mile away.

"Your back. You're going to need help with cleaning that up."

I step sideways and turn around. "Don't touch me. Stay away."

"I can help you."

"No, you can't."

There's something that might be concern in his eyes. But at least it isn't pity. I don't want either.

"The only reason I'm still here is to warn you that whatever you did last night was not smart. Whatever you drank or took knocked you out. Don't do it again. I really don't need to be back here fighting another bunch of those things."

He shakes his head, his hands hanging limply at his side. "I didn't take anything."

"Well, you had to. There's no fucking way you slept through all that without some kind of chemical assistance."

The reasoning doesn't sit right with me. People with that kind of goodness aren't predisposed to alcohol or drugs. But stranger things have happened, and I don't judge.

"No, really. The last thing I remember is having dinner."

"Maybe you were drugged." I shrug. It really isn't my problem, and my back stings fiercely. I need to get it taken care of.

"I cooked dinner and ate by myself."

Dude never fucking stops. "I don't know what to tell you. But I really need to get on the road."

I search for my other sword, picking it up and wiping the black, viscous liquid off the blade. Where the hell am I going to put them? There's no way I can just walk around with them, even in the city.

"Can I have a towel?"

"Sure."

He walks to the bathroom, and I crane my neck, admiring the muscle in his calves and hamstrings. He's got to be a runner. I lick my lips. Like any person with breath in their body, I like eye candy. Eye candy doesn't sate desire, but it sure as fuck looks yummy.

Coming back into the room, he stops short, not coming closer.

"Just toss it." I catch it and use it to toast him. "Thanks."

I leap through the wall and land on the fire escape. Wrapping the blades, I tuck them under my arm. My back truly feels as if it's on fire, and I grimace. I can't risk an infection. Running down the stairs, I get into the car and lay the back of the seat down. Damned if I'm going to have that leather touch me. I don't care how soft it is.

I head to Crofton Hospital. A few people who work there, all conveniently in different departments and on different schedules, work with me. Cash-only transactions and no records, with a little extra thrown in for their troubles. No questions allowed. If they even care. There're a ton of people in the field of caring for human beings who don't care about them at all. Maybe they did at one time, but that light puffed out long ago.

It suits my purposes.

I park the Ferrari in the underground garage and use the stairs to climb up the levels to the Neurology floor and enter the code I was given long ago. Security is so tight here that they haven't changed the digits in five years.

There's a doctor's jacket hanging on a hook in the closest office. With a small hiss as it settles across my shoulders, I stalk toward a corner office. I pull open the door and toss a bundle of hundred-dollar bills on her desk, stemming any type of protest.

"I need some first-aid care."

Dr. Alexandra Socs immediately stands up and comes around the desk. "Let me see."

I shrug out of the jacket, careful to let it slide down my arms and not my back. An inhaled breath is the only reaction, as they've all learned long ago that I will take my personal business elsewhere if they say anything at all.

Silence, and keeping any comments or small talk to themselves, is mandatory. I don't know what they think about my various injuries, and I really don't care. This is pure business.

Dr. Socs grabs an extra-large first-aid case out of the closet in her office. All the docs that work with me have one. My idea of first-aid doesn't come close to the commercial little kits most offices have, and they each stocked up after the first time they had to go and raid their pharmacies, coming up with flimsy excuses as I sat bleeding on their chairs, paranoid someone would come in and see me.

They don't need to know that I have excellent senses and that I'd be long hidden before anyone came in uninvited. Their paranoia leads to business being executed quickly and efficiently, which is just how I like it.

I hold my breath, fists clenched in my lap through the rinsing of my back, the application of ointment and bandages being taped on. I don't care what the doctors on my payroll think of my seeming disassociation with pain either. That's all I'm going to show, ever.

Once she's done, I walk to the closet and pull out a stored, locked chest. The heavy-duty lock can only be opened by my thumbprint and heat signature. And I'm rocking a cool ninety-five degrees. I pull out a spare outfit to change into, making a mental note to replace the clothing as soon as possible. I never know when I'll need it, like today. Be prepared for every contingency is me.

Removing a plastic bag, I gather all the bandages, wrappers, and blood-stained cloths and shove my clothes on top of it all, including the borrowed doctor's jacket.

Dr. Socs makes a brief sound of objection. I raise my eyebrows until she purses her lips. I close the bag, check to make sure I haven't left anything out, put my box back, and stroll through the doorway.

"Pleasure doing business with you," I toss over my shoulder.

Stalking out of the hospital and holding the bag as if it is the most natural thing in the world means I won't get asked questions. Blending in is a necessary skill learned early.

"Unlock."

A soft click lost in the sounds of a busy garage unlocks the Ferrari. Tossing my bag on the passenger seat, I head for home, hoping for a respite. And food.

After parking in my own garage, I unlace my boots and kick them into the pile starting to grow by the door. Damn piles. They never get smaller. Fuck.

The quiet of metal and contemporary lines grace my sanctuary. White-on-white walls. There's no art here. No distractions. The purpose of my home is to focus on myself. To heal the mind, to strengthen the body, to fuel my machine. To be the best that I can be.

And that's it.

I drop my bag at the door to the laundry room and continue to the kitchen. Grabbing my always-proportioned meals, I remove a container with a shredded chicken breast, ham, and several cooked eggs on top of a variety of lettuces, raw chopped vegetables, and cheese. Protein. Without it, I would not be able to function. I douse it with dressing because I need the fat, too. I don't bother to sit but simply stand in the kitchen, scarfing it down.

When I'm done, I wash out the dishes and head to my room. I don't shower, instead opting for a quick sponge wipe down to get rid of as much of the blackish fluids of Nightmares seeping into my pores as I can.

Like I need any more dark.

Back in clean clothes, I strap on another harness and gently maneuver it onto my back. A hiss escapes my lips as the leather settles in between my shoulder blades. With a weary sigh, I lay gingerly on the bed, my blades on the bedstand next to me. Always my constant.

I drop immediately, the colors swirling behind my eyelids.

My body jolts as a tan face with blue eyes wavers into my peripheral vision. I don't dream. Ever. I don't even sleep. Dammit, now I can't get any peace during my rejuvenation?

I rarely give much thought to it. It does its job. Like everything else in my life, the same, day in and day out. It's a necessary evil, mundaneness. I need to fight the Nightmares, and I need the color to balance it out, to absorb the remnants of dark, so I rest.

To save me from falling to its lure, turning me from a salvation to an instrumentation.

From saving the goodness of people for the betterment of the world to a collector of the liquid gold, stripping the good we desperately need as a humanity.

Unfortunately, golden boy's face lingers, the colors swirling around him. What the fuck does it mean? Even in the rejuvenation, my hands close into fists. Deciphering what amounts to daydreams would probably take days. Why do I feel like I don't have the time to figure it out? The thought barely crosses my consciousness when the screaming starts.

Chapter Five

I roll out of bed, wincing at the new skin stitching itself across my back, the pull and tug of it as it stretches. I heal fast, but not fast enough today.

Grabbing my butterflies, I shove them in the sheath on my back and punch the wall next to the doorframe. My GPS pings golden boy's apartment or very, very close to it.

What the fuck is with this dude?

I make a pitstop in my weapons room and strap on thigh and side holsters and belts, arming myself with a variety of ten additional knives. If earlier was any indication, I'm going to be better prepared this time around.

No more wounds.

I jump into the Ferrari, shoving a granola bar and apple into my mouth on the way. It takes me two minutes to get to his house. Grunting with each step, I run up the fire escape and rush through the brick wall with my blades drawn.

"Come on, bro."

The shadow stands there, its greedy anticipation of joining forces with me emanating like a sick version of a grin. It slips into me, and I lock down on its soul and wait for it to come out. I'm ready. The second it slides out and turns, pissed at the deception, my blades are already there, ready to slice into the insidious, wispy flesh.

Fuck!

My blade does nothing but clink on the armor it rapidly covered itself in. I throw myself to the side as it swings with a club. The skin, newly healing in my back, pulls taught, desperate to keep itself together. I roll sideways as a sword slams into the ground.

I hate when Terrors manifest as human-shaped. Most are easy to kill, but the bigger the Nightmare the more skill, and it doesn't need the advantage of opposable thumbs.

I jump up, feinting left and right, attempting to drive it back, but instead my blades crash against shadowy steel. The reverb echoes up my arm and to my shoulder. Reassessing, I kick out, catching it in the crotch. The crack and howl as it drops to the ground gives me great satisfaction. With two-handed effort, I rip one of my butterflies through its neck, severing the head.

"You want to be human, don't forget you have human weaknesses, asshole." My voice is no longer creaky and weird. I've talked more today than I have in the last six months.

I search the room for golden boy but don't see him. Nightmares manifest in front of their prey. Where the hell is he? Hiding?

I snort.

I can't believe he's made it to adulthood without losing that shimmery skin. I guess pure gold doesn't replace common sense.

The familiar feeling of dark stealthily slipping into me alerts me to this next one's ability to strategize. But it can't just fucking sneak up on me, and I separate it from its soul. It slips back out with a howl, and I'm ready for it, shoving my dagger right into its throat and giving it no chance to retaliate.

I search the room and finally find him behind the bathroom door. He was either getting ready for a shower or he has a propensity for being naked.

Another shadow slams into me. I'm getting really tired of wasting energy on one man. I always thought the golden ones were equal, but today? Not so much.

This one also comes out fighting in human shape, again. Shield and axe at the ready. As if it had communicated with the previous and knew what to expect. I know that souls call to each other, but Nightmares sure as shit don't talk. At least, not that I ever heard.

What the hell is going on?

The axe narrowly misses me, but the shield clobbers into the side of my head. I shake it, my ears ringing and my eyes watering. Dammit. I'm going to have to step up my own game.

I dodge it and, with a cold rage, furiously swing in quick succession, driving my opponent back. Satisfaction slithers through my mind. *Fuck*! The damn thing is calling the souls locked in me and planned this all along, pulling me to it like a puppet. I snarl.

It splits itself, and suddenly I'm fighting two of the damn things. The axe of the copy embeds itself in my shoulder. When it's viciously ripped out, a scream whips out of my throat. I duck, landing hard on my knees. The second incoming swing catches itself in the face of the first shadow. I jam my arms out wide and ram my swords into the sliver of belly that shows between the two pieces of armor of each shadow.

"Should've gone with a one-piece," I pant heavily, dragging air into my lungs. The two globs disappear.

I sprint into the bathroom, grabbing the replaced garbage can, and skip the water this time, spiking it right at his head. I hope it hurts long enough he doesn't think about sleeping—ever again.

Thank the Fates he comes to. I back out of the bathroom and all the way to the back wall, leaning precariously on my uninjured shoulder, careful not to touch the other one. Blood pours down my back. I may need to get some kind of bandage on it before I can get back to the hospital. A wave of lightheadedness washes over me, and I grit my teeth. There's no way I'm falling to the ground. Not here.

"Again? Ow!" Golden boy leaves the bathroom clutching his robe to his body and rubs a growing goose egg gingerly. "And can you stop throwing things at my head?"

He sounds disgruntled. Good. I latch on to the irritation floating through me, hoping it grounds me. Whatever it takes so I don't focus on the pain. That's the only way to get through without anyone knowing.

"Sure. Can you stop *fucking* falling asleep for two minutes?" I snarl, letting the anger coat my irritation. My blood flows faster and hotter through me, taking the edge off my thinning vision. Thank Karma, he's safe for the moment.

He shakes his head. "I don't know what is going on. I don't take naps. And I certainly don't pass out."

"Someone must be drugging you. Where did you go since I left you last?"

"Nowhere."

"Fine. Did someone come here?

"No." At my raised eyebrows and the disbelief that must be crossing my face, he reiterates. "No, seriously. The only person that's been here is you."

His countenance changes to suspicion.

Seriously? The bastard.

"No. I'm not setting you up just so I can beat their ass and save you. I can get my kicks elsewhere, thank you."

"I don't know." He drops to the bed with a sigh, still rubbing his forehead. "I honestly don't."

"Well, we have to figure it out."

"We?"

"Yes, I need time to heal, and it's not going to happen if you keep passing out and leaving yourself vulnerable. Obviously, you can't eat or drink anything here. Somehow, someone must have slipped something in your groceries or something. I'll go get you stuff from the store myself. But first I need to stop this bleeding."

"I can help you with that." He shoots up. The eagerness to repay his debt to me is evident in the outstretched arms, the gentleness of his eyes. All that yummy gold. I swallow hard.

"You can't touch me. Unless you don't want your golden goodness anymore?"

"I'm sorry, my what?"

"Your goodness. You know, what they are coming for you for?"

"I didn't know they were coming at all."

"How you survived this long astounds me," I mutter. He frowns and I wave him off. "Never mind. You got any bandages here?"

"No."

"Fuck. A first-aid kit?"

He shakes his head.

"Fuck. Fuck. Fuck." I huff out a breath.

His frown deepens. "You keep cursing. Is it necessary?"

My jaw drops. "Are you fucking serious?"

He nods, and I slap my hand against the wall to steady myself in the only outward show that something is wrong with me. I grip onto logic. Words. Yes, words are good. I focus on making the words come out evenly, and the concentration helps my brain pivot from the all-consuming pain.

"I'm bleeding out over your carpet after fighting Nightmare monsters that want to suck out your goodness and leave a vital piece of humanity missing, and you have a problem with me saying *fuck*? That's dumb."

He just keeps staring sternly, brows furrowed, condemnation in his eyes.

"You're really serious. Fine." I growl when he nods. "I'll attempt to curb myself. In the meantime, do you have sheets, or something clean I can use to shove into this wound of mine?"

"Thank you, and yes, I do. I can cut one up."

"Hurry, you don't want me dying on your floor or I can't help you." Or anyone else, for that matter. I almost choke on the vulnerability clawing at my throat at the words, but panic is now steamrolling through me. I fucking refuse to pass out and let out all the dark within me.

"My name's Blaze."

I snort. *Figures.*

"Arnica. And I'll need some peroxide and a needle. And the sheets should be one hundred percent cotton." *And can we now fucking skip the pleasantries?*

I nearly curse again at his muffled response.

"Did you just tell me the only thing you have that's cotton is your underwear? There's no way I'm shoving pieces of your ball holders in my skin."

He walks back into the room. "They aren't ball holders. I don't wear tighty-whiteys. I wear boxers. And it's the only thing I know for sure is a hundred percent cotton without searching through labels."

I raise an eyebrow.

"I break out if I don't wear cotton on my bum."

"Bum? Did you just call your ass a bum? What are you, four?"

I chuckle and suddenly can't stop. It's the funniest thing I've heard in a long damn time. Maybe I've already lost too much blood. Tears leak slowly out the corner of my eyes, and for a moment, I don't feel the pain. Blaze stares at me as if I've hit my head a bit too hard. It's probably not that funny. My existence is by its very necessity lonesome. The laughter dies off and agony replaces it. Damn endorphins didn't last long.

He shakes his head at my lunacy and walks to his closet, opening the door. How many clothes does one man need? He grabs a shirt and reads the tag. He hangs it back up again. He grabs another and repeats the sequence. He hangs it up as well. How hard is it to own cotton clothes? What the fuck are they made of?

I growl low in my throat. At this rate, I'm going to bleed to death. The wound throbs with a vengeance.

"Just give me your damn underwear."

"What was that?" He pops his head around the door.

"Give me your fucking underwear," I grind through clenched teeth.

"I thought you said you wouldn't want to use them."

A deeper growl is my only response. Sweat beads on my lip. He must notice it or the grimace scrawled across my face because he hastens with it much faster than I anticipate. The pull toward him is strong enough that combined with the pain, I almost vomit on his floor. I back away hastily, running my back into the wall behind me. Pain rolls through my body and my vision darkens quickly before clearing up.

I clench my fists hard and breathe through the jolts lancing through my shoulders and back. At least it cured me of getting sick all over the place.

"Can you just cut up a piece? I need to soak it in the

peroxide." I carefully make the words come out, slow and steady.

Never show your pain. Never let anyone see how they can force you to do their bidding. Never expose yourself.

"Yeah. I'm lucky I have some. My friend brought it to me. She, ah, wanted to make sure I had some here in case she hurt herself and needed saving." He waves his hands vaguely. "It's a long story."

I really don't give a fuck how they're there. But his soothing voice makes it easy to focus on it instead of the slight shaking of my hands. He heads to the bathroom, and the sound of drawers opening and closing breaks through the silence. I wince now that he can't see me and consciously count in between each word to sound nonchalant.

"Just cut it up and leave it on the remaining underwear. I can't have it contaminated."

Blaze doesn't say anything. Maybe that was too slow and he knows. But he does as I ask, and I focus on what methods I can use to get it on my body. I'm not sure there's a way.

Once he backs out of the bathroom, the wince drops from my face and I walk over, making sure my pace is normal. The room spins slightly around me, and I narrow my eyes, focusing on the door. I can't pass out. I grit my teeth, and when that's not enough, I bite the side of my tongue hard enough that a metallic flavor fills my mouth. If I fall out, the souls in me will escape, either consuming me or finding another source like him.

Neither option is acceptable.

I prep the stuff I need, dousing pieces in peroxide and cutting more pieces into smaller squares so that I have several layers. The air has a molasses feel to it that I know is slowing me down. I have to move faster, and the world fucking needs me to get out of here.

"Tell me you have cling wrap."

"I might have some, but I'm not really sure."

How the hell can he not know what he has in his own home? Fuck.

"I need it, so I hope to hell you have it. But hurry."

I could use some sugar or something with a quick hit, but I won't risk eating or drinking anything in this house.

I'm almost done prepping when the shadow slams into me.

Chapter Six

I 'm rarely thrown off-kilter, but I'm not expecting this to happen.

Fucking get your fucking lazy ass in gear. Don't sit there and let them walk over you. Do you have what it takes? Or are you a drain on this institution? Move, if you want to survive.

The words are a sick mixture of my own conscience and the Mother's, and I latch onto the soul at the last second before it can escape with the others, causing a much bigger problem. I bend over double, my fists on my thighs. I breathe deeply, concentrating through the agony ripping through me, over my back and down my arms. I harness the pain and use it to win the attack. There is no other choice. I fucking refuse to lay down and die. I refuse to let the souls go.

My swords were on the bed when I slipped the harness off and dropped it on my way to the bathroom. The daggers sheathed into the belt are on the floor where they dropped after the last monster disappeared. The little daggers I've got strapped to my thighs are going to have to do.

Whipping them out, I face the monster forming in front

of me. As it grows into something bigger, rage pushes aside the pain.

Fuck. This. Shit.

Ignoring the stinging sensations ramming into my shoulder, I give a feral yell and leap up, stabbing the thing in both eyes and burying the daggers all the way into the end of the hilt.

It drops and vanishes before I've even jumped off. I land hard on my ass, but I know I don't have time. I can't take too much more damage. I shove my conscious thoughts away—I'm done trying to compartmentalize—and I force myself to ignore everything. *I have no feelings. I have no pain.* I roll mechanically, standing up and running to the bed. I'm leaping over it and reaching for my blades, my hands grasping the handles before I even clear it.

Screams rip through my head, and I almost miss it. When I round the corner, the Nightmare hits me like a brick. Fuck me, but this one will be even fucking bigger. How is this possible? In milliseconds, I assess the kitchen while waiting for it to come out.

Grabbing for it before it solidifies is pointless. I'd be trying to catch air. I do so anyway. It grins at me as if I've made an amateur mistake, and I smirk, pulling my hand back out, holding a knife from the knife block on the monster's other side—right there on the counter. Just as my hand clears its shape, it forms. With a nearly confused look, it glances down at the handle in my hand, the blade obviously in its very solid mass. It pixelates and disappears.

Turning the spicket on, I yank the sink hose out as far as it goes and douse the eternally sleepy one. He comes to, sputtering, and I pointedly keep spraying him. Once I think he's sufficiently gotten it through his head that I'm pissed, I let go and lean weakly against the counter.

"I swear to anyone listening, if you eat or drink something

else before I'm healed, I will let them suck the gold out of you like they were slurping up the bottom of the best milkshake they've ever consumed. Do you hear me?"

I don't bother to raise my voice. If he can't tell my threat is serious, he doesn't deserve my assistance. I'm about fucking done.

"I drank a bottle of water. It was sealed. I didn't think." Blaze sits up and drags the robe around him while droplets of water cling to his hair and eyebrows.

"Exactly. You didn't think. How the fuck you have survived this long is beyond me. Now come help me before I pass out and you have bigger problems. And bring the damn cling wrap and a pair of tongs."

He doesn't understand what will happen to him if these souls get out and there's no time to fill him in. I limp to the bathroom without looking to see if he is following. Once there, I cut another strip of his underwear and resoak it. The only thing I can't do is stuff the peroxide-soaked cotton into my skin. I just can't physically reach it or rig anything. Stupid incompetency that I'm going to research the shit out of and remedy. Damned if I will find myself in this situation again.

"I need you to use the tongs to shove this into the open-ing. Whatever you do, don't touch me, unless you are craving death."

"I thought you didn't want me near you."

"Just do it. If I growl at you, run. Wait for my mark."

"Uh. Sure. I can do this."

I straddle the toilet, hugging the porcelain. I grip as hard as I can and set my teeth.

Not one sound, Arnica. You can do this.

You will not let the souls consume you. You will hold them. You will not break.

You will not turn into a mindless monster consuming the good in this universe. You will not do it.

41

You will complete your mission.

I channel the words of my teacher. She rode us like a bitch riding a monster, bringing it to heel. We hurt, many times did we hurt. But we won. Always. The outcome was worth the lesson. Otherwise, I was dead. I knew it, but I still hated it.

"Go!"

I clench my stomach muscles as hard as I clench the internal cage in my body. The souls inside rattle, sensing the gold. But I rattle the cage back harder.

Fuck you.

My arms wrap around the toilet as if my life depends on it. And it does. I refuse to give in.

He slowly picks up the soaked cloth. By the Fates, if he doesn't fucking move faster I'm not going to be able to help him. Or anyone.

I grit my teeth harder, hoping I don't break one.

Doing so keeps the scream in my throat. The pain burns through me as Blaze gingerly inserts the cloth. My back muscles clench and ripple with tension. Blood oozes down my skin.

"I'm so sorry."

I don't answer him. Sweat beads on my forehead and drips into my eyes. I scrunch them tight and ignore the burn of salt. I can't answer. The litany in my head can't break.

I will not move, I will not move.

I will not consume his gold.

I will not move.

He finally finishes pushing it in, and I sense him backing away more than I can hear him through the buzzing in my head. The pain slips from the realm of burning to a constant throbbing. It becomes so continuous, I can almost ignore it easier now. Like the quick loop of insert, extract of a tattoo gun.

I slowly let go and reach for the folded cloths I've prepared by tying them onto the cling wrap. I'm going to use it like a long and thin, albeit plastic-y towel. Taking one end in each hand, I pull it across my back as if I am drying myself until I get it situated. Toga style, I finish wrapping it around my body, as tight as I can make it. For a moment, my vision darkens until it matches my clothes, but then lightens. Safe. He's safe from me.

I crack my neck and roll my shoulders. I pull my shirt on, careful of the wrap, and push the renewed throbbing to the back of my head. I can't focus on it. I won't focus on it. I turn to Blaze who watches me with those blue eyes, his arms crossed at the chest.

"Get properly dressed. We're leaving."

His hands drop quickly and he steps forward. "Where are we going?"

I step back as I quickly reprioritize.

"To get something to eat. Then to the hospital. I need someone to look at this and clean it out for me."

"I could have done it for you."

I clench my jaw and then release it. "Get dressed or I'm leaving, and I won't be back," I repeat my earlier threat, hoping he doesn't decide to say no. In my current condition, there's no way I can survive another Nightmare.

His eyes travel up and down my body, but he finally obliges. I hiss quietly. He's going to piss me off more, I know it.

I collect my various weapons. Much as I don't want anything on my back, I need my swords more. Just in case Blaze continues his habit of passing out. Just in case I am wrong and there's nothing here causing his sleepiness. My head swims from a lack of calories. We need to move. Desperation makes my movements choppy.

"I'm leaving in two minutes, with or without you," I yell at his closed closet door.

He opens it and my jaw slightly drops. Thoughts of food

evaporate and the thought of sex slithers through my mind. The dopamine hit pushes my pain and my lightheadedness away.

I've never been a fan of tight jeans and tight shirts on a man, but hot damn. He had looked good naked. A buffet of rippling abs and lean, corded muscles for my hungry eyes. He had looked ridiculous in the Hugh Heffner, monogrammed, silky robe he insisted was a present, and it had been easy to overlook his pretty face as just another one. But dressed in slick, rich-boy clothes, he made my mouth water. Soft material and smoky colors...eye candy be damned. This is like staring at a fucking glass case of delectable pastries. I already know what's under the pretty topping.

And as usual, I can't touch. I turn away and force myself to think of a pizza pie dripping with melted cheese and hot sauce. My hunger returns with a vengeance, my stomach gurgles in sympathy, and the burn of my cuts screech back into my consciousness.

"Let's go."

Moving at a slower pace than I'd like, we walk through the apartment. This building houses four spacious apartments on each floor. He has a whole damn floor as a penthouse apartment. In the city. He must be someone important.

My eyes narrow as I take a better look at the furnishings. He *does* look like old money instead of new. The furniture is tasteful, classic. New money likes flaunting their newfound wealth. This is subtlety, a normal so normal that it isn't even second nature, it's ingrained.

I have no problem with money, I have plenty of it myself due to calculating the odds of all sorts of bets before I turned to stocks that had equally been more than profitable. But even my money looks like it might be a drop in the bucket compared to his. Hopefully, he doesn't have an ego to match. His carelessness with his life is already a hindrance; having an ego is a complication I don't need. I don't have time for that kind of bullshit.

At his whistle, I forgive him for his sleeping habits. I like anyone who likes cars. Especially my cars. Cause I'm picky.

We slide onto the buttery seats, me once again being careful not to lean my back against it. Pulling my seatbelt on, I stare at him until he squirms a bit.

"What?"

By the Dreamers. He really doesn't value his life.

"Put your seatbelt on, dude. Damn."

"Oh, yes. I forgot."

I shake my head. Who forgets to put on their seatbelt? Pressing my foot to the pedal, we peal out of the side street.

I head toward a hole-in-the-wall joint that I know serves fresh, hot food, fast.

As we pull up, Blaze looks around in wonder. "This looks like a crappy place. I love it."

I snort. "Yeah, you should. It will have the benefit of having untainted food."

We walk out and up to the counter. I swallow the grimace that wants to twist my face. *No weakness, no vulnerabilities. Show nothing.*

"Hey."

I nod to the bulky man who jerks his head back at me. We have a standing love-hate relationship. I love him and he hates me. But only because he's a sore loser. I can't count the number of times he's lost the bet that I can't eat everything I've ordered. Sometimes, I even come here hungry just so his eyes can bug out of his head.

"I'll take three Greek gyros, one with beef, one with chicken, and one all veggie, a side salad with beef tips, and the Greek tzatziki sauce, a burrito bowl with spicy chorizo, a large order of fruit kebabs, and two bottles of water, please."

He furiously writes everything down and then looks at Blaze expectantly. Blaze turns his head.

"Oh, that was all for you?" At my nod, he glances at the board. "I'll have the same, please."

Jeff and I glance at each other. I roll my eyes, and he laughs. "Okay, give me five minutes."

Standing at the counter, I let my eyes wander down Blaze's lean build. "You think you'll be able to eat all that?"

"No. Isn't the point so that I can take some home with me?" His nose crinkles.

Jeff comes back out, eyes wide, at my bark of laughter. He's never heard me laugh. I have now done so several times in Blaze's company. Even though it's *at* him, I'm still laughing. My heart flutters in my chest, and I frown. I just enjoy the high of laughter hitting my system helping me forget the pain. That's all.

"Yeah, no. I need to wolf all that down. I'm lightheaded from lack of food." At his glance down my own body, my temper notches up.

"What? Male bodybuilders can eat massive amounts of food and it's okay, but because I'm not bulky like a Hulk, I'm not allowed to?"

"Woah. That's not what I said. I'm completely an equal opportunity guy. I just don't know where you actually put it."

"I eat it. It goes in my stomach."

I shake my head. He's beyond oblivious. Or maybe I've forgotten what normal people are like. Maybe his money meant never having proper schooling. Even battling dizziness, my brain can still function right.

At his continued stare, I glare back. "What the fuck now?"

He frowns. "Nothing. I was asking figuratively not literally."

Huh? I don't say anything. I'm not convinced he's not stupid. Jeff comes up to the counter with a large bag of food.

Blaze and I move at the same time—me to pay out of habit, and he as well, I guess.

The souls straining against my ribs send a stabbing pain through my chest and I gasp. It's a last-moment saving mechanism. The knife is out of its holster and at his neck before he can take another step forward.

"I told you. Don't touch me."

Chapter Seven

J eff wisely says nothing. This isn't his first go 'round seeing me. We live in a world that some men still see a pretty face and nothing else. I don't know what it is about my dark hair and pale skin that calls to them. The emo look I channel with my dark clothing clearly doesn't help.

They see an emphatic woman whom they think they can catcall, and I'll jump at the opportunity, as if my clothing and my single aura screams a need for their attention. Whistles are answered with my usual flick of the middle finger. I don't bother turning around to see how they take it. Most will back off. Apparently, those men like the meek and obedient. I have a mouth loud as the day is long and the words waiting to cut like barbs.

Those who think my middle finger up in the air is an actual invitation to join me in bed take some misconstrued challenge and attempt to strongarm me. If the muscle under their hand doesn't give them a way to see reason, a blade at their neck does. I don't exert myself.

Blaze's eyes widen in shock, and he pales. This is why I

can't have a relationship. People crave touch. I crave their soul. It's not an even exchange.

I don't remove the blade, and he has no choice but to back away. I put the sword back in its sheath and pull money out of my pocket. Laying the cash on the counter, I pay Jeff. Always extra. Not because I bribe him or because he's not good, but precisely because he is. Great service and great conversation should be rewarded. This is the only way I can reward it. He lost the argument a long time ago.

I pick up the bag and turn on my heel, crossing the sidewalk and getting in the car. I wait thirty seconds. Blaze doesn't move from where he is standing. I let the window slide down.

"You can get in or you can live on your own luck."

He stares for another beat, and sighing, walks around to the side of the car and gets in. He remembers his seat belt this time.

The smell of the food makes my mouth water, but I won't dirty my baby. We sit in the car in silence, listening to the purr of the engine as I drive to the parking garage of the hospital. I pull in in the back and taking the bag out of the car, grab a blanket, and lay it on the trunk. I pull food cartons out and set them on the lip. The pain, excruciating though it may be, I can live through—passing out from lack of food, and setting souls loose, I can't.

Opening one of the gyros and pulling the silver wrapper down, I shove as much as I can into my mouth and take a big bite, barely chewing before I swallow. I take another bite and another. I throw the last bit into my mouth and ball up the wrapper.

I open a bottle of water and guzzle half of it. Reaching in for the next gyro, I glance up at Blaze. He's staring at me, his gyro open, not a single bite taken out.

"Hello? Earth to Blaze? You going to eat?"

Why isn't he eating? The calories I've already consumed

take away the spinning sensation. The pain has become constant enough that I easily ignore it. Practice has always made perfect.

"I am, yes... I just have never seen anyone eat so fast, nor put that much food in their mouth."

"So?"

"So...nothing, I..." He takes a bite, and a moan rips out of his mouth. At the sound, my own wants to come out. Shit. Butterflies flit in my belly. Who knew a moan could sound so good?

"This is wonderful. I've never tasted a gyro this flavorful. The spices are perfect, the temperature is perfect." He peers into the gyro. "It's simply amazing."

He takes another bite, moaning again. My stomach clenches. He keeps this up and I won't be able to rest next time I lay down. What is it about someone moaning that takes you right back into the memory of a sexual encounter?

"Can you eat? This isn't a make-out session, it's lunch. And I need to get my back looked at."

"This is just so good. I can't get over it."

"Well, get over it. I'm on a schedule."

He nods, and though he still slips out a moan or two, I focus on shoving food into my mouth as quickly as possible. If I let myself, I would concur. The food does taste amazing. It's one of the reasons I go to Jeff's.

His food is far superior to my lack of cooking skills. I don't have to moan and enjoy my food though. I need to eat and get my aching back fixed up. I desperately need a lie down, but I'm afraid it's not going to happen anytime soon.

Fucking golden boy is going to want to sleep and spend eight hours in luxurious bliss while I have to stay up and watch over him. Damn. Why are they coming after him so hardcore?

Most of the Nightmares I've encountered aren't real bright. Like a raccoon, they see something shiny and go for it.

Rarely do they hunt with such focus. But for Blaze, I never come back to the same person.

What was so special about him? Except for his goodness, which I have yet to witness. And his exquisite body with sprinkles of golden curling chest hair, which Nightmares don't care about.

This obsession of mine with his body irritates the shit out of me. I don't have time for this. I shove the last of the salad into my mouth.

"I hope you're done. We've gotta go."

I pluck the second gyro out of his hand, rewrapping it and shoving it into the bag.

"Hey, I wasn't finished."

"You are now. I need my back looked at, and you're coming with me."

"You know I'm an adult and don't have to listen to you, right?"

"Oh, sure. You want to go round with those things? Suit yourself. I'm going up." I put the food into the trunk and grab my bag, walking away.

"Lock."

I throw the word over my shoulder, grinning at the look of amazement on his face when the doors click on their own.

Striding toward the stairs, I wonder what I'm going to do if he doesn't actually follow me. I don't know, maybe force him at blade point. My priority must be my back. I swipe the badge at the door to gain entrance, and just as it's about to close, Blaze's hand shoots in and pulls it open wider.

I don't bother acknowledging him. I figure self-preservation won out in the end and I don't feel the need to rub it in.

"Where did you get that badge?"

"None of your business."

I climb the stairs two at a time. My back is screaming, and the cloth is starting to seep through. And now I'm seeing stars from the pain. I thought my dizziness was from lack of food, but it might be lack of blood. I need to move faster.

Blaze's footsteps run right behind me. Good to know he can keep up. Not a complete pampered ass then.

Punching in a code, I stalk into the Neurology hallway. I no longer try to stay incongruous. I hasten my steps toward Dr. Socs' office. When I round the corner, panic flares briefly, my heart pounding. Her office is dark. Damn.

I double back and hit the stairwell again. I cross the hospital to another department, a rush of relief flooding through me at the lights in the office.

"Fuck!" The room is empty. Where the hell is Dr. Rollins? I pick up the phone and dial another number.

"Dr. Fika, how can I help you?"

I get straight to the point. "It's Arnica." At the soft gasp, I continue, "Don't leave your office. I'm on my way and I have some severe cuts on my back."

I've never called ahead, but the situation's dire, and I hang up without waiting for confirmation. It's what I pay her for.

Leaving the office, I spot a drop of blood on the floor. It's got to be mine. I lower myself carefully and use my sleeve to wipe at it. With my other arm, I reach back and press my forearm to the edge of my shirt to contain the blood. Can't be leaving DNA all over the place. Ghosts don't have bodies. And I should've been dead long ago.

The throbbing in my back increases, splitting my focus. More attention than I usually need to keep the souls in me in check. My head's pounding, causing my vision to dim.

"Where are we going now?"

Blaze's voice sounds far away. I grit my teeth. The souls are rattling their cage harder, sensing a weakness.

Fuck.

I jog to an elevator. I don't care who notices me now. Shit is about to get real.

We get in and I punch the buttons for the Dementia floor. I grip the handrail. It doesn't help, and I drop to my knees.

"Hey! Are you okay?"

"Grab Doctor Elaine Fika. Tell her I'm here. Whatever you do, don't touch me. Don't. Touch me."

I slump against the wall. I can't lose consciousness. I can't. The souls will escape without my inner guard keeping watch. I set my jaw, remove the knife from my boot, and swiftly stab myself in the thigh.

Pain explodes in my leg. I'm careful not to hit anything vital, but it still hurts like a bitch. Just enough to bring my consciousness back into focus.

"What are you doing?"

I don't answer but then vaguely realize he's on the phone. Can't he follow directions? Spoiled brat. I don't care how *good* he is.

"Dr Fika, this is Blaze Davidson. I'm in the C elevator. Our mutual acquaintance is on the verge of losing consciousness. Bring help."

What did he say? "No," I whisper through the pain. "Only she can touch me. No one else or I swear, I'll stab you, too."

"Never mind that," he continues into the cell, his blue eyes like storm clouds again. "Just meet us, STAT."

I breathe a sigh of relief. The door pings open and closes several times until Dr. Fika rushes in. She looks at Blaze.

"Sir, I—"

He shakes his head. "Not now, Elaine. Help her up."

He watches the doc and I struggle but doesn't attempt to help. I force myself to stand. Every step I take sears pain through my leg, and it's just enough to get me into her office.

"I'll be right back."

Blaze heads for the door.

"Don't go far." My voice comes out in a whisper, and I

hate it. But he needs to stay close. "I won't be able to help you if you're too far away."

His eyes swim with emotion, which dammit, looks like pity. But he nods and walks out.

"Patch me up quick."

Her face tightens and her lips purse, wrinkles forming over her upper lip.

"I know it won't be good. Just do it enough so I can get going again."

"This is more than a scratch. These things take time."

She rushes around the office, making room for me and my bloody body. She's already prepared the suitcase with the necessities, but even I know she'll need more than what she has in there.

I gasp several times.

Stop it, Arnica. Stop making sounds like you're a pathetic, sniveling human.

My back spirals out electric spasms, and the itch of infection crawls along my skin. My vision dims again. Where the fuck is Blaze?

If he passes out again, I need him close by. I won't be able to help him if he's too far away. There's no way I'll make it in this condition. The room darkens, and I don't understand what the doctor's saying.

I jam my knife into my leg again. Hello, vision. I grit my teeth hard to prevent a whimper escaping.

"What are you doing?" the doc screeches, her arm reaching for my knife.

I snarl, my hand fisted tightly around the handle of my dagger. "I may look weak, but I promise you, you will regret it if you take this from my hand. Get to work."

"I need to go get more supplies. I don't have enough here."

"Just patch it up."

My leg burns in sympathetic agony.

"No. You need to wait..."

I wave the knife in her general direction. "Make it work. That's what I pay you for."

"I can't work under these conditions."

She shakes her head, wringing her hands.

"The fuck you can't. I'll double the money."

Her eyes widen, and my shoulders curl inward while I struggle to stay sitting up. This will be the last time she's on my payroll.

Blaze chooses that moment to bring in a cart full of supplies. How the hell does he know what to get?

Suddenly, I remember the name he spoke in the elevator, and my split-focused brain makes the connection. BCD. Dr. Fika's deferential 'Sir.' Crofton Hospital.

Blaze Crofton Davidson—CEO of Crofton Hospital. Board Member.

Fuck. Me.

Chapter Eight

"Just do the best that you can, Elaine."

Blaze brings the cart closer to her, his body angling weirdly to keep away from me.

"I'm sorry, sir."

She preps the bandages and opens a bottle of sterile water. The awkwardness in the room is palpable, but Blaze doesn't say anything to change it, just stands there with his arms crossed over his chest.

Weren't we all just fish out of water. I straddle the chair. My eyes droop, so I jab myself in the thigh again, gasping with the pain of it.

"Will you stop doing that?"

I never realized her voice was so high-pitched. It's irritating.

My own voice sounds weak, which pisses me off even more. "I need to stay functional." I don't tell her it's so that Nightmare souls won't be released from inside me like fucking bats from a cave. I doubt she would stay calm.

Dr. Fika nearly drops the cloth in her hand. "You can't— you can't just—"

"Just focus on her back."

Blaze's soft words pierce through her shrillness. His arm stretches out and he hands me a towel. I use it to cover my breasts, just as scissors snip the last of my shirt away.

His poise screams quiet authority. Why did I not notice that before? I whimper at the stinging in my back, but then bite down hard on my lip, cutting it off. The souls rattle in my cage a bit lighter. They're dying off slowly but surely. Thank the Dreamers. My strength's scraping the bottom of the barrel.

A scream echoes in my head, and I reflexively move. "Shit. This has to wait." I stand up. Too fast. The room spins, but I reach for my jacket anyway, one hand still on the towel.

"Where are my butterflies?"

I swivel my head, my eyes searching the surface of the desk next to me, but they aren't there. Where did I leave them? I shake my head, begging my eyeballs to work right.

The doctor tilts her head. "There aren't butterflies here. I think you're hallucinating."

"What's wrong?" Blaze steps forward, arms outstretched again. The souls slam around inside me as if they're trying to break free at his nearness. I tighten the cage, mentally and physically, focusing on each internal muscle.

"What part of *you can't fucking touch me* don't you understand!" I snarl, stepping back quickly. My knee-jerk reaction causes my foot to slide on the bag collecting my blood on the floor, and for a moment, I flail. The last time I wasn't sure-footed I was a wet-behind-the-ears thirteen-year-old.

He fists his hands but keeps them at his side. Dr. Fika reaches out and steadies me.

"You're in no shape to be going anywhere. And I'm not done." Her voice is uncharacteristically stern. She's trying to be assertive. A doctor. Well, she can take that attitude and shove it.

"I have to go. I have a job to do."

I glower at Blaze. He of all people knows exactly what my job entails.

"I don't think you're in any shape to go." He shakes his head. "I'm sorry, I must insist you stay."

He plants himself in the doorway, wide-legged, hands on his hips, elbows jutting out, knowing there's not enough room to get past him without touching.

Bastard. And would he have wanted someone to stop me from coming to his aid? He damn well wouldn't have.

I grip my head with one hand, the other fisted into the towel. I want to hit him. The cries are hysterical, reaching a fever pitch. Hope for help fading. Tears prick my eyes at the despair in the sound. My chest aches.

When fear mingles with terror, it snuffs out everything else and creates a scream that's indescribable. It's ripped from the throat in a last, desperate bid for salvation.

Silence. The sound dies off, strangled like everything else. Goodness stolen by evil, leaving a dark hole that will scab over and heal. And humanity loses more purity that could've saved it.

I straddle the chair again, slumping over the back. This is the second time I've failed today. Guilt wraps its steely hands around my chest and squeezes. It hurts to breathe, and I struggle to draw air in.

"You have no idea about shit, apparently."

"Please finish cleaning up her back, Elaine," Blaze's voice rings with conviction.

I close my eyes. Another failure due to my body's vulnerability. If I could replace my entire body with titanium or some stronger metal, I would. But for now, only Wolverine has those small advantages, and I'm not part of that comic club.

Dr. Fika stands frozen for a moment, and pressure on my

back is the only warning I have before the sting starts again. I clench my fists and bite down hard on my lip.

Ten minutes later, I'm sure she's taking her good old time. There's no way it should take this long.

"Okay, doc. I've had enough fun. Wrap it up."

"There's still some more cleaning up to be done."

Her voice sounds tight, probably with disapproval. Who is she to judge me?

"No. I'm done. The rest will have to wait. And shoot me up with something to numb it for a bit."

I don't hear any movement, so I look up to see Blaze, his eyes roaming over my face. She's fucking waiting for him! This is unacceptable. I'm the paying customer here. After a few seconds, he nods, and there's a small humph from Dr. Fika.

But she steps back, and I peel my body off the chair, my bones protesting as if they're ancient. Before the doctor has a chance to say anything, I snatch up a gauze pad and roll and expertly wrap my thigh, one-handed.

It's stopped bleeding, the blood congealing around the slits in my pants, but I don't want questions on how that's even possible. I don't want to talk, period. Still holding a towel to my bare breasts, I gather up the bloody bits of cloth and the cut shirt pieces and open wrappers from the bandages.

"Leave it. I can have someone dispose of it."

Blaze steps forward as if his authority binds me as well. But I'm not a damn lackey at his beck and call.

"The hell I will. I clean up my own messes and I leave nothing behind."

I jerk my head in the direction of the doc, who stands well away from me, peeling her gloves off her hands. She tosses them into the growing pile in a plastic bag. Her face pales as she notices Blaze's tight lips.

There'll be repercussions here, I suppose. Not my problem. She's paid well for her work—and was given the option to turn my offer down. She knew the risks of accepting my business.

But I'll have to get new business contacts in another hospital. It's a shame as this one is closest to the city center and their cafeteria is open twenty-four hours a day. The food is palatable if not hot. There are other hospitals as well as walk-in clinics I can tap, even if they aren't convenient. It won't hurt me to help her. I shrug.

"I won't be bringing my business here anymore. You don't have to worry about it."

The lines in between Dr. Fika's eyebrows smooth out, until Blaze speaks.

"On the contrary, you're welcome to the hospital and any of the staff if you require their assistance. Please, anytime. Free of charge. Consider it repayment of my debt to you."

Dr. Fika lets out a gasp and her cheeks redden. It doesn't take much of a leap to know what she thinks I did for the CEO. I growl low. I don't trade in skin.

"No. I'd rather keep that debt handy."

I stalk to the doc's closet and pull out the familiar box. I slam the lock with my fist, breaking it, not caring she'll see a bit of strength that's not normal. Petty, but satisfying to hear the hiss of inhalation from the judgey doctor. There's a reason I pick those who can be bought. But the sting of never being good enough for people never really goes away.

I pull out a black T-shirt and drop the towel. Another inhalation. This time from Blaze. I glance over my shoulder and am unprepared for the look of admiration written so plainly on his face, he might as well purse his lips and whistle. The jolt of need rushes through me and temporarily stops the throb of pain in my back. Instead, it takes up residence elsewhere. I deliberately look away.

What is wrong with me? The image of his naked body, muscles corded tight even in sleep, dances in my head. It's like a carrot on a fucking stick. Like I can even think of having sex with him. Sure. If I want to take that gold that floats out of him like pixie dust.

I close my eyes and, taking a deep breath, dive headfirst into the shirt, biting hard on my lip to silence anything that might come out of my mouth. The instant pain of the soft cloth on my open back removes any hints of a throb. The fire is no longer between my legs but consuming my skin from the spine out.

I shudder and turn around, pinning Dr. Fika's glare down with my own. "I'll have something for the pain now, too."

She hands me an unopened bottle of a generic painkiller. I'd made sure years ago my contacts in the hospital knew better than to give me open bottles or cups full of pills that could be literally anything. I make sure what I take is cleared only by me. Though they could still perform some sort of trickery, I'd made it clear they would regret it.

It hadn't taken much. Loss of their jobs was usually enough of a threat. No hospital liked doctors taking cash on the side. How would the hospital make any money if they couldn't take a cut and overcharge for a room and some bandages?

I pull out a thick roll of hundred-dollar bills and toss them at her. She deftly catches it and puts it into the pocket of her doctor's coat. Blaze clears his throat, and her cheeks redden once again.

I point my finger toward him, wagging in admonition without even looking in his direction. "Don't make her give it up. I'll only find a way to give her what she's due. We had a deal, and I don't break my word."

I don't catch whatever facial expression he makes because I

don't care if he likes it. I pack up the rest of my things and wipe down the chair.

"Are you...cleaning the furniture?"

Shock colors the tone of his voice.

"I don't leave anything of me behind."

I haul up the waste bag and gesture with my box toward the door. "Let's go, golden boy."

Chapter Nine

We walk toward the elevators, every step pulling my shirt against the slices. Most people hate this part, but I need the pain to remind me of one thing. Off-load Mr. CEO with a fresh batch of groceries on his doorstep and get some damn rejuvenation. The rattling in my cage has stopped, with most of the souls absorbed by my body by now, but it doesn't make me any less of a threat to him. If anything, it makes me less human, more Nightmare.

The physical pulls of them, attempting to force me to him, may be gone, but I'm still dark. How can I not be when their very soul splinters into pieces in me? The color of my rejuvenation washes away the last vestiges of black floating in me, but what about the pieces that embed deeply into my body? For surely they do over time. I'll become more violent. My mood, tone will all be darker.

"I meant what I said. You can use my facility, free of charge. And I'd still be in your debt. No amount of money can clear the fact that you saved me at great cost to yourself." Blaze waves at my back.

"I don't want nor need your staff questioning my every

word, as she just did, waiting for your approval. I don't have the time nor the inclination to wait for your minions to go running to you every time I need something done. I'll buy my loyalty, thanks," I sneer and grip my box harder. Plus, people who are inherently good, even without the gold that spews out of them, can't touch me. I'd remove every little bit they have.

I'm no better than the monsters I kill. My saving grace is that I rid the world of the insidious gold suckers.

Electric streaks add to the throbbing in my back as my flesh slowly repairs itself. I force one foot in front of the other, going down the stairs as fast as I dare without jolting my back unnecessarily.

"You don't need to waste your money. I'll tell them your instructions are to be followed without question."

Why does he have to be so tenacious? Not used to having his every whim met with complete compliance? He doesn't own me. And I don't have to listen to him.

"Nothing I buy is wasted. And the answer is no."

We're almost to the Ferrari. It never looked as good as it does in this moment. The metallic tang of blood forces me to ignore the fire burning in my spine.

"Unlock."

The Ferrari opens, and I throw my things in the sheet-lined trunk. I'm always prepared for blood.

"That's kind of a cool, useful feature." I don't bother to respond, and he clears his throat.

"I never properly thanked you. I know you must be in pain, even though you are barely complaining. Your back is...a mess. I don't know how you do it so stoically."

Blaze's voice is tight with some emotion I can't identify.

I scream.

I always scream with that first cut of the whip into my back. No matter how many times I bite my lip, blood pooling into my mouth, I scream. Why can't I just keep my mouth shut?

The screams erupt one by one in the room as each girl in my dorm receives their own lashing.

"If you can't contain your pain, your sisters will receive punishment. Is that what you want? You want to hear them scream?"

I stumble, rounding the car, as the memory burns through my thoughts. It hadn't taken me long to learn how to control my mouth. But it was too late. The girls would never forgive me.

"It's fine."

If I keep talking, I won't be able to hold my own scream in. Sliding into the car seat, I'm careful not to lean back. Blaze gets in next to me and snaps his seatbelt in.

I scrutinize the bottle and its intact safety seal. The dosage is fairly low, and I break the cap open, spilling three of the pills into my hand. A bottle of water appears in my peripheral vision. Blaze hands it to me, careful not to touch me. I nod, both my thanks and my approval. He's learning.

Hopefully, the meds kick in fast, driving sitting straight up is damn awkward. I want to melt into the soft leather and close my eyes. I'm tired.

Instead, I drive to the nearest supermarket and pull in a spot as far away from the store as possible. There will be hell to pay if someone scratches my baby.

"Couldn't park any farther away?" Blaze says drily.

"You afraid of exercise? Or you just *that* used to door-to-door service?"

How much longer am I going to be stuck with this spoiled man? I get out and slam the door harder than she deserves and take a moment to swipe my hand down her hood in apology.

"I was worried about how you're feeling actually. Do you ever let people finish talking?"

I nearly trip over my own feet but straighten hastily. When was the last time someone cared about me? Enough to ask?

"Why would you worry about someone you barely know? You have more gold than brains. Speaking of which, who wants to piss on your golden flakes?"

I'm sure he's got enemies. Rich heirs always do. I ignore his last question. I'm not used to talking to people at all.

Blaze raises an eyebrow. "Do you have an obsession with gold? You keep saying it, in regards to me. I assure you, I don't have any gold that someone would want to steal."

I forget that humans can't see their own goodness. And the chances of him seeing someone else's are slim to none.

"You have an...aura, for lack of a better term. A gold one. It's what the Nightmares are trying to steal from you. It's what your soul screams in fear of. It's why I came to protect you."

His blue eyes widen and turn into a raging ocean. I've never seen eyes that shift like elements of the weather. Dramatic. "An aura? Gold? Can they just take it?"

I shake my head, both as an answer to his question and to free my mind from getting caught in a trap. Curiosity will get me nowhere except dead. Everyone knows what happens to those cats.

"It's not actually your aura. It's just the best way to describe it. The goodness in your soul. It shines out like a beacon, calling to them. They take it and destroy it."

Blaze stands in front of the cart line with his mouth slightly open. I guess this is why humans so easily lose their goodness; they don't have the sense to know what they've got.

I yank on the first cart and push it, the loose wheel pulling the cart to the left. I hate broken carts.

"Here. Your groceries, your cart. Push."

He grabs the bar and pushes, the muscle in his left forearm bunching with the tension he uses to keep the cart straight. I jerk my eyes away. Painkillers must have hit me a bit too hard.

I've had sex with manly-men with big, brawny muscles,

with girlie-girls with smooth abs and sleek thighs, and every variation in between.

Yet this man, with his lean, corded muscles and tawny hair flopping over his eyes, with skinny jeans and a metro chic wardrobe has my eyes glued to a small ripple of movement. I need a fucking vacation. And maybe an orgasm.

The image of the two of us fused on his bed, the silk sheets sliding around my skin, taunts me. My nipples harden, but it's not enough of a tingle to overpower the pull of my open skin, zigzagging its way to closure.

Screw relaxation, I need my punching bag.

The downfall of pain is...need. I need to be soothed, to be grounded in a reality that doesn't include feeling wounds. Pleasure, even when it packs trouble, is an elemental need that can erase pain. Or at least put it on hold.

Unfortunately, my pleasure won't be found with him. My tongue slides over my lower lip, briefly. Shame, that.

I bet he'd be up for several hours of fun. But not worth siphoning his gold. And I'm in no shape to control the urge to steal his soul even if I didn't have dark pieces parasiting their way through my system.

But a round in the gym will suffice. Endorphins are endorphins. My fists hitting canvas, sweat, and the pump of adrenaline has long been my source of comfort in a home where the Mother caused my suffering. Where the Sisters would offer a knife to my chest instead of a hug around the shoulders. Brothers found plunging your head into a basin of water, pulling at your shirt to cop a feel or yanking your pants down, intent on letting you know what can happen out in the real world, if you can't stop it.

None of them familial, yet I was forced to call them so. Hard lessons taught.

Fuck family. Fuck anything that will warm your heart.

Around there, anything that warmed your blood instead was acceptable.

Those lessons learned, while harsh and solitary, have never failed me.

We walk up and down the aisles with him putting in far more food than necessary. I carry the few things I need. No sense wasting a trip to the store. I stay as far away as possible from him to ensure the souls stay put. We finally wrap up in the grocery store, bagging items that he's picked out for himself. I don't understand why he needs so much variety. I can't comprehend the need to eat things that have sauces on them, or foods that will make you fat, like ice cream. Such a waste of money.

My own bag contains the things I need to survive. Healthy fats like nuts and chicken, eggs and milk. Protein, always protein. So what if he raises his eyebrows at my five dozen eggs. I don't explain myself to him or anyone. He can think what he wants. I know what I need and what I don't.

In unspoken agreement, he loads his bag in the trunk of the car, and then I load mine. I appreciate that he has a brain. Repeating myself fifty times gets old. Obviously, he can follow directions.

That's the kind of people I like. Keep quiet and follow the orders I give them. Nice and easy. Once he gets in the car, I guide the sleek machine onto the main road.

Neither of us says anything. The quiet vibrates on the air. My nerve endings tingle and the hair on my arms lift slightly. Maybe those painkillers were a bit too good. I nearly jump when he exhales loudly.

"Are you going to say anything?" His fingers fidget on the armrest.

"About what?"

"About your back? About that goodness you see? About

people not touching you? About how you stopped talking and refuse to say anything at all?"

His voice tightens, something probably only I can pick up on. Extra-sensitive hearing is one of the bonuses bestowed on those of us who need it to become finely-honed weapons.

"I didn't know you wanted to kill the lovely silence with nonsense."

"People don't generally talk about auras and then shove carts at them and stalk off. They don't usually not talk to someone they are with for almost an hour. Doesn't it make you uncomfortable?"

"Why would it make me so? Silence is comforting. It's peaceful."

What is this obsession humans have with always filling the air with noise? You have something to say, that's great. But speaking just to talk is pointless.

He throws his hands up in the air. "Nothing about today has been peaceful. How can you be so nonchalant? Doesn't your back hurt?"

I snort. What does he think I am, superhuman?

"Of course, my back hurts. The painkillers have dulled it down to someone slinging a hammer at my back."

"But you haven't complained one time. If I hadn't seen it with my own eyes, I would never guess that you're even remotely hurt. Honestly, I don't know how you're walking around like that without a major intervention. It's kinda freaky."

Is it? I run my tongue over my teeth. I can barely feel the ridge of them and only because I'm concentrating. I never stop to think of what my life was like before I saved my actual sister. Before I signed a contract. Before I screamed with the numb terror of losing my soul. I shrug.

"You can complain, but nobody fucking listens. So, what's the point?"

The movement of his arm in my direction catches the corner of my eye—that damnable need humans have to touch in compassion—and I hiss. At the sound, he lowers his arm and sighs but doesn't say anything.

"I don't need any of your sympathy or pity or whatever it is you think you feel for me right now. Your goodness can't save me—and you don't want to do that anyway. I wouldn't be great at my job if it did."

He jerks at my words, but I don't explain further. There's no need. I know where my priorities lie, and it isn't amongst those who have pure hearts. Protecting them so they can make a difference in the world is where I belong. The world needs me just the way I am.

Soulless. Dark. Alone.

We pull up in front of his apartment building. When he gets out, Blaze turns around and leans back in.

"Thank you for everything you've done for me. I appreciate it."

I nod but keep my gaze straight ahead. I don't want his gratitude. Nor his indebtedness. He shouldn't be feeling anything when it comes to me. I don't need some human male thinking about me. And I don't need to be thinking about his stunning eyes and sexy stubble.

There's another soft sigh and he shuts the door. Like he's fucking disappointed. I definitely don't need that. My eyes cut to the rearview mirror. His toned arms lift the trunk and shortly close it. *Eyes on the road, Arnica.*

I count to fifty. He should've made it to his front door. I focus on him, and my ears pick up the shutting of it and the muffled footsteps. Then I tune it out. The silence in my head is a faint echo of my chest. Nothing beats there. I may have a physical heart, but it doesn't do anything but force blood through my veins. It has one job.

Just like me.

The pedal hits the floor when I stomp on the gas. The Ferrari growls in response, and I apologize again. No reason to take out my frustration of the day on this beauty.

I once again pull into my garage and trudge up the stairs, stopping only to grab three protein bars, and head straight to my room. I drop my butterflies on the bed. Waiting only long enough to finish chewing, I slowly ease onto the mattress. With a wince, I roll to my side and close my eyes.

Silence. It's dark. My heart accelerates and then slows back down, when finally, the rainbow colors creep in and swirl behind my eyelids.

Too many dark soul vestiges lingering with their toxicity? Consuming me? I hope to fuck not.

Every Nightmare Killer knows what happens then. The end. Finished.

The harshest truth has always been the knowledge that I'll be hunted down and extinguished before I can wreak havoc on everything I've ever accomplished.

A Killer turned Nightmare is lethal. Smart, trained, with the ability to heal? Mindless dark is bad enough. A mindless me is worse.

Chapter Ten

The colors finally do their job, whisking away dregs of black. Wisps carrying them like ants with picnic food. Overloaded. Too many shadow souls. I never thought I had a limit, but this rejuvenation episode jars me. What happens if I have too many in me? Can they overtake me? I have no idea, but I better fucking find out. I've never heard of one of us having to kill so many in one session before...

An incessant sound blares and jerks from a deep sleep, my blades already in my hand. My head's fuzzy, but I wildly scan the bedroom and land on the annoying alarm clock. What the fuck is happening? I read the time and date, and I tighten my grip on the handles as the blood pounding through my veins clears the brain fog.

It's noon. Hours have passed. I open my senses carefully, searching my home, but there's no one here. It doesn't matter because I'm not leaving anything to chance.

I turn off the clock, slowly lift the covers, and quietly slide out of bed. The damn thing is only set to remind me to make the bed...if I have time. Not to wake me from a sleep I never take.

Soundlessly, I walk to the door of my room and plaster myself next to it. I duck and roll across the floor of the hallway and end with my back against the wall in the living room.

My blades are still in hand, and I crouch in my bare feet, my breathing shallow and controlled. I search the room and slowly stand up to peer into the kitchen.

Nothing.

I move from room to room, methodically checking each one visually. Until every inch of my home has been searched, I don't stop to think about the why or how. The thought of losing my abilities, of not being able to trust the accuracy of them, terrifies me. Thank the Fates they were spot-on. They haven't failed me, and now that I've done a visual confirmation, I slam my sword on the counter and pull up my security system on the pad by the wall to check the cameras. Again, nothing. No one has been in or out.

Something's horribly wrong.

I slept for sixteen hours. And while blissful and restorative —I roll my shoulders back and stretch side to side, confirming my back has indeed fully healed—I've never slept by accident.

I schedule my sleep once a year, like all Nightmare Killers, and sleep for a glorious twenty-four hours straight.

When someone else can pull double duty and cover my area.

Oh, shit.

I run to my office and login to the county and state police departments. My fingers twiddle with a pencil while I scan police reports for the last sixteen hours, searching for any assaults or violent crimes committed by usually nice kids. The ones that victims or neighbors say would never do that.

But they did. 'Cause some fucking piece of shit Nightmare sucked the goodness right out of them.

Five of them.

My grip tightens on the slim wood in my hand. Those bastards slurped up five children's gold halos while I slept like a baby. On my watch. On my turf.

The pencil snaps in two. A frustrated scream rips from my mouth, and I throw the pieces across the room. Two events in the last twenty-four hours that are out of the norm. This is no damn coincidence. I stomp to the kitchen.

Hating the need for fuel, I stand in front of the open fridge and grab anything that's already cooked, cramming food in my mouth. I chew, swallow, and repeat until I've eaten enough to replenish my caloric deficit without emptying the fridge. Contingencies are always on my brain. I chug two bottles of liquid electrolytes. My body hums like the forsaken machine it is.

The brakes squeal in protest outside of Blaze's apartment, and I stalk toward the entrance. I wait impatiently for the elevator, shifting my weight from foot to foot.

Rules ingrained deep into my psyche about violating privacy of people who aren't in danger is the only reason I don't blur my ass into his place. The elevator opens to his floor, and I approach the door with as much finesse as a bull in a china shop. My fist pounds on the gleaming wood.

"Blaze!"

I wait a minute and pound some more. "Blaze, open this fucking door."

Silence. I finally open some of my senses and don't pick up any kind of heat signature on his floor.

My skin prickles and the hair on my neck stands up. What if I'm wrong and this isn't his fault? He's supposed to be *good*, and I assumed he's connected to the cause of my failure. But what if he's not and is instead a victim? What if he's lying in a pool of blood in his room? Dead? An image of his naked body devoid of that stunning gold, cold as ice and still as a statue, laying limply on that massive bed flits through my head and the air catches in my throat.

Fuck protocols.

I kick the door until it splinters and move through the hanging pieces. Frantic, I blur in and search each room. He's not here. I kick the coffee table in his living room, and a deep crack appears in the wooden leg, listing the furniture.

I broke a rule for nothing. I have no problem bending them when they're needed, but this was just a fucking waste of time. The fear I'd felt a minute ago evaporates.

My jaw clenches. If he's not a victim, then he's a part of it. My nostrils flare. Because I'm sure he's slept in the last sixteen hours and his soul hadn't screamed. Something isn't just wrong; it's straight-up twisted, and I'm going to unravel it. Blaze will wish he never met me.

The elevator dings and my head snaps up. I run to a wall and pancake myself against it. That's all I need, someone seeing me and calling the cops. I can wipe the cameras here, as well as the police call log and records, but I need to know which station I'm hacking into. And it's a colossal waste of my time.

Notes of cedarwood oil, eucalyptus, and lemon reach my nose. I narrow my eyes and push off the wall, my arms crossed. My fist curls in, the short nails digging into my palm. He will make a perfect punching bag.

"What the?"

Blaze's face pops up at the door and he peers in, his mouth slightly open, until he spots me. His lips compress and he uses a key to open the doorknob on a remaining sliver of wood in the frame. The golden color shimmering around his body is all the proof I need.

He doesn't bother shutting the ruined door. His arms rise at his side before dropping back down. Relief washes over me.

"What happened here?"

I rock back on my heels. How dare he act innocent? Anger curls through my gut. I can't believe I was worried about him. I should know by now that everyone has an agenda. My jaw clenches.

"What did you do to me?" I say the words slowly, deliberately. He better answer in the same fashion.

His eyes widen innocently. "I didn't do anything to you. What are you talking about?"

I cross the room so fast, he has no chance to move. I shove myself into his space, careful not to touch him. I can't guarantee that I won't steal his soul, as angry as I am. I've never had to control myself this pissed-off before.

"Don't fucking play dumb with me. Humans have two hundred and six bones in the body, and I know how to break every one of them, five different ways."

Blaze pales and his body jerks backward. I step forward.

"I'm not going to *fucking* ask you again."

He puts his hands up, and I step back to avoid contact.

"I honestly have no idea what you're talking about. And I would never do something to hurt you."

His brows are raised, pleading with me. If he's lying, I can't tell.

I take another couple of steps back and cross my arms. "I'm not convinced. You still have your gold prostrating itself around you. How have the Nightmares not come back when you slept?"

"I haven't slept."

I snort but take a second to search over him. Now that I'm searching minutely, there are smudges under his eyes and his five o'clock shadow is more of a ten o'clock, the golden stubble thicker than yesterday. My eyes narrow. He's wearing the same clothes, too. My nostrils flare. Under his scent, I can't smell fresh soap. I uncross my arms.

"Fine. I believe you."

I stalk past him. I'm going to find answers elsewhere. I'm almost to the elevator when he yells.

"Arnica! Wait!"

My head swivels. He stands in the doorway, palms on the frame, like he's stopping himself from running out.

"What happened to you?"

"None of your business."

He's wasting my time, and I step into the elevator.

"I need your help."

His tone pleads with me, but I'm no charity. "I already have a job."

I jab the elevator button to shut the doors. I won't have to deny him if I can't hear him.

"I'm afraid to sleep."

The whisper floats on the air, the words pathetic in their simplicity. Dammit. My hand shoots out, preventing the doors from closing.

Why me?

I sigh and step out. He's still standing in the doorway, but his shoulders sag and he looks for all the world like a damn lost puppy.

Fuck me. I'm going to regret this a million times before my next vacation.

Blaze formally gestures in invitation, ignoring the pieces of the door hanging drunkenly off the hinges. The rich always think they can raise their noses and act like everything is normal. I grin at the silliness of it and then let my lips fall back into their normal shape. There's no way I find it endearing.

"If it was just me they were after, I would sleep. But now I know you'll come, too. And get hurt or worse. And you won't let me help you, and I'm so...tired."

Blaze closes his eyes and his shoulders slump. My mouth pulls into a grimace. He feels bad I'll get hurt? Damn do-gooders. Always being so...nice.

"You don't have to worry about me. I'm fine. See?"

I swing my torso in a few side twists, twisting my lips into a smile. I probably look like a clown, but I only have to convince him I'm not in pain anymore. He doesn't have to know that my healing kicked into overdrive because I actually slept. He won't know my back's fully healed in a superhuman-ish way.

Blaze shakes his head. "But you could keep getting hurt. And I can't allow that."

Now heat climbs in my face. "You can't allow that? Who the fuck turned time and made you my liege?"

My jaw clenches. I had been *allowed* to do things once before, like eat. I don't ask permission anymore.

Blaze puts his hand up, palm facing me. "I don't mean to offend you."

"Too late. You don't own me."

I spread my legs in a wider stance. He wants to go a few rounds, I can accommodate him. His eyes travel down my body and back up, sending tingles into my muscles. I ignore them.

"I'm not sure what you're preparing here for, but I just want to talk to you. I have a business proposition that you might be interested in."

He waves his hand as if encompassing all of me. His propensity for nudity flits across my thoughts. Now that's something I can consider. I raise my eyebrow and cock my hip. I have another proposition entirely if he's game. My tongue flicks out to lick my lip. I'm capable of keeping his soul and gold to himself after all the sleep I got. Probably.

"What proposition?"

My voice comes out huskier than I intend, but he flushes red, and I'm suddenly okay with it. He looks cute with it riding his cheekbones. Much like I want to. Looks like I need an orgasm sooner than I thought.

81

"That's not what I meant. I would never offer to pay for... anything like that. Besides, I could take my pick if I really wanted to."

The blush on his cheeks deepens. My brow rises higher. I like a cocky man. When the attitude is done right, it can be downright sexy.

Blaze clears his throat. "I wanted to ask you how I can get around the Nightmares. And I'd pay handsomely for the information."

"Well, I'm not going to say I'm not disappointed." I shrug. "But I can't help you. If there was a potion to prevent them from coming after you, I'd bottle it up and sneak it into every good person's food."

But there isn't. And I will always be there to kill them. Rage clouds my mind. Except for last night. Someone knocked me out, and I will get to the bottom of it. Blaze's eyes dart away for a moment. My own narrow. What's he up to?

"Actually." His weight shifts slightly to the balls of his feet. "There might, hypothetically,"—he clears his throat several times—"be a potion."

My body stills. "What the fuck are you talking about?"

He moves to the sofa and sits down, indicating I should do the same. I stomp over and sit, my back straight. The muscles in my body tense. I want to know what he thinks he knows. Humans and their tendency to think they've got a superior brain to everyone else.

"You know how you rhetorically asked how I've survived this long yesterday?"

It wasn't rhetorical, but I keep my mouth shut. Blaze sits with his elbows on his knees, his hands clasped in front of him, and his head bowed. I frown. This seems far bigger than it should be. Maybe he thinks he's come up with some superhero thing and wondering how he should check his embarrassment. He looks up, his jaw clenched, and his blue eyes burn with a blue light. I lean back, exhaling hard.

What the *fuck* just happened?

Chapter Eleven

My thigh knife is already in hand. So this isn't your average human after all. And I had no fucking clue.

"What are you?"

He blinks and the fire is gone. Just normal blue eyes. Except I'll never forget what they looked like. Blue flames flickering in the orbs, obscuring the pupil.

Blaze stands up, and I react, a knife in each hand now, rising to a half crouch, half standing position. Do I need to fight, or do I need to run?

"I won't hurt you. I just need to get water."

I snort. He could try. But I pull up to a standing position, keeping an eye on him as he walks toward the kitchen. Is he going for a weapon? Is he trying to throw me off? He already has. I don't want to admit it, but a sick feeling's churning in my gut and it has nothing to do with hunger or sexual attraction.

"The last time you did that, you had trouble keeping awake. Think that's wise?"

"It's one of the bottles that I bought yesterday."

I continue to stand, alert and ready for battle in case he does pass out, until he walks back and sits down. Only then do I slowly lower myself, sitting on the edge, ready to jump back up. I don't understand what's going on here, and I'm fast losing patience. I gesture with a knife.

"Continue with who the *fuck* you are and what the *fuck* you're talking about."

He winces, no doubt at my ramped-up language. He can kiss my ass.

"I'm Blaze Crofton, as you know. CEO of Crofton Hospital. I'm also the leader of Healers. I'm a Magical, Arnica."

I lean back into the sofa, sinking into the cushions, the soft black leather warming my back, and study him. His nose, straight and a bit thin, ends in a slight point. The golden-brown brows are heavy above his stormy eyes. He looks like any other human.

Except for the blazing blue light, which he apparently activates on command.

I'm a Dreamer myself, and there's been bad blood between the two years ago. You'd think with the Guardians killing off Magicals and Dreamers, we'd band together, but we haven't. It doesn't matter to me. I give no shits about the branches of Infinites in the Guardianship. In my book, you're either decent or a dick.

To be fair, most of the Guardianship look human because we are. We just have supernatural abilities and talents that make us different. Each branch has their own special abilities. As far as I can tell, Guardians herd people with their Destinies and Fates and shit. Dreamers deal mostly with the subconscious, and Magicals...are magical. I'm not surprised he's got a title. His posture and bearing gave that away. I wave at his words because none of this matters. It's imperative I learn what potion he's talking about, if it's real, how I can get some.

"I don't care if you're the prince of dogs. I want to know

about this so-called potion. And if you Magicals have one, why the *fuck* you haven't shared it. Do you know the good that gets siphoned every day? There aren't many of us who protect you."

I'm getting angrier with every second that passes. Countless souls screaming, countless opportunities lost for humans to regain some humanity. My hand curls around the handle of the knife so hard my palm throbs. Seven people without their innocent gold since I met him. "And you have the nerve to ask me how to protect yourself from the Nightmares?"

I lean forward and slam my fist into the crooked leaning coffee table. The other leg breaks and one end hits the floor. I don't blink.

"If I wasn't in the business of saving your golden ass, I'd tell you to fuck off."

I jump up, suddenly edgy, and pace the living room, the flat side of my knife tapping my thigh.

Blaze sighs loudly, and I want to punch him. How dare he be exasperated? As if what I do is insignificant.

"First, it's never been my call. Second, we have limited supplies to make more. We have to pick and choose who we dole it out to."

I pause my pacing to stare at him, jaw dropping.

"You're fucking choosing who to give it to? What's the criteria? How much money you have? How pretty you look?"

My body's vibrating with the urge to hit something. I force myself to sit back down, and it takes effort not to scream. I throw my hand up when Blaze opens his mouth, and I grind my teeth hard.

All those people I've not been able to make it to, that I haven't been able to protect the last couple of days. All that wasted goodness that could be used to change the world for the better.

Suddenly, weariness slithers through my body and my

shoulders slump down. I dip my head, my eyes tracing the edge of the blade in my hand.

What's the point of it all?

What's the point of me?

Everything I've done. The pain. The loneliness. Eternally without a soul. I shove the knives into their holsters and my hands curl into a fist in my hair. I give a tug, the quick sting failing to stop my thoughts. My head snaps back up and I gaze into Blaze's eyes.

"You have no idea what we Nightmare Killers do. What we give to do it. And all this time, we could've utilized a stupid fucking potion. A simple solution to all the aches and scars we bear. The pain we've endured."

My heart stammers and then pounds, racing faster till I think it might explode. The phantom pain of multiple emotional knives slam into me. The invisible stabs in my back. The gut-wrenching sorrow of those who should have loved me and instead twisted me into a killing machine. The years of abuse and the building of thick skin.

I chose this life because I didn't know there was a different path. My breath hitches and it's hard to drag in air. I jump up and pace—an animal trapped. My head whips around wildly.

There must be something I can hit.

The muscles in my body are strung tight till I'm stalking the room like it's a cage.

I can't take it anymore, and I blur through the wall into the next room and into the next. On and on until I'm outside on the fire escape ladder.

I grip the railing. Twisting my hands down, stretching my tendons at the wrist until I'm afraid they will snap, and then up to the opposite side. If I had superhuman strength, I could rub the paint off the metal. But I don't because I'm not like the others with a plethora of gifts bestowed upon them.

I earned my strength, because I've always been broken.

The door opens. I keep my head down and don't acknowledge him. He stays silent for a few more moments. I close my eyes. He has no sense of self-preservation.

"I'm sorry. I've grappled with the knowledge for years. With my own conscience. In the end, we can't just make up a bunch of the potion and give it away. We need to protect those that we do. Please, you have to understand that."

His voice, smooth like butter, cuts across the sound of traffic below. My shoulders tense, and I push against the railing, using the momentum to spin around.

"What I *understand* is that you keep knowledge that could be used to save thousands of people. That the *Magicals* care only about themselves and not the good of the world. No wonder everyone in the Guardianship hates you people. Selfish bastards sitting on your damn thrones, pretending you're gods of the humans. Fuck you. You don't deserve the gold oozing out of your head. Too bad it won't last long enough to choke you. Even gods must sleep."

I vault over the railing and land on the concrete below, hard. A sharp pain lances through my left leg, but I straighten up and stalk to my car.

This is what I get. How many times do I need to feel an emotion for someone for it to get through my head? Emotions cause scars, every time.

I don't need any more of them.

I haven't driven more than a mile down the street when screams echo through my brain. I need the distraction. It's been weirdly quiet, and the thought crossed my mind that something was even more wrong than just unscheduled sleep. I focus on the location.

I groan. Why? Why is he doing this to me? My internal GPS is pointing due south. About one mile behind me.

I grip the steering wheel and drive forward another ten seconds. Dammit! I'm just not capable of letting those inky things take more good out of this world. Even if I haven't seen him use it myself, even if I don't think he deserves it.

Abruptly, I yank the steering wheel to the left, leaving several cars honking and slamming on their brakes. I accelerate and am long gone before the cacophony of pissed-off drivers dies away. The Ferrari barely stops and I'm running up, blurring through the wall and landing on the other side. My weapon's out when the Smudge slams into me. The sensation is oddly familiar, like breathing in ice. I must've had too many souls in me yesterday after all. The blade slides right through where the heart should be milliseconds after it pulls out. The soul inside me rails at its loss of a host.

I hate that I'm comforted by the heaviness it feels. Kinship with the thing I despise the most is the ultimate slap in the face. Turning, I tense, waiting for the next shadow, wondering where Blaze finally passed out.

The bark of laughter escapes before I can clamp my lips shut.

He's lying on the couch, a bucket of water next to him. There's a sheet of paper taped onto the plastic.

"DON'T LET ME CHOKE."

I dump the water over his face and chest. Did he purposely wear a white shirt? He sits up, sputtering and shaking his head. Droplets cling to the stubble on his chin.

I clasp my hands together to keep from wiping the dripping strands of hair off his forehead. Fuck, I need to get laid. I'm more than pissed-off at him, yet I want to quench my thirst and lick the damn drops of water.

"Thank you for coming back."

Blaze's voice, rough from too short of a nap, vibrates on the air. Tantalizing and sexy. Stalking to the kitchen stops me from jumping him. My body, used to combat and to constant energy expenditure, has my muscles vibrating from the need to move. And right now, the movement I'm focusing on definitely can't happen.

The pull of the soul inside me messes with my emotions. I turn and face him, an entire counter and sofa between us. The gold spilling around his shoulder looks shinier. Ethereal.

Focus on something else, Arnica.

My eyes drift down his chest, his nipples pushing against the white shirt.

Oh, for fuck's sake. I yank open the fridge to get my mind out of the gutter and into anything else. The contents baffle me. Condiments and sauces in various bottles. How many different types of vinegar can one person use? Frustrated on multiple levels, I slam the door shut and sigh. "I didn't do it for you."

"I know. I was hoping that your own code of honor wouldn't let you let the Nightmares take advantage of me."

I snort. My code of honor is tenuous at best. Even now, my body desperately wants to plaster itself to him and ride him to oblivion. The soul taking up residence inside me wants to perform a different kind of suck. Namely the gold shimmering around him, sweet and pure. I slap my palms on his counter hard enough that the skin stings. I can't focus. And that's dangerous.

"Look, much as I'd like to yap about codes, I need rest. This soul inside me needs to go. Can you stay awake long enough?"

Blaze nods. "Is there anything I can do to help?"

"Yeah, stay the fuck away from me. And stay awake."

I head down the hall, looking for a guest bedroom. I'm sure he has one. I was intent on finding a body earlier and didn't pay much attention to the contents. Each room I pass is spacious, filled with various furniture but none with a bed. An office, a game room, and what looks suspiciously like a torture room.

My brow lifts. I need the rejuvenation, but this is interesting. Kink? I step up and peer through the glass doors of a hutch-style cabinet. Various tools lay on open boxes lined with red silk cloths. Most of them are foreign to me, the use of which I could only imagine. Some are a little more obvious upon closer inspection. A mortar and pestle, made of some kind of jade-like stone, glitter in the light.

Fancy.

"My bedroom's down the hall."

"I had to sate my curiosity. I thought for a moment there that some of your gold might be tarnished."

Blaze clears his throat. "You, ah, sound disappointed."

"You have no idea"—I turn around and lean my hip against the cabinet, eying his lean body, and a soft blush creeps along his cheekbones—"what I like. So don't make assumptions."

His white shirt, still wet and still stuck to his chest like a second skin, may as well be invisible. The blond curls on his chest darken the farther south my eyes travel. Wouldn't take but a swift flick of my blade to cut the belt on his pants. I swallow hard.

I need that rest. And then maybe a cold shower. I wave my hand in the direction of his bedroom.

"You've got a spare bed so that I'm not in yours?"

I clear my throat. A guest bed for colors and dark soul removal, not his bed for sweat and slapping skin.

I've got to get a grip on myself. If I walk by him right now, I'll either steal his soul or his gold. As much as I crave it, it's not something I want to do.

"I don't have a guest room. My bed will have to suffice."

Right. Cause that's going to be helpful in keeping this lust down.

"Fine. If you'll just move out of my way, I'm going to go there. In case I fall asleep, wake me in an hour."

"Isn't that what you're doing? Taking a nap?"

His brows pull forward and the tiniest frown line appears. Dammit, he even looks hot when he's confused. I shake my head but don't bother to explain. He backs out of the room, and I move forward quickly. The faster I get this soul out of me, the better.

Blaze's bed is perfect. Of course, it is. Why couldn't it be lumpy? Or have thin pillows? Instead, the mattress is soft but firm. For the first time, I cringe at the idea of lying down fully clothed with weapons handy. The silk sheets would slide against my skin, warming to my body heat.

Perils of the job.

I lay on my back, the harness a familiar lump in between my shoulder blades, and cross my feet at the ankles. The pillows cradle my head, and the entire bed smells faintly of lemon and cedarwood oils, of eucalyptus with an undertone of male skin.

A faint throb pulsates between my legs. What is it with this man? Sure, he's handsome, and the blue fires within his eyes kinda sexy. And that voice, butter smooth with just enough of a rasp to keep him from sounding younger than he is. But he wouldn't be the first to catch my attention and nothing can come of it anyhow. He's out of my reach.

Gold never mixes with steel.

Chapter Twelve

My eyes flutter down, and I hold my breath. What if the colors don't save me? But they swirl behind my eyelids, and I exhale softly, relieved.

Pinks chase yellow across my mental landscape, mint green pulling out shards of black and gray. For the briefest moment, my torso jerks, and there's a pang at the loss of the soul, a still emptiness that once was full. I don't like the despair, the sadness, the smidge of evil that festers inside me when I take a dark soul, coloring my attitude and intentions. But the hole that's left is fucking lonely.

I made a choice.

My body relaxes, my breathing shallow. I jerk, heart pounding, the throb between my legs no longer faint. His scent invades my nostrils. Every time I inhale, I might as well be shoving my nose into the crook of his neck.

Fuck.

I sense him in the doorway, but I'm not ready to face him just yet. I swallow hard and work on breathing normally.

Blaze's soft voice floats on the air like a caress.

"Arnica. Are you awake?"

His feet whisper against the wood as he readjusts his stance. And then he takes a step forward.

My eyes pop open. He stops awkwardly, like a kid caught doing something he shouldn't.

"I'm up."

I swing my legs over the edge, and out of habit, scan the area, making sure there's no one else here. Except he is. His heat signature registers in my mind, warmer than I am.

He's hot. One corner of my lip lifts in a small smile. He is that, and still really, really off-limits.

Standing, I lift my arms overhead, knowing full well my skintight clothing stretches against my skin.

I sheath my swords and saunter over to him. There's nothing more fun than pushing boundaries. I stop in front of him. He's showered and changed clothes, something I should've heard, but didn't. My eyebrows draw together. He makes me weak in ways I don't want to examine closely.

My eyes travel slowly down his body, smoothing out the crease in my forehead, in appreciation. He really is good-looking with a body he clearly keeps in shape.

"There's something to be said for an hour in bed. You ready to get in?"

His sharp inhalation means he isn't unaffected by me either. Good. I shouldn't be the only one that suffers. I smirk, but then stop.

Can't means I shouldn't. Why do I have to always be so heartless? The muscle at my jaw jumps when I clench it. Why can't I just be better?

"I need to refuel. And we need to talk, now that I'm not inclined to steal your pixie dust, Tinkerbell."

His fridge is full of the things we bought yesterday. But most of it doesn't make much sense to me. I like the taste of mushrooms but don't know how to cook them. Instead, I reach for the egg carton.

I don't feel right taking half of his stash, so I only take out three eggs. I search each shelf, looking for another source of protein.

"You have any chicken?" I yell without lifting my head from my perusal of the contents.

"There's some in the freezer."

Blazes' voice sounds much closer than the living room, where I thought he was sitting. I pop up, my eyes narrowed. I'm so used to turning off my senses when I'm home that I didn't realize how much I rely on them when I'm around others. Just because I'm always alone doesn't mean I shouldn't be aware of my surroundings—a downfall I'll need to work on.

He's on a stool on the other side of the counter, elbows propped, fingers linked and leaning against his mouth. His hair has dried and flops over his forehead. There's a hint of color on his cheeks, and it takes me a second to realize golden boy must've been checking out my ass.

Without invitation. Without me attempting to be sexy, roping in some willing one-night stand participant. And I don't want to stab him. Huh.

My heart stutters. No. He can't possibly want me. And I can't possibly think it's wonderful that he does. He's a Magical, for fuck's sake. A Healer. What would he do with a killer? And why would I want any kind of entanglement?

"You want to keep those cool blue eyeballs of yours? Stop ogling. You'd think you never saw an ass before, damn."

The pink on his cheeks darkens and his brows draw down, but I plunge ahead.

"If you're thinking with your dick, tell it it doesn't have a brain." His atmospheric eyes turn frosty. A sharp stab centers near my chest, but I forge ahead. "I don't fuck clients."

"I wasn't thinking anything. I thought you couldn't... what do you mean by client?"

One of Blaze's brows wings up, his voice as cold as his gaze. Ah, there's the CEO.

I rest my hip against the counter and fold my arms.

"You're in need of protection from Nightmares. I can do that. But I'm not doing it for free. There are contingencies. Payment to be discussed."

"Of course. Payment isn't a problem. What kind of contingencies?"

He leans forward, his hands on the counter and clasped loosely in front of him. I've thought about this a million different ways since he told me there was a potion. I tick each item on my fingers.

"My contingencies are as follows. You do what I say. My rules means you don't get hurt. Two, you pay me one million dollars if I get you to some kind of safety, gold intact."

Blaze's back straightens.

"That sounds like payment to me, not a contingency."

"I won't guarantee that I can get you to safety without you losing what makes you good. I can't. There are too many variables, far more than you are aware of. Far more than I'm aware of."

I haven't forgotten that I have yet to hear a scream from anyone else since I've met him. Something strange is fucking going on. I'm going to find out what it is, and Blaze is going to help me, whether he knows it or not.

"What is the payment?"

"The recipe for the potion."

He doesn't say anything, and I let the words linger between us. I gently suck in air and hold my breath.

He leans back against the seat and steeples his fingers, looking over them at me with his piercing blue eyes. The small line forms between his brows. I quietly let the air back out. He's golden boy. He's got to do the right thing.

"Honesty forces me to tell you that the ingredients aren't

easily accessible and are limited. The responsibility that flows from that is heavy. Painful even."

His voice, quiet and somber, the timbre of it dropping, rasps on the air, and a chill skitters up my spine. I'm not sure if it's from anticipation of his acquiescence or the pure sexiness of the sound.

I focus back on what he's saying. Yeah. He has no idea what pain is, has probably never felt much discomfort in his pampered lifestyle. I've got years of torture under my belt. I shrug.

"I'm no stranger to pain. I can take it."

"It's not that simple. It also can only be revealed to the Matriarch of the Leaders."

"Who is she? Your life must have value. Maybe she'll be willing to make an exception in this case."

I crack my knuckles. Creative threats and the keeping of such promises are skills I've mastered. Surely, someone will realize this.

Blaze's eyes close. Like blinds shuttering windows exposing the outside, the room seems suddenly darker. I drop my hands and tense. There's something I can't identify swirling.

I don't move a muscle, using my peripheral vision to glance to each side. Everything seems the same, but the hair on my skin stands on end. I keep my breathing even and slowly reach for my knives. If there's something here, it will meet cold steel shortly. The room seems to be getting even darker, the gold around him shining brighter. Is he falling asleep?

Every muscle screams to get up and move, but I remain still, watching Blaze. Like a wrap, the gold moves and slithers over his body, much like a caress. My eyes narrow. I had no idea it was capable of movement. Is he controlling it? What else don't I know?

It slides along his forearms, dimming into his skin. Then coming out stronger. What the fuck?

Just as I think I can't sit here any longer without bursting with tension, he opens his eyes. The room brightens and the gold shimmers against his skin.

He eyes my fists curled around my knives.

"I'm sorry, I needed a moment. My mother would have been the Matriarch. She's...dead."

Those damn blue eyes swim with moisture.

No.

What the hell do I do with a grown man who is going to cry? Shit.

Why me?

I clear my throat. "Uh, my condolences."

Do I pat him on the shoulder? I'm sure I could manage that small contact. But do I have to? Dammit. Grieving men aren't part of the lessons at the Weaponry.

"Thank you."

His gruff voice settles over me, and something warms the center of my stomach. I can't do this.

"Who's the new Matriarch? You have a sister or something?"

I try not to look at him, instead glancing at the wall directly above his hair, behind him.

"That would be my wife."

I jerk, my eyes locking onto his. He's married? I glance down at his ringless left hand and back to his face.

"Which I don't have," Blaze continues.

My heart did *not* just stammer in my chest. And I did *not* just breathe in deeply.

Fuck me.

Blaze lifts a hand up, the palm facing me. There's a faint curlicue design in the skin, maybe golden, almost scar-like. Was he branded? Is it his magic?

"This skin tattoo is only half formed. It will become brighter, more visible. The other half forms with the one I will marry. A type of soulmate. The knowledge passes to them during the formation of the symbol."

"You've got to have someone in mind? Aren't heirs, I don't know, prearranged to other heirs? Marry them so I can get the potion recipe."

I shrug, but the idea of Blaze marrying someone pricks my skin. Like a splinter working its way out. Why? I have zero connection to him. And though the sex would probably be amazing, that's about it for me. Till death do us part? I'd kill him. I shudder.

"You don't understand. They are the only ones that will have access to the potion recipe. The magic of it prevents them from just sharing it."

My eyes widen. Magic is fucking shady. And I hate rules. They're used to conform you, force you into something that you're not. Chiseling off pieces until you aren't yourself anymore. Add magic, something you can't control, and you're stuck. Like a mindless fly in a pinwheel. I narrow my eyes. There's got to be a way around this—rules are meant to be broken.

"Fine. They can make the potion every time I ask them to. No questions asked."

He shakes his head, and suddenly fury boils through my veins.

"No? Why is everything I ask for a no? Don't you value your own skin?"

Blaze gets up and walks around the counter toward me. I resist the urge to back up. He doesn't scare me, and since when do I run from a fight? There are no dark pieces in me now, and I'm nearly positive I can control myself and not leave him soulless. I ball my fists and stand my ground. He stops three feet from me, and I release the breath I'm holding.

His eyes scan me from head to toe. "I don't expect you to understand."

I stand straighter and raise my chin. What the fuck does he mean by that? Does he think I'm actually *lacking* something? I snort. Fuck him and fuck this. I turn on my heel and stride out.

I'm halfway to the elevators when Blaze dashes past me and stands in front of the door, throwing his hands up when it dings.

"You don't ever let anyone explain anything, do you?"

My eyes sting, but damned if I know why. "I don't have time to play games. You either agree to my terms or I'm out. I've got shit to do."

"You didn't let me finish. I was going to say that I don't expect you to understand. Because you weren't raised like a Magical, with the responsibilities that a Healer has, let alone the son of the Matriarch. You can't just do whatever you want. And I don't mind paying your price. It's just a matter of whether *you* will accept paying the price."

I want to scream and yank my hair. Why is he making things so complicated? This should be easy. Instead, I kick the potted palm next to the shiny silver doors that keep dinging open and closed. "What the *fuck* does that even mean!"

It's small of me to overemphasize the word fuck, but I get an electric shock through me when he frowns. His brows draw nearly together, and his expressive eyes shine. Just a small glimmer of blue flame.

"Marry me."

Chapter Thirteen

The flame flickers again, momentarily blocking the dark pupils. My nostrils flare. What the fuck did he just say?

"Excuse me?"

The blood drains from my face, leaving a faint tingle over my skin. He can't be serious.

"Marry me, Arnica. You'll have the recipe for the potion, and *you* can decide who to help."

"Is there something wrong with you?"

Blaze straightens, his body tensing. I hit a nerve. Something's wrong with him. What is it?

"There's nothing wrong with me—"

"Yeah, right. Your brows are damn close to covering your eyes, your fists are clenched, your body rigid. Your eyes are shooting flames in my direction. You're pissed I asked. Besides the fact that you just asked me to marry you, which happens to be a big no-no in our world." I point to myself. "Dreamer." I point to him. "Magical."

He waves his hands, as if he can just poof the facts of our

lives away. The two branches don't interact, let alone marry. Guardians try to hunt us down, and we all just do our best to disappear from their view and ignore our only possible allies— each other.

"There are ways around that. It's simple, you want the potion, you'd get it. Why are you objecting?"

He moves closer, an arm moving toward my back as if he's just going to guide me into his apartment. I step back, my jaw dropping, and then I quickly shut it. Spitting and spluttering is not my thing. But the idea of marriage, of having a normal life sits like a poisonous seed in my thoughts.

He steps forward again, and I sidle sideways and then stalk into his home. He keeps trying to maneuver me. Of course, I can outmaneuver him, but I'm tired of the dance. I can pace in his living room, and he can sit his ass on the couch. One of us has to be the rational one here.

"Absolutely not."

"Why not? Give me a reason."

I pause and glare. Has he not listened to anything I said? Why is he pushing this so hard? We aren't from the same branch of Infinites, and we don't know each other. Is this a transference thing? He likes me because I saved him?

He doesn't strike me as someone who'd so easily fall in love. And he'd said that he could have his pick. My eyes narrow, my fingers tapping against my thigh. I can't think of a single reason he'd want to attach himself to me. I cross my arms.

"You give me a reason why."

"So you'd have the potion recipe, of course."

"No. The reason *you* want to marry *me*."

Blaze's face pales a bit, and he leans back into the couch cushion, his fingers mimicking mine. "Because I need a wife."

He's deliberately annoying me. I pull the knife out of my pocket and throw it fast enough that he doesn't have time to react. He jerks, his eyes wide and horrified, and turns toward the knife quivering into the back of the couch, inches from his face.

I sweeten my voice so that he can't purposely misunderstand my sarcasm without me questioning his intelligence. No more games. "And you pick *me*? I'm flattered."

He pulls the knife out of the cushion, and turns it over in his hand, inspecting the blade. He acts like he's testing the weight, and I nearly laugh at the idea, until his arm moves back in a throwing motion and I duck.

I stand back up and turn to the blade embedded in the wall. I whistle loudly. It's exactly three inches from my face, just like his had been. I raise my eyebrow and reassess his body.

"You're not the only one that can throw a knife." His voice is irritatingly even.

"But I'm faster."

He nods in acknowledgement. "You are. We'd make a good team."

The word ends with a questioning lilt. No. We wouldn't.

"Sorry, I'm all out of sportsmanship. I won't be as generous with the spacing on the next knife. Answer the question."

"You'd be Matriarch..."

He trails off as if I'm supposed to jump with joy at the idea of ruling people. "Have you seen my people skills? Each time you don't answer, my knife's target gets closer to your skin."

Blaze sighs loudly and deeply. I swear he's attempting kitten eyes. Does that shit work on anyone? Well, maybe it could. I pluck the knife out of the wall and he throws a hand up.

"Without a Matriarch, I don't have the recipe for the potion. Without the potion, I'm a sitting duck. You've seen how they've come after me."

I sheath the knife, considering all the possibilities. I'm not going to agree to his proposal, because that's just fucking ridiculous. And I'm the best Nightmare Killer there is. I can protect him with my eyes closed and one hand tied behind my back.

"I had no idea this is what they are like. I've taken the potion my whole life. And now, I..." His voice falters and a tear leaks out of his eye, slowly trailing down his cheek. I stare at it, mesmerized. It's gorgeous. Pearly, luminescent. Glowing? He reaches out and catches it, the droplet balancing on his finger.

He rolls it between his fingers, round and round, until it becomes a smooth ball looking every bit like a pearl and just as shiny. He flicks it, and instinct has me catching it before I can force myself not to. I don't want it. It's warm, and I'm not sure if it's because of his body heat or if it has its own source. There's a hole down the middle as if it's ready to become part of a necklace. The idea that I'm holding a tear, one full of magic or not, freaks me the fuck out and my stomach rolls. What am I supposed to do with this?

"That's my promise to you." He rises and comes closer. The urge to bolt briefly runs through my mind. Contrariness has me digging my heels in. He stops close enough that his body heat warms my skin.

"That I'll give you whatever you want in exchange for marrying me. It's binding."

Whatever I want. The words bring so much emotion rushing through me that my knees buckle, and he reaches out. I sidestep out of reach. I can't think straight. And what I want isn't possible anyway.

I stalk toward the sofa and sink in. "Soulmates. Binding. All this magical shit. It doesn't apply to me for a variety of reasons. I stand by what I said. I'll take you to wherever you need to go, protect you the best I can. And I get the recipe for the potion at the end. I don't care how you make that happen. Whip up some magical shit then, okay? And if the answer is no, then you can take this...thing back."

"I can't give you the potion, I've already told you."

I lob the tear at him. "Then we have nothing to discuss." I move forward, intent on leaving. There are so many other things I need to get to. Like why the fuck haven't I already been summoned by a scream?

"You'd let them take my—what did you call it?—goodness? Doesn't that go against your code or job description or whatever it is you do?"

Irritation puckers my forehead. He's really pushing his luck.

"I don't have to take side jobs."

"I don't have to leave. And I have to sleep at some point. Are you going to ignore me then?"

I tried that once and I couldn't and he fucking knows it. I've battled with compassion my whole life. It never ends well when I give in. I'm regretting it now. If I had just let them take his golden aura when he purposely fell asleep, I would be home. Working out and eating real food and fighting Terrors. I despise being pushed into a corner and I growl low.

Fuck.

If I marry him, I'll get the recipe for the potion. And if then our marriage gets broken up, I'll still have the knowledge. I shrug. I could just divorce him. Unless they're into mind wiping shit, I'll have everything I want. I'll take my chances. I lift my chin and walk back to him, keeping my palm up.

"Fine. I'll marry you. Give me that thing."

Blaze drops it into my outstretched hand, and I close my fingers over it. It's still warm. Where the fuck am I supposed to put it? I pat my leggings, but I don't have those types of pockets.

"Let me just..." He reaches out and plucks out a strand of my hair and I hiss at the move. His hands move over it, and gold shimmers across the black. The result is some kind of halo around the piece. He threads it through the hole in the tear, still laying on my palm without touching me. Does he have a hawk's eyesight too? He holds his hands out, each one holding an end. The tear shimmers like a pearl in the middle.

"May I?"

I turn my back to him, my stomach clenching at the uncharacteristic move willingly exposing the parts of me I can't see to a possible threat.

His arms come around my head and my heart jumps. There's no reason to fear him. I could take him out with a few calculated moves, but the need to fight burns like acid in my throat. Is this what I've become?

I can't see the thing when it's on my chest, but the warmth seems to burn into me. It should be getting cooler on my cold body, but the opposite seems to be occurring.

I turn back around, breathing easier now that I can face him. I can't decipher the look on his face.

"It looks like a full moon against the dark sky." He gestures at my chest. "The tear against your black shirt."

I jerk slightly. A moon?

Fuck me. Why must there always be riddles. That Destiny at Club Ferraro had told me to watch the moon. Is this what she was talking about?

Do I walk away? Was it a warning? My current inclination to run away from all of this, to say no to this ridiculous scheme rolls strongly through me. Is it my intuition nudging me to back away, save myself? Or maybe her words were positive? Am I supposed to be here, in this moment in time, taking steps to marry a stranger for the greater good?

Fucking Destinies. Fucking Karmas and fucking Fates. Can't they just be normal people? I want to stomp my foot.

Maybe hit something. Why can't they just leave us all alone? Or if they're gonna meddle, tell me what I'm supposed to do! I huff out, my breath moving a few strands of my hair that had pulled loose when he'd taken one out.

This had better be the right damn choice. "When are we getting hitched?"

Chapter Fourteen

R elief flits across his face, relaxing the muscles around his lips, which quickly turn up in a grin. "You won't be disappointed. I'll be the best husband. I may have had a different upbringing than yours, and I've got my fair share of antiquated customs that have been passed down to me, but I consider myself a current man. You'll have every right you've had your whole life."

Shit. Maybe we should've talked about these things before I agreed to this. I don't care about politics or wars or stupid grudges between the various branches of the Infinites. I do my job and keep away from people. It's how I like it. This...this is not going to go well.

"I'm not following any of your rules. I make and break my own. I live by my own codes. Let's get one thing clear. I don't like you. Don't take it personally. I don't like anyone. Stay out of my way, I'll stay out of yours. When can I have the recipe?"

His fucking eyes twinkle with blue, and I want to tell him to cut that shit out. This isn't cutesy win-her-over time. I meant what I said, and he can take his gorgeous blue eyes and...and close them. I can't even think of a proper insult in my own head. I stomp to the fridge and pull out the last of his eggs. Pretty soon his things will be mine too, so I might as well make myself something to eat.

"There are some ceremonies we will have to partake in for you to become Matriarch."

I whip the eggs with a little more frenzy than needed. I have zero desire to be part of anything ceremonial or involving attendees.

The only reason I'm doing this is so that I can sleep more. Sleeping once a year sucks, and if I'm able to dole out the potion to those who might be attacked, then I'll be able to take more time off. I can cover the rest of them. My eyes close at the sheer bliss the idea of sleeping invokes.

I open them when a shuffling sound reaches me. Blaze's swaying on his feet, exhaustion evident on his face. I lick my finger where I grazed the butter and motion him off. "I've got your back. Go sleep."

Once the eggs land on my plate, I grab a fork and a napkin and the jug of milk he bought yesterday and take it to his room. I can eat there, and I'll be closer to him when the Nightmares come.

The chair and other room furnishings have been replaced since the dragon Terror was there yesterday. Was it only yesterday? He must have a cleaning crew and servants. I haven't seen anyone, but I can't imagine he's doing it himself. I chew thoughtfully while contemplating the idea that one of them spiked his food or drink. It's not out of the realm of possibilities. With thoughts of politics and such recently on my mind, I guess traitors and spies isn't too far off. Fucking people.

He snorts lightly once and moves his head, facing me. Some people might feel strange watching someone like this, but I'm kinda fascinated right now. I know people sleep every day, and I vaguely remember doing so myself when I was kid. I remember fighting with my parents about bedtimes. I remember sitting with Angelica, whispering long into the night and giggling when Mom yelled for us to go to sleep. That was before she started sneaking out at night. Before I started covering for her.

There's something soothing about seeing his vulnerable state. The eyes moving lightly behind the lids. The almost pink of his lips, barely parted. One could say kissable even. For a moment, I allow myself to think about planting mine on his. Just to see if they're as soft and smooth as they look. I swallow hard.

Marrying him does not mean I can start acting like a normal wife. I'll have to be extra careful that my constant presence in his vicinity doesn't distract me. Doesn't make me forget that I can steal his soul as easily as the ones I protect him from.

A short moan sounds on the air, and the hairs stands straight up on my neck. Yeah. A visit to someone to ease the sudden ache between my legs is going to have to go on the schedule. I can't keep this up for long. The man sounds sensual even while sleeping. Must be some good dreams. The resulting picture runs like a porn film in my brain, and I punch my thigh. *Stop it.*

Movement out of my peripheral view has me reaching slowly for my butterflies laying on the chair next to me, between my legs and the chair wall. I'm slightly horrified by the way the Nightmare slips in, like a waif on the breeze. I've only ever seen them slurping up the gold from their victims or swiftly coming at me, desperate and aggressive. It moves around Blaze as if trying to figure out where to begin. The gold that shimmers beautifully just above his skin must taunt it.

But it continues fluttering in the space above his head, peering at him. It's more than a little creepy, and I can't sit still anymore. Honestly, I'm surprised it hasn't reacted to my presence. They usually want to unite with me, grow bigger and stronger maybe. I rise swiftly, feet planted and ready to take the hit as usual, but it twirls around me and...disappears. My jaw drops open. What the fuck just happened? I stomp my foot lightly because kicking the chair might wake Blaze up. Why are things changing? What's causing it?

Waking him up won't change anything because then the Nightmares definitely won't come. And he needs the sleep. I push back into the wingback, thoughtfully sliding my finger down the curved blade. Every once in a while, there's just a hair more pressure, and a quick sting reminds me that I'm playing with razor-sharp blades. The cuts are shallow and quickly close up.

Three more shadowy mists slide in, hovering and staring. What kind of sick joke are they playing? I'd never have pegged them with having more than two cells in their bodies let alone capable of thinking, but clearly they aren't mindless creatures. Two seem to confer together, but then just slide out. None of them pay any attention to me. This continues for another eight hours, with shadows coming in and out but not doing anything.

I don't know what is going on, but maybe this is why there is no screaming in my head. Are they no longer thieving the gold of good people? I highly doubt it. Centuries of the inky things and they just randomly decide they don't want to slurp up the decency in the world? But what else could it be?

No. Something is going on, and I'm going to find out—right now. I stand up and inch closer to Blaze. Maybe his gold isn't calling to them anymore? Nope, the pull is there, even if it feels a bit different than usual. Like it's familiar, but I could just be getting used to it. I'm never around the golden ones for more than it takes to dispatch Nightmares. And certainly not without dark shards invading my body.

I refuse to acknowledge the hope that briefly flares in my

chest. If you don't want shit, you don't get disappointed when you get shit. If I'm not touching him, I'm going to do my best to mimic an annoying alarm clock. I lean close enough to his ear that the scent of his skin, warm and slightly lemony, wafts in my direction.

"BEEEEEP, BEEEEEP, BEEEEEP! Time to get up, golden boy."

He jerks up and my quick reflexes are the only thing that saves me from the nuisance of a bloody nose and him from the tearing pain of a bloody soul. I shudder as the memory of mine getting ripped out gives me goose bumps. I shouldn't take chances with his, and guilt weighs heavy on my chest. I sigh.

"What's wrong?"

"I have to go, so you gotta get up. I need to find out some things. Meanwhile, I don't think you're gonna have to be saddled with me after all. None of them bothered you." I remove the tear from where it had rested against my skin after slipping under my shirt. I drop it on the nightstand, the necklace making a strange sound when it hits the wood. I almost feel naked, and shiver as if fingers dance up my spine. No, I can't have been used to it already. I can't have wanted it there.

I'm tired of all the strange crap, and the tug deep inside me has got to be relief that I'm leaving. I stop in at home to workout, change, and eat. Not because I'm amping myself up for the visit.

But because I want to be in top mental shape before I head back to years of hard memories.

Chapter Fifteen

The Weaponry is a gorgeous building that reminds me of a castle. As a petrified young teenager with a second chance at life, I had stood in front of it with the romantic thought that it represented honor and nobility. That it was going to protect me. Instead, it had symbolized pain and terror. Maybe if I had known the name of it then, I wouldn't have gone in. Little good that would have done—I had already given up my soul, and I wanted no parts of the pain returned to me.

I carefully close the Ferrari. I've parked far enough away that the stench of the place shouldn't seep into the leather. But the closer I get, the more potent the smell of sweat and fear, of blood and tears, of broken dreams pervades the area like a low-lying fog. You can't outrun it and you can't escape it. It's the material the gray block is made of. Hours, days, years of young Nightmare Killers layered upon minutes, weeks, decades of Mothers. The flayed skin and feverish screams found a home and became something twisted and beautiful.

I control the shudder that wants to rack through my body.

I beat them all at their own game years ago, and fuck if I would allow them to think they didn't lose.

I pull down my shades when I step into the darkened foyer. The echo of my boots flits ahead of me, giving them ample time to prepare for my first and hopefully last arrival in years. I breathe in deeply through my nose. The stench twists through me and settles into my lungs. A reminder that I don't ever want to come back willingly, unless they carry me in dead. And even then they can go fuck themselves.

I've already made a pact with a Guardian, one of the few who know Dreamers are still alive. He's under orders to burn my body. Scrape it into a bucket and burn it again. And then take me out to the four widest corners of the oceans and sprinkle me everywhere. I'll be damned if I'm gonna become a block in the continuation of the Weaponry. They may have made me a weapon and a damn excellent one, but only I will be able to wield and control it ever again.

I eye the bench outside the Mother's office and snort quietly. What is this, a principal's office? Anybody getting sent here and told to sit out there was probably shitting themselves with fear.

I shove the door open, not bothering to knock, and barely glance over at the girl stone-faced in the corner. A single dried-up tear track shows on her cheek, and she doesn't move a muscle or acknowledge my presence. Good for her. My heart squeezes in my chest, but there's nothing I can do. Any favors I give her would end up not being a favor at all.

"I see you still haven't learned manners."

I hate that her smooth voice can make my blood boil. I hate that it's soft and deceptively soothing. Like a chameleon snake right before it's strike, you'd never know what's coming.

"I see you still haven't learned I don't give a fuck."

Her lip curls, presumably in disgust. How can I *still* feel guilty for not being dependent on their so-called mercy and suitably thankful? That I hadn't stayed where any compassion and feeling had been beaten out of me?

"One day, child, someone's going to put you in your place, and you're going to regret turning your back on us."

I'm so tired of this stupidity. As if she can possibly hurt me any more than this entire place already has.

"I stopped being a child the moment I arrived here." I lean forward, putting my hands on her precious desk. The childlike urge to swipe everything off it briefly flickers through me, but that would be pointless and wasteful. "I'm sure you wish it was you, but we both know you're not capable, don't we?"

Her eyes move quickly to the corner of the room. There. I've done what I can for the girl. If she's smart, she'll play that card right. And if she's not, well then, she's not cut out to make it on her own.

"What do you want?"

I lean back slowly, masking my eagerness to stop touching the wood that pulses with depressive life. I should've known better than to think it wasn't imbued with the same essence permeating from the stone.

I straighten, purposely standing as tall as I can stretch my spine, just to piss her off when she has to crane her neck. Fate forbid she actually has to stand up and concede anything.

The grin on my lips taunts her, and satisfaction weaves its way through me.

Oh.

Fuck this building and its games. I drop the smile and force myself to focus on the task at hand. My soulless body feels at home, and for a moment there I almost slid down the slope of sickness. I will not let it corrupt me.

"Have you heard anything...different from any of the Killers?" There's no way to make the question innocuous. No way to not raise suspicion. Anything out of the ordinary is always analyzed.

119

She stands, for once, thinking she's got the advantage, the strange glee on her face making her no better looking than some of the Nightmares I've hunted.

"It seems that your lack of discipline is coming to the fore. What did you mess up now?"

The desire to please, to avert punishment rises like bile into my throat. But I'm not a defenseless, unknowing student anymore. Rage burns through me, but I have zero desire to end up with the girl's death on my conscience, and that will most certainly be my punishment now.

I lean forward again, toward the smell of disappointment, and pitch my voice so low only she can hear me. No small feat, considering we all have superhuman hearing.

"If you think you can make me submit, I'm willing to give you another try. But until then, back off with the posturing because you're pissing me off."

At the door, I don't bother looking back. I got my answer —she doesn't know shit, but unfortunately, it doesn't help me at all.

Instead of leaving, my feet move toward the library. The Librarian is deaf and blind but somehow always knows exactly what's going on in her domain. And more importantly, how to help. I wasted months of my life fearing her, judging her based on what others said.

When I enter, I nearly freeze. Two of my Sisters are whispering in the middle of the room. They turn as one and stare. We should've been able to band together in our misery. But that was the first thing taught at the Weaponry. You never rely on anyone. And certainly not the ones you think you can.

"Anne. Azalea." I nod toward them, wondering if they're going to speak to me. The last time I saw the twins, I tried to tell them I was sorry...for everything that was coming. I was sure they'd receive punishment for my win.

"Oh look. It's the failure. Come back to beg for us to take you in?"

The sweet voice, the innocent posture hides the nastiness, as usual. I don't know why I bother. I wish I could bury the compassionate nature deep inside me and never let it out. It never, ever helps and always makes things worse. Of course, they must've been told I was booted. Well, fuck them for not being smart enough to use their own brains.

I snort. "If by failure you mean I get to live a nice, normal life while you're stuck here. Yes, yes I am. And you couldn't pay me to reside here."

I turn, looking for the librarian, effectively dismissing them. If they are still assholes, then I don't want anything to do with them. They'll die here, chained to the Weaponry and all it stands for.

A rustling sound around the corner is my cue, and I head to one of the many rows of books, until I come to a sudden stop when a book is shoved into my face.

Magical Myths, Memories and More

The tiny black, leather-bound book looks almost exactly like a million other books in this room with one difference. The edges of the pages. There are some specks of gold, and when I rub my thumb over it, black paint or something rubs off, revealing more of the color. I shove it into my pants at the small of my back. No one would dare to get that close to my butterflies. I lift out a book closest to me and hide the wrapped candy behind it. The librarian will sniff them out. She's never acknowledged any of the gifts I've left over the years, and I've never acknowledged her help. Speaking those words out loud would result in a swift death sentence. I've often wondered if there was something she would want or crave, but even though she doesn't communicate, I get a sense

121

that she doesn't mind being here. Sometimes I've left a trinket, sometimes food. But always to let her know she isn't alone. That I see her.

The thought of staying here forever makes me shudder and I quickly leave, heading for the comfort and peace of my car.

I drive far enough away that there's no way anyone from the Weaponry can see me and I pull in on a shoulder. The pages are yellowed with age and so crispy, I'm afraid to turn the paper in case it just crumbles away. There are huge chunks of empty space, as if someone was leaving room for updates or to add more information. What is written down is clearly in code because I don't understand any of it.

I toss the book on my seat and sigh loudly. If only it had been that simple. I'm more than halfway home when the scream startles me after not hearing any for so long. I push the car as fast as she'll go to make it back in time to save someone's goodness. It doesn't take long to sense I'm headed for Blaze's apartment, and I push the pedal down as far as it goes, but it still takes me two more minutes to get there, and a sick sensation twists my insides.

What if I'm too late?

Chapter Sixteen

I blur into the apartment, blades drawn, and nearly choke with anger. They're clearly toying with him. Five shadowy shapes circle him, taking turns. They move in and...and *nibble,* for fuck's sake, on the gold aura that lays like a second layer of his skin, before retreating. His soul continues to scream inside my head, drowning out the city sounds beyond the walls.

His body lays limply on the bed, unmoving, unable to defend himself. And those things are fucking taking advantage of him, the gold-sucking scum. Guilt sits like a stone in my belly. Why did I leave him unprotected? Acid rises from my stomach and rage pours into me. Maybe it's the whisper of my blades or the dark gurgling inside me, ready to spill over, that finally alerts them to my existence. They turn as one and rise above me like inky ghosts. I swivel my wrists, the butterflies slicing through the air.

Bring it, you nasty pieces of shit.

And then the five merge into one large turd. It rises even higher, bending the top of itself so it's angled over me. Acting like it's going to force me to cower in fear is the last mistake it'll ever make. I brace myself, planting my feet and willing them not to move. I can't imagine that when it enters my body from such a height, in this proximity, that I won't at least stagger. And fuck if I'll give that concession.

Instead of trying to merge with me, the Nightmare attacks, a large hand materializing out of its misty shape and clobbering me on the side of my head and shoulder. The move throws me across the room, and I'm left flat on my belly, gasping for air. The shock of the hit reverberates through me, my ear ringing, the telltale tickle of blood trickling down my skin. I waste seconds lying on the ground my mind attempting to process what just happened.

A large fist hits me in the middle of my spine, and my agonizing scream rips through the air. Pain mixed with embarrassment weaves through me, and for a moment, pity too. Why do I always have to get hurt? Haven't I suffered enough? But I finally have the sense to roll away, just as another fist hits the floor, the wooden boards creaking before splintering under the weight. The Terror follows me, its arm elongating, slamming another fist into the floor, and I roll faster.

When I reach the wall, I jump to a standing position, cursing the headrush that accompanies it. I don't have time to get my dizziness under control and my vision back, so I blindly dart back the way I came, hoping I don't run into another punch.

When I've regained my equilibrium, I counterattack, slicing and hitting anything I can reach. Seconds pass as the blades swing seemingly through it. They're not completely futile as the thing howls in pain or irritation, I can't tell which. But if it won't enter me by choice, I'm going to force it, kicking and screaming. My senses expand and the taste of the Nightmare floods my tongue and mouth. Like strange exotic spices, the darkness has a spicy taste, but I focus and blur myself into it.

I'm confused at the familiar sensations, at the memories of siphoning gold that spreads their allure, and my fists clench with need. I force years of muscle memory to kick in, and after fully absorbing into the Terror, of forcing myself to take over and devour all five souls, my hungry cage locks them in. My body trembles with the effort of forcing myself to blur out instead of staying, and I gasp in heaps of clean air, while my arms make slicing motions until it finally disappears, and I vomit all over the floor.

Swiping a hand across my lips, I slowly move toward Blaze. He hasn't moved much if any, and I'm concerned about the color of his gold. I've gotten used to the brightness and cheeriness of the small children I usually save. But his is slightly different. Mature if you could call a color that. Just as shiny and nearly as bright, it pulsates with a different...rhythm? Something I can't quite explain. I don't typically stare at a person long enough to decipher their color. When I come into contact with them, I slay their Nightmares and extricate myself—and the dark growing in me—from their vicinity.

This is different though. It lays on his skin like a sickly version of itself. Not moving much or with any type of beat. It looks feeble, and that scares the shit out of me. It shouldn't look like that.

Guilt nearly drowns me. I shouldn't have left him. I shouldn't have relied on my years of knowledge and thought it would apply here. Nothing has been the same since I met him, and I have a sinking feeling it never will again. What is wrong with me? The days of old are gone, and I nearly snort.

They weren't that great to begin with.

It doesn't take long for me to realize that pull I'm so familiar with, the one I'm always fighting against, is nowhere near its usual size. It's barely there. Was I too late? Did they take too much gold? Does the rest of it die off? I've no experience with the creatures toying with their food or whatever it is to them. And obviously no experience with gold myself, so I don't know if it can repair itself or rejuvenate or whatever the fuck it does when some goes missing.

But I should be able to touch him while keeping myself under control and not be the cause of his golden loss if I don't feel a pull like normal. Right? I have no idea. My hand trembles when it reaches out toward him. I may have told him earlier that I didn't like him, but I lied. He's growing on me, dammit.

Grazing his foot with my fingertips, I'm drawn in toward the spark of gold that leaps from my skin to his aura. I don't move my hand, but bend down, nose almost touching his toes to stare at the light dancing between us. It's like a comical lightning bolt bursting with waning and ever-increasing color. Suddenly, it glows bright, and I turn my face, accidentally placing my hand on his body, and the charge rips through me.

Pleasure and pain spark and rolls down my body. Joy floods me and sadness drowns it. Pure white blinds me, and then darkness settles like a shroud. Panic replaces all thought, and through sheer will, I move my feet backward, one step. Two.

Like a cord stretched between us, I'm being yanked toward him, but I don't allow it, pulling back another step and then another. With a gasp, Blaze shoots up in bed just as I fall down to my knees. The connection, or whatever the fuck that was, is broken.

I'm broken.

I almost killed him. Or me. Or both of us. Fuck. I cradle my head in my hands. I should be killed. Taken out. I can't be trusted to not steal from the very thing I've pledged to protect. I'm a gold thief.

"Arnica?"

The bed rustles and the smallest sounds of the springs reaches my ears. Eucalyptus and lemon waft into my nose before I scramble up, moving faster than he does, almost blurring out of the room in my haste to remove myself from his nearness.

"Are you okay? They came for me didn't they? I didn't mean to fall back asleep."

The words are soft, maybe full of disappointment, I don't know, and I'm not going to listen too closely. I'm going to have to tell him what happened—my role in any extra loss of gold. Guilt nearly blows me back down, but I lock my knees. I don't want to look at his face, see any disgust when he hears the words, but it's what I deserve. I glance up into blue flames dancing in his eyes, and my own widen. The apology dies on my tongue.

The gold slithers and moves over his body as if verifying it is, in fact, whole. It's back to its original beautiful color and beats like a heartbeat in its fluidity.

I don't know what happened, but thank the Fates I didn't slurp it up myself, like some horrific monster. I don't know how he got it back and I don't care. The words pour out of me before I second-guess myself.

"How fast can we complete the wedding ceremony?"

Chapter Seventeen

I f I marry him, I can give him the potion. Shove it down his throat so neither I nor anyone else can steal it.

The electric-blue flames flicker faster in his eyes before dying out, and it's like a shutter closed. The loss of them echoes in me, and I wonder if the soul in my cage is capable of feeling regret.

"Are you hurt?"

I shake my head and point toward the doorway. "I need my rejuvenation. To get rid of this darkness—there's a lot in me right now—and we'll talk."

His stare nearly unnerves me, but I won't even consider casually chatting until I can be sure whatever just happened won't happen again. And I can't do that if there's a shred of doubt about being able to control myself. I keep pointing at the door until he sighs and walks out, closing it softly behind him.

When I lay down, I'm unprepared for the emotions that rise to the surface, thinking I may have lost him, only to know I'm going to do something that will always protect him. And there's something intimate about lying down in a bed that's still warm from their body, their scent in your nostrils. A hot flush flashes through me.

Again, I'm reminded that I may need release before I tackle the journey of getting hitched. It just won't be with the groom. His scent reels me in. The thought of fucking him grabs me.

I reach down and slide my hand under the bands of both leggings and underwear. Even with the battle and shock of nearly killing him, I'm wet with desire. I close my eyes, bringing the memory of his naked body that first day to the fore and insert a finger and then two. His satin pillowcase slides against my cheek when I turn my head, and it takes everything I have not to moan aloud. My other hand cups my breast and I pinch a nipple, softly tugging, wishing his lips were doing the same. I don't have time for a leisurely orgasm, and instead of playing with my nipples, I gently rub my clit, both hands comically under my clothes. But that's the advantage of stretch material.

A sigh whispers out of my mouth as the orgasm builds and crests. I hope that now I can concentrate on protecting Blaze. And not banging Blaze.

My eyes flutter shut and the colors swirl quickly and brightly, whisking away the dregs like they're short on time. My body feels lighter, and sleep drops over me.

I'm floating on a cloud. It's warm and comforting. The slight scent of lemon and spice, of male skin and sex sends shivers down my spine. The dreams fill up my head, crowding me with visions and thoughts I've never seen. Blaze striding down the aisle, clearly getting married. Blaze playing with two little kids, lovingly staring up at me, each one a replica of him. Joy spreads throughout me, and there's an ache in my chest at the cozy domesticated scenes. My heart beats faster. Blaze moving above me, his forearms plastered to either side of my shoulders. His scent becomes stronger until every breath is full of him. Waves of happiness flow through me as we snuggle in a big, inviting bed.

I gasp and kick out, connecting the side of my knee and thigh to a set of abs.

"OOF." Blaze bends over double, clutching his stomach. "Damn that's a hard side kick. Even in your sleep."

"What is wrong with you? I've told you repeatedly not to touch me, and you think you can while I'm asleep? Do you have no sense of self-preservation? At all?" The waves recede, and I'm left with guilt and the sudden urge to kick him while he's down. To stop him from getting closer to me, figuratively and literally. It's too much.

I don't bother to ask him if he's all right. Not only does he deserve it, but maybe if he gets a small taste of pain he won't do it again. I roll my eyes. If he only grasped the idea of what would happen if I took his soul. Let him think I'm heartless. I don't mind being the bad guy—especially if it will keep his soul intact.

"I'm gonna shower."

I hop over a couple of holes in the floorboards and grab my spare bag I brought from the car and stroll into his bathroom. The towels are fluffy, and the soap is thick, but unless I want to smell like golden boy, I'm not using any of his stuff. I'll only end up wanting him more. Another great reason for keeping my own shit with me at all times.

The hot spray moves around any lingering soap and shampoo on the tiles and it's like a fucking aromatherapy session got started in here. Doesn't his staff clean the bathroom? Eucalyptus floats on the air and settles on my skin. Damn. I scrub harder with my own soap, but when I sniff the air right above my forearm, the scent is still there. It reminds me of the visions while I slept, and I frown. Do all people dream so vividly? Sleeping once a year doesn't give me the opportunity for dreaming, or if I do, I don't remember them. But I've now slept three times in three days and remember everything I saw.

There's a tug low in my belly at the memory of some of them, and I'm surprised to identify it as yearning. I can't possibly want a family? Kids? I shudder hard, the sensation skittering up my spine. Is it fear? Or envy? Nothing is making sense. I scrunch up my eyes and tilt my face into the hard spray, letting it pound out the emotions, the homey scenes, until all I can focus on is the hot water and my lungs screaming for air. I push my limits until I think I might die.

I finally fling my head back, gulping in oxygen. And nearly scream aloud. Blaze stands on the other side of the glass wall, hand poised to knock. He quickly turns around and walks toward the door.

"I'm sorry. I knocked and hollered because I was gonna order pizza, but you didn't respond, and when I came in your head was underwater. And I noticed that massive bruise on your back and I was going to ask you if you were okay, but then you stayed under the spray for too long. I was...worried... about—" He sighs. "I don't know what I was worried about."

He's babbling. And embarrassed. A light shade of red. And cute as fuck. Oh, shit. The self-maintenance did nothing for me. And everything for him. Instead of satiating some of my horniness, all I did was stoke the embers. I turn off the water and pull down the towel I hung up.

The towel's ridiculously luxurious on my skin, and I put effort into scrubbing myself dry. He's worried about me more times in the last couple of days than I have by anyone in the last thirteen years. And it's causing a soft spot in me for him and that's dangerous. I push my cloth-laden fists into my chin and rest on it for a moment, the material hanging in front of me, nearly long enough to brush the floor.

"Thank you."

I could probably count on one hand how many times anyone had warranted those words from me in the same time frame. "And pizza would be great, but let me order from a place I know. That way we know it'll be edible when it gets here."

Chapter Eighteen

"This isn't edible!"

Blaze yelps, his mouth hanging open while he fans it.

"Sure it is. Pizza's only salvation is when it's so hot the cheese slides off when you lift it and then it burns the roof of your mouth."

We're sitting in his living room, steam wafting from four boxes of the best delivery pizza this far south of New York.

"I think I'll wait till it drops several hundred degrees, thanks." He wipes his mouth with a paper napkin, grease quickly seeping into the crepey stuff.

I shrug. "Suit yourself. We need to discuss this whole marriage thing. When do we do it. Where? What ceremonies need to take place? Will there be an audience?"

"Luckily, there's a Magical that can marry us, right here in the city—that part is simple. And there's no audience. The hard part is...the Fasting."

I choke on a piece of crust and wave off the concern on his face. I know how to use a chair to give myself the Heimlich, if it boils down to that, but it takes two bottles of water before I stop the hard coughing and the tickle in my throat.

"We have a problem. There's no way I can fast. For any length of time."

He nods, a blue fire glimmering in his eyes. "It's part of the trust process. You need to trust me to provide you with food."

"Excuse me?" My throat hurts from the coughing, but I can't help laughing. "You haven't really been managing to provide food for yourself, let alone me."

"I'm not sure it's an actual fast. I think it's more about the...symbolism. That I'm worthy of providing for the Matriarch. But I don't know. There's no record of it, and nobody discusses it because of the nature of the Fast. I'm guessing it's also different for every couple."

I snort. The idea is preposterous and antiquated. I can provide for my own damn self.

"It doesn't matter. If it's a real fast...well, the problem lies in the actual fasting. I can't do it. My metabolism burns through fuel at a rate that would astonish you."

"You don't say?"

He eyes the three empty boxes as he finishes his first slice.

"I'm serious."

"So am I. It's not negotiable. The ceremony won't start without it. The tattoos won't burn into our skin without the evidence of trust."

"How long is this Fast?"

Maybe I can stockpile on calories and hope I last however long the fucking Magical requirements are. The potion could help hide so many do-gooders, in addition to Blaze. And I'm supposed to be the best at protecting them. This means doing whatever it takes. That's the only reason I'm doing this.

"Until you trust me to feed you. I honestly don't know. The fast is different for everyone."

My stomach drops. There's no easy way out of it then. "I

guess you're gonna have to carry me down the aisle. 'Cause I won't be conscious."

Is that sadness that flits across his face? There's no way this means so much to him. I don't mean anything to him. Just a means to an end. Saving his own ass. A couple of days ago, I would've thought that selfish. But not so long ago, I would've considered it survival. How is it that I became so judgmental in things that I did myself? I have no room to talk.

"It's not a reflection of you. It's an unfortunate side effect of my existence."

If it's possible, his face falls even more, and I bite my lip. I don't know how to reassure him, so I stand up and wash my hands in the kitchen, using the action to get out of trying to be nice. Clearly, it's not working.

Blaze's cell rings and a conversation ensues. The hospital staffer on the other end is whiny and annoying. I've forgotten he's the CEO and probably has to deal with a ton of shit like that. Why in Karma's name would she call him to discuss the discipline of a surgeon though? That falls under Human Resources. It sounds more like the unknown female on the other end wants an excuse to call him and vent. Or maybe just to call him. My eyes narrow. Is she an ex? A friend? An old lover?

The sour emotion burns in me unexpectedly and I jerk.

Get your shit together.

I'm already acting like a jealous wife or lover.

Ew.

My head tilts as I study him. His response, quiet and firm, simultaneously treats her with respect while probably secretly rolling his eyes. He's got to be, right? There's no way his good-ness is *that* good that he can listen to that drivel without once thinking it's stupid. Can it? I've never spent a lot of time with anyone who had even a glimmer of an aura for fear I would strip them of it. If their life was this mundane, I wasn't missing anything.

But the man underneath the aura might be someone I'd like. Even being the exact opposite of me, I think I could get used to that gentle confidence. My breath catches in my throat. Since when does authority, no matter how sexily packaged, sound attractive or worse, something I might crave? Horror rolls through me. Maybe it wasn't the food that was drugged here, but the air?

Oh shit.

The possibility makes me fully open my senses, every single one. GPS, heat signature, and energy tracker. The ability to analyze all the data quickly. My activated hearing, taste, smell, and vision assault me. I'm overloaded and stagger the few steps to the stool, falling into it.

Blaze's, "I have to call you back, Olivia," and the slide of the phone into his pocket reverberates through me. His footsteps pound in my brain and I clap my hands over my ears. The woman faking her way through sex three floors down echoes loudly in my head. A bird pulling up a worm—it's squeaking its own protest, elongating its body—is like nails on a chalkboard.

The intricate fibers of a piece of dust mote against the chaotic background of the paint on his walls forces my eyes closed.

I rarely open myself in a setting where there are so many people and so many sounds in the vicinity, and even more rarely, fully. My system attempts to categorize, process, and prioritize every motion and decibel.

Sweat beads on my forehead and slides down my back as I focus on each thing. My body trembles as I deplete my energy, and the calories from the pizza dissipate as if they'd never been there at all. But I have to continue.

Blaze's voice, loud in my ear, finally disappears as I move

on to the next systemic item. When I shut off those senses I don't need, when I mute the ones I use in everyday situations, until there's blessed silence and normal vision, I lift my head, knowing that I'm paler than normal. That my eyes seem large in my face, haunted even. That my breathing is shallow and faint. That my body has shut down all but the necessary bodily functions to conserve energy.

A cloudy bottle of water appears in front of me, and I weakly drink the liquid. The energy output requires far, far more than this, but it stops me from feeling like I'm going to pass out on the floor.

He's stripping off the familiar wrapping from a granola bar and quickly opening the next one as I shove the first one in my mouth.

"I took the liberty of going through your bag when I noticed your blood sugar dropping. Is this what I have to deal with when we Fast? I hope it's not really about food."

I don't bother to respond but help him rip off the wrapping from three high-protein bars. Once I'm done eating them all and my body feels solidly here once more, I punch the counter.

Ever since I met him, everything's been fucked up. I rushed into checking for danger without taking the time for any precautions. I didn't think about the fact that I would need calories, that I can't rely on much that's here. I didn't think at all.

And not thinking, scoping out the probabilities, keeping detached and calm almost fucking killed me. Again.

Have I not learned that feeding off emotions, of reacting blindly is the most dangerous thing I can do?

Now I have to keep a close eye on Blaze and on myself. Double check my actions, second-guess myself. And protect everyone else. How much can one person take? I've always been broken, something wrong deep down inside. I lost my sister when I gave her my soul. But Angelica had been pure and good and my soul, black as it was, no matter how hard I tried to be good, poisoned her. Just like arnica does. I poison everything, including myself. Fuck.

Have I not paid the price for that many times over? Has the Weaponry not done its duty?

I'll have to marry this man, in order to do the best I can for humanity, to atone to the best of my ability. Stay close to the one possible thing I want and can't have. A soul coated in gold, shimmering with its ability to do for others without pain —simply because they want to. Much as I need to, I can't keep the emotions from rolling through me, draining me even more.

"No. I just haven't been eating enough and I was...trying to figure out if your home was being drugged. Like something in the air."

A frown creases his forehead, and he looks around as if he could possibly see something here.

"I couldn't sense anything, so we don't have to worry about that at least. But we do have to seriously stock up on food. Or..." Did I want him at my house? In my sanctuary?

"Or be stuck getting delivery all the time." Soon-to-be husband or not, I'm not willing to share my personal space. Yet.

We're on the way to the grocery store when the insistent buzz of Blaze's cell becomes super annoying. But he doesn't even glance at it. His face nearly pressed against the window looks like he's lost in thought.

"I think someone is trying to get a hold of you."

"Hm? Oh. Hello?"

Even without superior hearing, I wince at the loud hysteria in the woman's voice, and I bang a sharp, illegal U-turn in the middle of the road to the honking of several drivers. I flip them my middle finger and keep going.

"Thanks. Just pull up in the Emergency lane and I'll make sure you don't get towed." He's already jumping out of the car, and I wave him off. I'm sure I'm capable of finding him. There's no way I'm leaving my baby where she can get nicked by ambulances, so I drive around to the parking garage and use my regular entrance.

Following the signs toward the Emergency Room, I stop by a vending machine and grab some packets of nuts until I can get something else in me. The closer I get, the louder the woman's screeching becomes, and I nearly mute my own hearing to save my sanity. Really, she probably just needs a good slap in the face, but I know such things would get me tossed out.

I stiffen when Blaze puts his arm around her shoulders and guides her to an office where he shuts the door. The group of people who had been standing around in the hopes of seeing some kind of drama unfold, disperse.

I nonchalantly stroll to the door, but it seems I've been locked out. I turn up my hearing and stiffen.

"I don't know. She went completely crazy. She's always been the nicest person in Surgery, but now she's just a total bitch. But the last straw was when she decided she wasn't going to finish the patient she was working on and went to take a nap!"

"Olivia. I promise I will take care of it. Please take the rest of the day off and tomorrow too. We will be firing her posthaste and she'll be escorted off the premises."

I step aside as Olivia runs out, chest heaving, and then lean against the doorjamb. "Who's getting fired and why couldn't your staff take care of it?" I don't understand why Blaze needed to be here.

"Dr. Desben...used to be nice and thoughtful." He frowns, eyebrows scrunching together, his jaw set. It's obvious he doesn't like what happened. He sighs softly. "Not anymore though. It's a shame."

I jerk at the name. She was one of the docs I didn't bother approaching as my personal emergency carer because she didn't have a streak of the dark in her that I needed. My eyes narrow and I push off the wood. But there's also no way she had a golden aura. I'd have seen it.

"What happened to her?"

At his sigh, guilt whips through me as my suspicions are confirmed.

"She's one of mine. A Healer."

"I swear to you, I never heard her scream. Or I would have protected her."

She had to have had her gold cloaked by whatever potion the Magical had because I also never saw a golden aura. Anger replaces guilt, and suddenly I can't take this shit anymore. The past days seem intent on ruining any peace I'd built for myself in the last several years. I'm a kick-ass Nightmare Killer, excellent at my job. There isn't anyone better than me. I'm faster, deadlier than all the other Killers. I've survived and made the best life I can with what I was given. Now, my world's crumbling apart, and the only reason it's doing so stands in front of me.

"Ever since I met you, everything's wrong. You're the common denominator."

Flames flicker in his eyes and his jaw sets, a muscle jumping. "Don't lash out at me because you're feeling incompetent."

Chapter Nineteen

Red tinges my vision and my hands visibly shake. I step back and pivot on my heel. I have to leave or I'm going to strangle him with my bare hands and show him how competent my skills truly are.

"Arnica!"

His words drown away as I move quickly through the building. He follows me, but I know the hospital and all its corridors and staff sections better than he does and I lose him.

The Ferrari does nothing for my mood, even though I take her out on the highway and push her as fast as her stock is capable of going. I speed past commuters and police officers who attempt to give chase, but my car has been modified far beyond her specifications, and I quickly lose them all. I end up at the coast, an hour and a half drive that should've taken four.

Staring at the sand dune, memories pour through me. I'd forgotten about this place. About the summers I'd spent here with my family. Sun-drenched days filled with laughter and ice cream, seafood and fries. Mom and Dad, Angelica and me.

Before the shadows entered my life. Before my sister died.

I rip off my boots and socks and storm out. By the time

I've stomped halfway through the sand, I'm staggering. It's too soft to walk in anger, and I probably look like a fool. I drop to my knees when I get to the wave-sodden sand and dig my fingers in. The ocean laps at my hands, and when I lift them, the wet mess runs through. I can't hold it any more than I can hold my tears, and for the first time in years, I let them run unchecked.

I haven't allowed myself to feel pity, since the day I realized that the more I cried and railed at the Weaponry, the harder I tried to do what I was told, the more I failed and the more gleeful the Mother would become and would administer punishments. That moment of clarity when I was bloody and beaten, when my Sisters and Brothers in our warped Family, as they called themselves, eyed me with hatred and vengeance, when I realized that no one was going to help me but me. That I was in charge of my own destiny. And that I could be whatever I wanted to be...after I figured out how the fuck to leave.

I wanted to be the best. Show them I was better. Show them they were wrong. But maybe the best isn't what I'm meant to be.

The waves retreat and rush forward again. Over and over. The symbol of endless energy, of endless consistency and repetition. Sometimes, the tides are low; sometimes, the tides are high. But the water is always moving. Fuck.

I have to make a choice. I can sit still in the same space or move forward. Reinvent myself again. Recapture the essence of what I am and try to do the best I can for that moment in time. I hate failure. And I despise feeling sorry for myself. There's really no choice to make at all. Forward it is.

Now that I've made a decision, unreasonably, indecision plagues me. Do I go to the hospital or to Blaze's house? Shit. I'm an idiot. I'm all, sure I'll marry you, but the only thing I do is worry about food and being horny? About being the best at everything I do? If I thought beating myself up over this is worthwhile, I'd do it, but clearly that's not worked in the past.

I have no idea what his phone number is, where he'd likely be or what his schedule is. I know nothing about him, and he knows nothing about me. It's about time to rectify that.

After stopping at my house for a quick shower to remove the sand and tears, I load a cooler full of the perishables from my fridge. There's not much left, but it'll tide me over until we finally go shopping.

Parking the Ferrari at his apartment, I take my time going up. There's no heat signature on his level, which means I picked wrong, but if I head to the hospital, I might miss him coming here, so I'll just wait. Maybe figure out how to eloquently apologize for my abrupt departure. I don't say sorry often, and when I do, it's always stilted and awkward. Rarely saying it hasn't helped improve the delivery.

I'm just finishing emptying his fridge of everything, cleaning it out and replacing it, adding my meager food haul, when a car door slams shut and I peek out the window. There's a limo out front, and I'm sure that's his ride. And here I worried about how he was going to get home. I snort and step back when the driver comes around and quickly settle myself on the couch. There are books to read, but I'm not the sit at home, drop into a fictional world sort. The elevator dings and I whip out my blade, using the tip to pretend to clean out my fingernails.

My jaw drops as the driver, Blaze, and another burly man who looks suspiciously like he stepped out of an FBI building, walk in, all three of them carrying about six to seven bags of groceries on each arm. The meme about never carrying groceries, 'but when I do, I take every bag in one trip' floats through my mind, and I bite my lip to keep from grinning. They do look kind of ridiculous.

They deposit the bags on the counter and, though the

alphabet man narrows his eyes at me and my blade, the two men leave without saying a word, leaving Blaze and me and a shit ton of groceries alone in the apartment.

Did I think I could actually do this without being awkward? I clear my throat and move to stand, but Blaze puts up his hand. "You never let me finish what I'm going to say."

"I'm sorry," I blurt out quickly before he continues. I'm not going to let the do-gooder take all the blame. I can be nice, too.

A smile lifts his lips, and it's as if the sun came out and shone on me in a dark room. I can't possibly be happy that he's happy with me? What the fuck is wrong with me?

"You still don't let me finish. I wasn't implying that you were incompetent. I just meant that you were lashing out at the wrong person for what you were experiencing emotionally. Because it's not my fault. And it's also not your fault. Your world isn't the only one changing. There are so many things going wrong that I don't even know where to begin."

He starts unloading the grocery bags and, curious as to what he bought, I come to help him. It's the least I can do.

"I'm not used to...people." I wave my hand, making a shooing motion. I'm not used to words either, apparently. "I don't like people." Ugh. "I mean, both those things are accurate but not what I want to say."

I stare at the jar of pickles, mayonnaise, ketchup, relish, and mustard. Why do people need these things? A waste of space, honestly. I shrug. It's his money and food. The next bag reveals protein bars, protein powder, and protein cookies. People like their desserts way too much.

"This protein powder any good?" It's a new brand that I'd been meaning to try, but every time I went to the store, they were out of stock.

"I don't know, I don't use that stuff. But the stocker told me that it's in high demand, so I got it for you. I didn't know what kind you usually get. Or what protein products you like, so I just picked random ones that looked good. There's a couple of other items in here somewhere. If you don't like it, we can return it. Or donate it. I can buy other ones."

He rustles around in a couple of bags, searching for whatever he wants to show me. Warmth pools in my chest. He bought this for me? Even after I took off? The ache builds in my chest again, making it feel like it's going to burst open. My throat thickens.

"That's the nicest thing anyone has ever done for me."

He stops perusing the groceries and stands still. Blue flames erupt in his eyes, and I don't know why I can't stop staring at them. The warmth continues to spread through me, and to my horror, I just know my cheeks are pink. I blink rapidly, focusing on his hands fisted into the plastic bag.

"What kind of life have you lived that picking up some groceries that take your tastes into consideration is something unique?"

Probably not the kind that he can fathom, and it doesn't matter. It just matters that he did this—for me. I shake my head. He doesn't need to know the things he can't do anything about.

"How did you know what to get? After stupidly leaving you, I came to the conclusion we don't know anything about each other. I don't even have your phone number."

He motions with his hand. "Give me your cell. I'll program it in." I lay it on the counter and slide it over to him. "Every time we eat, you consume a lot of calories, but almost half is protein. Chicken, cheese. I figure you need it. Plus, I *am* a Healer. I do know that you need high protein and high fat to combat a high metabolism that burns through calories."

He pays attention to details. And he likes taking care of people. And he's considerate. And hot. And I'm going to be married to him, no matter how briefly.

I'm screwed.

You'd think I'd be used to torture. But torture was never packaged this temptingly. After we put away the groceries, Blaze rolls up his shirt sleeves and begins making dinner, and I sit at the counter watching in fascination. The way the muscles bunch in his forearms and biceps while chopping mushrooms, the way he handles the knife and rubs spices on the meat. I'm most definitely screwed.

After eating a dinner of steak, roasted potatoes that have a crispy skin and a soft center, and sauteed mushrooms and onions, I nearly moan with ecstasy. The man can cook, too. I'm royally fucked, and I'd be thrilled if I actually could be. But there's no way I'll get that lucky. I sigh.

"Everything okay?"

Oh, yeah. "Mm, the food was perfect."

He beams and begins washing dishes, waving me off when I protest. "After this, I think we should go ahead and start."

I jerk. Start what? Did I say I wanted to be fucked out loud?

"There are only a few words. I'll need to formally ask you to marry me, and you'll need to formally accept. Then the Fasting can begin at any time. Neither one of us will know when it starts."

My face pales. There's nothing worse than anticipation of something unknown. Panic rolls through me. This isn't like the Weaponry though, and no one's planning on hurting me.

I breathe deeply and evenly, attempting to curb my fear. Blaze wouldn't harm me. No one can. I won't let anyone hurt me ever again.

"Sure."

I can do this. I'm fucking Arnica, the best Nightmare Killer the Dreamers had ever seen.

Chapter Twenty

We're in the living room again, and the coffee table has been miraculously replaced. I'll have to remember to ask Blaze, who does it all. I'm not comfortable letting just anyone in here now that my own food supply might be corrupted. But he looks so serious and solemn, and I know now's not the time to ask.

"That place you went to earlier. Did they answer your questions?"

I snort. "No one at the Weaponry really answers questions. I should've known better than to go there in the first place."

There's a soft gasp as his eyes flame, then smolder. "You went to the Weaponry?"

What the fuck does he know about it? "Yes."

"You shouldn't have gone there alone. Something could've happened to you and—"

"Nothing would've happened. I used to live there. If I didn't make it out alive, I don't deserve to."

His eyes widen, and too late, I realize I've told him more

about myself than I ever wanted to. Shit. All the relaxation has fled, and I stand up and pace the room.

"There's a lot I don't know about that place, but the things I do know... I'm sorry. For everything you must have endured."

I don't want his pity. Or his apologies.

"I'm fine. I survived."

"Survival doesn't mean you're fine. Let me heal you."

Anger rifles through me. I'm not a patient of his.

"You can't heal me, Blaze. There's nothing inside of me but holes. Put in a dark soul, and I'm full of black shards forming the very thing I kill. Take it out, and I'm a bunch of puzzle pieces that don't fit right. No amount of healing will fix me."

"I don't want to *fix* you. I want to heal the wounds inside you. Remove the pain. Soothe your scars."

"I don't have scars. I'm a fast healer, remember?" I shrug. Why won't he let it go?

"Not ones on your skin, but the ones so deep within you, you don't even know are there."

"You can't heal those, either. You think I don't know about them? That they were put there by others? No. I've caused them all. Every one a reminder that I'm soulless, unlovable. I'm okay with that. It keeps people safe from me."

Blaze steps up to me, his face mere inches away, blue eyes like the ocean with a storm raging above it.

"You may have no soul, but you're far from soulless. I've seen you put yourself in danger to protect me time and time again."

I shake my head. "It's my job—"

"Bullshit."

Blaze just cursed. What is happening here?

"You want people to think you're a badass, but really you're a softie, with a heart bigger than your blades."

I hiss. Did he just call me a fucking *softie*?

I lean back. I can't think when I'm around him, and I won't risk him.

He steps forward. "What are you so afraid of?"

I snort. If only it was that easy. Fears can be broken. Molded to the shape of you until they are a second skin, part of you in ways that can be controlled by you.

"I'm not afraid. I can handle fear, whip it into submission. Control myself. Fuck fear."

"I'd rather you not."

I almost laugh. His dry one-liners are unexpected. I back away and turn around.

"There's definitely something wrong with me. I will always take what I want, even if that's not good for you, for humanity. There's something irreparable inside me. I was this way even when I had my own soul. It's why my training took so long. Always wanting more at the least touch. So much *more,* it consumes me and that's all I can think about." I whisper the last words, hating them. What the fuck am I doing? Exposing my weakness like an untrained killer.

I don't need to open my senses to feel the heat of him as he comes closer. I scrunch up my eyes and ball my fists. What have I done to the Fates that they keep testing me over and over?

"You tell me you can control yourself though. To me that means that whatever you think is broken inside you desperately wants to mend."

If only he was right. But it's my own willpower that keeps me from doing so. And it taunts me every day. What happens when I can no longer direct it?

Blaze's breath moves the wisps that have escaped my bun. I stand rigidly and wrap my willpower around me.

I will not steal his soul. I refuse.

"May I touch you?"

I nearly shudder at his words. What would it be like to have someone do so because they want to? Not in anger or in lessons. Not humans with very little redeeming qualities because they're safer from me. And not because I've seduced them to scratch my own itch. But of their own violation, their own need to touch me.

Need and want fill me with warmth, rushing over my skin, lifting hairs until I'm tingling all over. I inhale and nod, pulling the strands of my will tighter around me like a fucking impenetrable coating. A damn prison for my body's curse. But I can do this. I *want* to do this.

His fingers trail along my neck, so softly most would barely feel it. But I do. Fuck. The tears of ecstasy gather in my eyes, and I squeeze them tighter. My nerve endings burn as his skin caresses mine. Emotions, unrecognizable, fill me up.

Blaze slowly walks around me, fingers seductively moving over my tank top and down my shoulder. I bite my lip and swallow the gasp that wants to escape.

I will not steal his soul. I will not steal his soul.

"Open your eyes, Arnica."

I shake my head. I can't. I've seen his naked body. I've wanted it. I've wanted *him*. I can't risk taking him. All of him, body and soul. And I'm very much afraid that if I watch him stroke me, watch the desire deepen those expressive eyes, I'm going to devour him.

He continues down my arm to my fingers and starts back up again. A moan rumbles in my throat, and my body trembles. I focus on my will, my only shield.

I will not steal his soul.

His thumb grazes my lower lip, and I finally let it go, his finger sliding across the wetness left behind.

My eyes pop open and I gaze into blue fire dancing in front of mine. The heat of skin, the look in his eyes and the desire flushed on his cheeks, breaks my concentration as I knew it would.

My breath huffs out in a pant. My nipples tighten and I inhale hard. Karma, I want him.

I will not steal his soul.

I jerk slightly, attempting to move back, but Blaze's hand moves from my lip to the side of my face, cradling it. My eyes flutter closed, and I sigh. Heat rolls through me in an odd mixture of hunger and satiety. I want to fuck him, but I also want to stay here, just like this forever. The tenderness with which he holds me, never stopping. Just the two of us suspended in time. I can do this. I *am* doing it.

"It's okay. *You're* okay." His voice sounds like liquid honey.

Maybe it is. Maybe I can have both. I lean my face into his hand, inhaling the scent of lemon and cedar. I *can* do this. I press a small kiss into his palm, my tongue darting out, tasting his skin.

And my body erupts.

The need to fucking *take*, to slide up against him, throw him down and straddle him whispers through my mind. The tug pulls me in. He's mine.

I move forward and push him into the wall, my lips capturing his. They're firm and soft and everything I thought they would be. Sparks rip into the air, but sexual attraction *should* be this way. His hands trail down my back and over my ass, pulling me to him with desperation. He's hard, his erection arrowing heat through me.

The ache between my legs intensifies until all I can think about is him pulling me off, flipping me over, and ramming his dick into me, fast and hard, his hips pumping against my ass cheeks, my hands fisting on the edge of the counter.

YES!

I nip his lip and line kisses down his jaw, his stubble rough under my mouth. Fuck, yes! He moans and frames my head, pulling me back to his lips, kissing me with a ferocity I didn't expect but sure hoped for.

I inhale deeply, his scent drenching my nose, flowing into my mouth, he tastes so sweet. Like nectar on a honeysuckle. Warm and intoxicating. Sparks sizzle and I sigh, sucking on his lower lip. A strange silkiness soothes my mouth.

NO!

I rip myself away and lean over, hands planted on my thighs, panting.

The whisper of his body sliding to the floor echoes loudly in my ears. I back away to the far end of the room. He's nearly gray but breathing. I watch as color slowly returns to his pale face. For a long moment, my heart stutters in my chest. And the gold leaks back out of his body, enveloping him, and retreats to his skin, giving it a warm glow. I slump to the floor.

I'm broken beyond repair. I know this and I keep hoping it's not true.

Wanting it to not be true does not make it so.

Chapter Twenty-One

He sits up carefully and scoots closer to me. Reaching for me. I ogle him for a second before I shove myself farther away, sliding to the floor myself. My legs can't seem to hold me up.

"Is there something wrong with you? Are you trying to get me to hurt you again?"

"You didn't hurt me. And I'm capable of healing myself too, you know."

His gold aura shimmers brightly before dimming again. Is that what it was doing? It doesn't matter—he shouldn't have needed it to. Did I take some of his gold? I don't feel different though, so maybe I did imagine those sparks.

"But you were...gray. Not a good color on anyone."

"It's fine. I'm fine. I promise. Speaking of which."

Suddenly, he sits up on one knee in front of me, and for a moment, butterflies wing around my stomach and I remind myself this isn't real. He isn't asking me to marry me because he loves me, but because he needs protection from me. And I'm not reciprocating love. I'm marrying him so that I can protect him and people like him. I want to cry at the irony of it all.

He holds out the tear he'd made me, the promise shimmering on a golden-coated black strand, and says, "Arnica. Would you do me the greatest honor of marrying me, of becoming the Matriarch of the Healers? I promise to provide for you, everything you need and desire."

He never can, but that's okay. I don't think the ceremonial words are all about specifics.

I stare into his face. The slight blond stubble growing back after he shaved yesterday. The blue of his eyes moving like flames in a fire. His hair on his head curls slightly in his own version of a halo, and his gold aura emanates from his skin like an inner glow. His lips part, but he doesn't say anything. Does he worry I'm going to decline? It's almost ridiculous.

The rich Healer, used to having others jump at his command, the do-gooder who has his world at his fingertips begging me, my family's deepest regret, the black sheep, the rule breaker, to be his wife. The one who just tried to steal his golden soul from him. Two people who were never suited to each other to the point that we are complete and utter opposites.

"Yes. I accept. It's my honor and my pleasure to become the next Matriarch."

He stands up quickly and steps forward, bending down and placing the necklace around my neck once more. My stomach flip-flops, and the tear burns against my chest, but the pull isn't there anymore or I don't pay any attention to it. Finally, my selfishness shows some restraint. Or maybe I'm just too disgusted with myself.

There's a tugging sensation on the thread, and I glance up into the deepest blue flames I've yet to see in his eyes.

"I tied it in a magical knot. You won't be able to take it off again. My promise is permanent."

His breath moves across my face, and I close my eyes. I have no business wanting any of the things I want to do right now. Not if I want to keep him safe.

"Thank you." He better not thank me just yet.

"Uh, you're welcome."

I crawl over and push up onto the couch, twisting my hands in my lap. I've never been so idle in recent years, and I'm fidgety. I don't want to talk anymore about what happened. I refuse to acknowledge the tingle of my lips or how badly I burned when I kissed his. Anything but that.

"How long till we Fast? Does it start now?"

"I have no idea. But we can go talk to the Magical I was telling you would marry us tomorrow and see if he has any insight."

We talk, stilted conversation at first. I'm not used to talking to someone so much, let alone about any personal things. Blaze asks questions nobody has ever cared to know about and that I don't have the answers to.

"What do you mean you don't have a favorite movie?" He sounds frustrated, and I wonder if he thinks I'm withholding information. I shrug, but at the same time, it bothers me that he might think that.

"It's not like I had time when I was at the Weaponry. And since then, I've been busy. You know, protecting people like you."

His eyes widen and a flame erupts and darkens in them. If I was a normal person, I would be scared of the violence I see in them. That can't be right. Golden boy can't possibly be capable of being mean. But his fists clench and a muscle moves at his jawline. Butterflies float about in my stomach.

Stop it.

I can't keep thinking every damn thing he does is a turn-on or I'm never going to survive this marriage. I shrug again.

"It's okay. I don't feel like I'm missing much, and I happen to *like* my life."

There. Now he'll stop feeling whatever it is that's he's feeling and making little movements that make me want to lick him.

Blaze nearly chokes on his drink. "What do you mean you like your life? As far as I can tell, you don't have any fun, you don't eat but the most basic things, you don't have any pleasure in life on any scale. What kind of life is that?"

I stiffen. How dare he think his way is better? Not every one of us gets the luxury of sitting around and just having ourselves a good 'ole time.

"First off, kicking the ass of some Nightmare piece of shit is *exhilarating*. And I love protein, okay? And there's only so many ways to cook it. Plus, it literally fuels me. You think a body like this comes naturally?" His eyes follow my hands as I run them down the sides of my tight torso and dammit, no, I won't pretend they're his hands stroking me. "And also, I get pleasure. Lots of *fucking* pleasure." I'm careful to enunciate the word. "I can't count how many orgasms I get. I have a high sex drive and no problem getting laid. And *fucking* is always fun." I'm nearly panting and trying desperately not to get in his face. Killers always control their emotions. And I don't have any at all. Or I didn't until I met Blaze.

Get a hold of yourself!

But for some reason, it's important that I'm more than a mindless killer. That he thinks I'm more than that. I clench my teeth to stop more nonsensical words from spewing out of my mouth. I don't need his approval. I don't need anyone's. That shit stopped when I learned not to bow to the demands put upon me. When I learned I could be my own person. And that I needed no one's approval except mine. Fuck. I hate how quickly my self-assuredness seems to vanish with a few innocuous questions from a confident man.

I raise my hand to forestall any more words from him, and I use the late hour as a flimsy excuse.

"It's bedtime for you, sleeping beauty. But don't worry, I'll make sure no one takes your goodness. And I'll have a shit ton of fun doing it."

He frowns, those lines forming on his brow, and I know it's been all the curse words he hates being used. Good. He needs to know who I am. And take me as I am. 'Cause like it or not, we're gonna be hitched for a while, and I'm not going to walk around and pretend I'm some ladylike sheep.

Bleh, instead I'll be watching him sleep and battling my own desire for him—like any proper...pervert. Ugh. I stand abruptly and stomp away before I throw out any more double entendres his way. Stupid, stupid double meanings. Plopping myself in the chair, I bring my knee up and loop my arms around it. Keep it casual. Nothing weird about any of this.

Once Blaze gets ready for bed, he stands at the side of it, an indistinguishable look on his face.

"You know, you can lay in bed with me. I'll even wear some clothes while sleeping, if it makes you more comfortable."

Blaze's whisper floats on the air, causing the hairs on my neck to stand up. No, it damn well doesn't make any of this easier. Fuck. I swallow hard and clear my throat before the huskiness of my voice betrays my wants. Why must he be so nice? Especially after my outburst? Keep it professional, for fuck's sake.

"No, I don't sleep on the job."

There's a sigh, and I close my eyes at the whisper of his clothes dropping to the ground. I don't need any more reminders of what I'm missing.

My foot gets tingly, and I switch it with the other, leaning my cheek on the top of my knee. This has all-around been the strangest experience. I've only done a few jobs outside my norm of reacting to screams. I haven't had the time to do much else. Hunt Nightmares. Kill Nightmares. That's been my life. When I can, I grab the first willing sexual partner after coercion and drinks. The people I've slept with have never had a conscience. Have never been considered good people. But that's all I've been able to have. The few times I hadn't, I'd been far too caught up in making sure I didn't suck out their soul that I didn't have nearly as much *fun* as I'd alluded to. Fun, but not fun.

My eyesight, always excellent, improves even more as I adjust to the darkened room. The blanket has been thrown back, and that insanely sheer sheet lies across his very naked body.

I groan quietly and get up, moving out of the bedroom. There's no way I can continue to sit in there without either jumping him or worrying about my apparent creepiness.

Several hours pass as I sit in the quiet of the living room. I don't know what to do with all this time. Years of constant fighting for first survival and then work has whittled me down till I'm a hollow version of the person I once was. None of the things on his shelf tempt me, and I pull out the thin black book from the Weaponry from my bag and flip through the pages again.

My heart races as it becomes obvious that some of the empty spaces have become more filled in. Something has changed to make it so. Is it time away from the awful stench of bodies that have sold their souls? Has it been under some kind of spell? Magic and all the intricacies of it are beyond my scope, and I can only guess as to what happened. Either way, there's more information in between the covers. Unfortunately, it's still in another language.

Blaze pads out of his room, and I shove the book in between the cushion and side of his leather couch and pull down the blanket, quickly pooling it at my feet. He walks in, running a hand through his hair and yawning.

"It feels strange waking up and knowing you're here."

It's weird being here, but I don't think that's what he wants me to say, and I fumble for the right words, finally sticking to the least offensive ones.

"It was quiet all night. No Nightmares."

"I figured, since my bedroom was in one piece."

Is he trying to be funny? I frown and get up, conveniently leaving the blanket over the side.

"I've had a couple of protein bars while you were sleeping, but I'm starved. Want anything?"

The damned blush flushes lightly over his face, and I smirk, overexaggerating the sway of my hips as I walk to the fridge. It seems I just can't help myself.

He clears his throat, and a small smile accompanies the warmth spreading through my chest. There's nothing wrong with a little bit of flirting, right? Especially when the pull of his soul is barely there. My brows draw together, and I bite my lip. Have I forgotten what happened when we kissed yesterday? But —and this is a big but—I had actually let loose and dropped my guard and my willpower. I've been fine around him before and feel "normal" now. Control is key—being around someone with goodness in a controlled exposure environment. Had I always been able to be around souls but just never long enough? Had that part of my training been inaccurate? I wouldn't put it past the Mother for lying about that. Human contact, nurturing would be against everything they stood for.

Son of a bitch!

Fury rolls through me at the thought, and I slam the egg carton a bit too hard and a telltale crack pings in my ears. Fuck. Does it matter now? I can't change the past; I can only look forward to the future. The constant tightness in my chest loosens, and I gasp in a breath, as if it's easier to consume oxygen. And it could all be correlated to why I don't hear souls screaming. And I could actually have zero control. My thoughts racket from one extreme to the other.

"Here. Let me help."

His voice and breath move the air enough it's like a nearly invisible caress across my skin, and I suppress the shiver of pleasure that rolls through me. I shouldn't want help. I'm a strong, independent woman. Capable of feeding myself, dammit.

Before I can say anything, he's in my space, and I have no choice but to move so I don't touch him. My feet did not drag too slowly away. Nope, not at all.

He reaches into the fridge and takes out other vegetables, the muscles in his forearms moving like water. There are worse things than watching a handsome, sexy man cook me breakfast, and I lean back against the counter, crossing my arms over my chest.

"You want to start the coffee?" he asks.

I catch the sigh before it leaves my pouty lips. Can't have golden boy knowing I'd much rather be ogling him.

The aroma of roasted coffee beans punches the air after I grind them, and once the pot is percolating, I head back to my observation post. I'm not there more than two seconds and he's pulling out another cutting board and knife and placing it right next to the one he's using.

"If you don't mind, can you dice the bell pepper?"

The red is vibrant against the wooden board. Ugh, fine. It can't be that hard. I move it over so I'm not as close to him and then slam the knife down through the middle of the pepper.

"I'm pretty sure it's dead already."

Blaze sounds like he's choking on a laugh, and I glare. Smart man turns his face and, after a few seconds of silence and making sure he's not judging me anymore, I turn back to the offensive food. I've never seen the seeds on a plate or in my food, so it must have to come out, but the shape of it makes it kinda hard to cut out. Putting the knife down, I thrust my fingers into the roundness and pull. Triumph flows through me when the seeds are in my palm and no longer in the pepper. Not so bad. I pick a couple seeds off my skin. And the knife. And the cutting board. And my fingers, again. I flick one and it flies across the counter. Why the fuck are there so many seeds? And why won't they stay off me?

There's a strangled sound and Blaze erupts in laughter. That's it. I'm done. Moving to the sink, I thrust my hands under the water until all the little bastards are off and dry my hands. My movements are pissy, but I can't help it.

"I'm sorry, I'm sorry!" But he's wheezing as he says it, and irritation boils in me.

I swivel on my heel. I don't need this. His fingers flutter against my elbow when he reaches out, and I jump out of the way much like a cat getting spooked. I haven't forgotten how I nearly took his gold yesterday, even if he has.

"I'm not laughing at you."

"Mm. Hm."

"No, really, it's just the look on your face...when the seed flew across and stuck to the wall." His laughter echoes around the kitchen, and try as I might, I can't stop it from affecting me. I want to hear it over and over. I want that same level of happiness. To be overjoyed at dumb things.

My lips lift into a smile, and I walk back to the cutting board. "They're so annoying."

He grins, a few curls flopping over his forehead, and my fingers itch to smooth them back. To slide down his muscled back and pull him to me.

"Let me show you."

He cuts the pepper in the other direction, and the knife

moves smoothly through it, creating even slices. After motioning to the other half, I mimic his movements and am pleased to see something resembling red sticks. Not nearly as perfect as his, but still.

"What else needs chopping?"

The happiness at completing such a mundane kitchen task that I'd never really had the time for before is addictive. I want more.

Blaze places a bowl of scrubbed mushrooms in front of me, and I contemplate the roundness. Placing one stem down doesn't work because it's top heavy. But upside down doesn't look right either.

I can sense him eyeing me up, and suddenly I don't want to seem helpless, and I expertly twirl the knife in my hands and attack it like I would a Terror, until the thing looks like a sodden mess.

My eyes sting and I clench my jaw. I will not cry over a stupid fungus. Closing my eyes, I inhale deeply before whispering my embarrassment.

"I've never chopped vegetables before. Not like this."

His lemon and eucalyptus scent wafts towards me, and I open my eyes. He's inches from my face, and my heart races at the anger in the tight lips and drawn brows. His eyes flame an icy color I've yet to witness. I hate that I have to force myself to not back down. I'm not afraid of anyone. I angle my chin, daring him to say anything negative.

"I despise...no, I hate that they've made you think that just because you don't know how to do something that it must be a flaw or weakness. That they made you want to flinch, yet you stand your ground. I rarely want to hurt someone, but I'd like to beat the *shit* out of whoever did this to you—give them the same pain they inflicted on you."

The raw emotion in his voice lowers it to a timbre that can't be, shouldn't be, anything but deadly sounding, yet the soulless dark in me finds it incredibly sexy, and I pull in some of my lip, biting down so I don't say something I can't back up. I haven't learned how to control myself sexually with him, not since yesterday. I need more practice, but this soon is not the time.

His eyes lower, caught up in the action, and the flames change, burning low until they've nearly disappeared. His hand moves up, and he catches my chin, turning it sideways. His lips hover near my ear, but all I can focus on is his touch. The delicate, barely there touch on my jaw. The silkiness of his skin, the *heat* of it makes my heart stutter in its rhythm before resettling. Did I think I couldn't control myself? I can. I have to just to keep experiencing this.

Leaving my chin, his hand falls down to his side, and disappointment rolls through me at the loss of contact, but his whispered breath sears the thin skin of my ear. "I want to kill the person that made you think you're anything less than an incredible woman. I want to drop to my knees and thank the Fates for the strength you exude. I want to kiss every inch of your skin until you're showered in love. Until you see yourself as I see you."

His confession snatches the air from me, and I can't breathe. I can't think. I shouldn't keep standing here, inviting trouble. The ache begins again, like a warning sign I should heed. He's a drug I can't get enough of, and I lose all common sense when he's near. I swallow hard, knowing he can hear it— the desperation and need.

"I can't. I can't fuck you. I won't risk it." Not that I don't want it. I can only be honest so far.

He doesn't respond but angles his head, his nose millimeters from my skin. He's going to kiss me and I'm not going to be able to control myself again. The fear that I could hurt him, make him lose his gold, drops into my stomach like a boulder. But his lips only hover over me, moving down my neck and over the hollow of my throat. My body betrays me, and I tilt my head, giving him full access if he should want it. Wetness dribbles out of me, soaking the little bit of fabric of my thong. My breath quickens in the anticipation I should be fighting.

Blaze continues to the other side of my neck and up to the other ear.

"I have never wanted someone as much as I want you. To delve in between your legs, to your very core, tasting you and lavishing attention onto your clit until you orgasm. Over and over into my mouth until you have no choice but to know how much I want you. To not want to touch me until you *need* to. And then to bend you under me and bury myself deep within you until you can't deny how much I want you, exactly for who you are. I don't want you to *fuck* me. No. I want to lick you. I want to kiss and suck and move inside you until all you can think about is me and how I'd never treat you badly."

Chapter Twenty-Two

F uck. That may be the hottest thing I've heard. Ever. I'm not sure I can do more than squeak right now, so I place the knife I've been holding this entire time on the counter and keep my mouth shut—the better to hold my drool in. If only.

I clear my throat and pretend I don't think the blood tinging his skin pink isn't hot as fuck right now. The sweet, golden man who used only simple words to turn my knees to jelly and start a heartbeat pulsating sensation between my legs. I want him so bad I can taste it, and the part of me that's supposed to be responsible really doesn't want to. Fuck. I breathe in deeply.

"Start by teaching me how to dice mushrooms."

That's the last thing I want to say, but he does. As well as onions and raw bacon before frying it all together and adding scrambled eggs and cheese. He finds small ways to barely brush up against me, heightening my already high arousal. His beautifully sculpted ass stretches against his pants when he leans up and reaches for plates. He's trying to kill me.

Halfway through eating, I consciously slow down my pace to match his. I'm not used to the absence of the screams, but I know that I have to relearn some things right now. I don't have to race through a meal. It's odd.

Blaze yelps, his fork clattering against the plate, and I jump up, blades out of their holster, and turn on my heels searching for whatever startled him.

"Arnica."

I stop at the reverent way he says my name and turn. He holds his hand out. I sheathe my butterflies and sit down, staring at the fully formed tattoo on his ring finger.

"I...just. It's here."

My own hand is still tattooless. "Does that mean because you made most of our meal, you are able to provide, but because I couldn't chop some fucking veggies, I can't provide for you?"

My stomach churns, eggs and vegetables sitting heavy. I knew his sweet-talking was wrong and I was right. I'm not good enough for shit like this. I clench my hands into fists and hide them in my lap. His Fasting judged me on my weak chopping skills. I want to cry.

"No, it means you don't trust me."

His eyes look sad, a flame spluttering, pain lancing through his voice, and I feel like I've kicked a puppy.

"I..."

He stands up abruptly, and my words trail off because I can't lie to him. I don't trust him, but it's nothing to do with him and everything to do with me. I don't trust anyone. Any time I've ever trusted anyone—brutal pain.

"I understand." He nods and picks up his plate, carrying it to the sink and dropping it loudly. "I'm going for a walk."

And now it's like I not only kicked a puppy but kept kicking it. But he doesn't understand. He's never been through the Weaponry. I sigh and wish, for the first time in my life, that things were different. That I was different. Maybe this has all been a mistake.

I'll find another way to get the potion. Marriage is not the answer. I'm never going to trust anyone—I'm incapable of it.

When he returns, he doesn't say anything, but heads to the bathroom. When the shower turns on, anger rises in me. What, he's just going to ignore me? Or not let me say anything in my defense? It's not my fault that trust may as well be a fucking unicorn.

I storm into the bathroom, and for once, his naked body does nothing for me.

"You can't be mad and not allow me to explain myself. It has nothing to do with you. Trust doesn't come easily to me. If it will ever at all. I have literally lived more than a decade of my life in a Dreamer-made place of torture. Trust doesn't exist there. And if I had, I wouldn't be here."

"I offered to heal you, but you won't take it."

I twirl to the open shelving behind me and grab a towel, chucking it over the shower and onto his head.

"You can't just fucking heal me, Blaze!" I screech, and the rational side of me cringes at this display of emotion. "It doesn't work like that!" The physical scars are nothing compared to the emotional.

He kicks the towel aside and opens the door, as if the glass is preventing me from hearing or seeing his frustration.

"You don't even know what it works like! You're not willing to try and see." Anger stains his cheeks while he yells back.

"I'm here trying to marry you! Doesn't that mean some-thing to you? Isn't that enough?" Why can't it be for him? I'm trying to save humanity the best way I know how.

"Why would it be enough? I'm marrying you too, in case

you forgot! It's not enough. You're marrying me for the recipe for that stupid potion. So, no, it's not." He kicks the sodden towel out of the shower and toward me, as if it would even make it far enough to hit me.

"That recipe isn't stupid! It's important and capable of saving so many of you thick-headed, stubborn do-gooders!" I raise my voice louder, hoping to get through his head that I'm not doing this for myself. This is save the world type of shit.

"That recipe is barely worth anything! The true value lies in other recipes—like ones that will enhance my healing abilities!"

I inhale hard. So. He *was* marrying me for reasons of his own. How dare he sit on his proverbial high horse and accuse me of not trusting him when he's done the exact thing that would spawn that feeling.

"Wow. I guess not trusting the honeyed words that slip through your mouth was my intuition being spot on. You know, you almost had me fooled. I really thought you were different. You had me questioning my life and wanting things that I've never wanted before. But you're just a user just like everyone else. Your precious gold isn't enough to change that very base flaw." I should have stayed in my lane. Maybe my life had been mundane and cyclical. But I had honesty in it. Nobody to twist words or my feelings.

I pull at the strand around my neck, yanking on it hard enough that tears sting my eyelids, but the thing won't break.

"Take this thing off me. I don't want it, and I'm not marrying you anymore."

"I told you—it's my promise to you, and I don't break my promises. I'm not taking it off."

I gasp and step back, so I don't push him into the shower and pummel him with my fists. "You fucking collared me?"

Blaze sighs, and it only makes me want to hit him even more. "No, I just made sure it won't come off easily and you can't take it off in anger. Because even trusting you, I know you enough by now. You're not getting rid of me so easily."

The fight seems to have left him and he shivers, the cold air hitting his wet skin and leaving goose pimples everywhere. I'm nowhere near the end of this argument, but it seems wise that I leave and reevaluate my position. And I'm nothing if not up on the ways people want to fuck me over.

I don't bother to respond, but blur out, taking a second to pack some protein bars and shove some other things into my bag, including the book, and blur out of the apartment before he can get dried and dressed. There's no way he's going to follow me naked.

I'm just sliding onto the seat of the Ferrari when he comes out on the balcony in all his glory. "You never let me finish!" he yells down.

A woman jogger passes me and glances up, stopping dead in her tracks. "Oh. Hello there, handsome."

"Move along. There's nothing to see here." I shove my bag in and slam the door a little too hard.

"I disagree. Plenty there to look at. And if you're not letting him finish, well, I'll gladly take him off your hands, honey, and do the job for you." She licks her lips, and I force myself to keep my hands to myself. The fuck she will.

I bare my teeth and step forward. "Move."

She laughs and picks up her pace again as I angle my face upward.

"Will you get inside? Everyone can see you!"

"Not until you come up here and let me have my say!"

The glances are now being thrown my way, and I'm sick of the attention. Fine. I stomp my way up the ladder and shoo him in, shutting the door behind me. Hurt and some other emotion I can't identify churns in my stomach, and I'm almost dizzy with not knowing what to believe.

"I actually don't want to listen right now. I need the space to think." I throw up my hand to stop him when he opens his mouth. "You went for a walk. Now, give me a bit. You're going to work. I'll stay here and I promise I won't leave. But I need a couple of hours to wrap my head around...everything."

He backs away and finally gives me a curt nod. "Fine. I'll get dressed and be back this afternoon."

After he leaves, I pace the room, my thoughts swirling without being able to land on any significant thing. Honestly, it shouldn't matter why he's marrying me. It isn't as if we love each other or have the stereotypical relationship. We barely know each other. And it's not as if I don't want something from him. Yet the need to be accepted for *me* burns through me. The damnable need for someone to want me, just because. After years without compassion and love, after years of solitude, suddenly I want *more*.

My cell vibrates on the kitchen counter, and I contemplate not answering it. It's probably Blaze. No one else would call me. And do I want to speak to him?

I answer before it can go to voicemail.

"You have to go. Wherever you are, you have to leave right now and hunker down." The voice, pitched low, means there are others around—a risk to call. The adrenaline moves through me, and I automatically reach for my blades, stroking a finger down the cool metal.

"There's been a break-in at the Weaponry. Word has it that there's an army coming for you."

Fuck. They must know I took the book.

"How much time?"

"You should've already been gone. Good luck."

And the line goes silent. I have to get out of here. The promise I made to Blaze whips through my mind, but there really will be a small army coming for me—they can't beat me on their own—and I don't want to—*can't* worry about his safety if they come here and he comes back.

I blur through the door only to blur right back again. The ding of the elevator echoes loudly between my ears. I withdraw my deadly butterflies, and for the first time in my life, I send up a nearly silent whisper to the Fates.

I beg them to keep Blaze at the hospital till this is over.

Chapter Twenty-Three

They come in twos through the door, dressed all in black with swords and knives strapped to their muscled bodies. There's a deadly look in hooded eyes when viciousness no longer phases someone, and even the most innocent person wouldn't make the mistake of thinking they can escape. They split off until they form a circle around me, and then finally, she enters the room.

"*Mother*. I'm shocked. Really."

I twirl my blades one time. I have no reason for theatrics. I beat her once before, but the dark within me cherishes the ability to piss her off.

I know first-hand how much pleasure she takes from hurting people. The way her lips twist into a cruel smile, anticipation layering happiness on her face. I won't give her the satisfaction she craves.

"Oh, Arnica. You didn't think you'd get away with stealing from family did you? Now, be a good girl and put down your weapons. It'll make all of this so much easier. And you can come home—where you belong."

"I don't know what you're talking about. But I'm wondering why you seem to think that I'm dumb enough to fall for that. Or why you think that twenty of your...*children*, are enough to bring me in. Or why *you* think I'd be willing to go back to that hellhole. Or really, why you even came here. You know this isn't going to end well."

I twist my wrists back and forth, the metal whistling lightly on the air. If I learned anything from my time at the Weaponry, it's how to mimic her tactics. I may hate them myself, but I'm not above using them. It's why I will win every time. I don't have a problem with stooping to her level and using her against herself. As well as her minions. They've been raised by fear just like I have, and I know every movement calculated to instill it.

"You know I'll beat you. Again." I make sure my voice is imbued with silky venom.

The words echo around the room and my Sisters' and Brothers' gasps, though nearly silently from fear of repercussion, are loud enough to be heard by even an average human. The barely-there shifting of feet causes me to grin. But it's feral and lethal and everyone there knows it.

"Arnica. Don't you dare talk to me like that or I'll make you suffer through a thousand deaths. You might be out here working, but I'll yank you back so fast you'll lose your grip on your precious blades."

I nearly choke with laughter, but manage to keep it in. None of the warriors here will take me seriously if I don't.

"Who the fuck are you kidding?"

But the nod has been given, slight though it is, and I catch it. My superspeed kicks in while I pivot on my heal, crouching low and slashing at the knees of the ones that had been behind me. I cut through four pairs before I violently twist my torso and surge upward and forward, my right butterfly sliding to a stop at the base of the Mother's jaw. It took seven seconds to put her in this position. She swallows hard and fear glimmers in her eyes. I have nothing to lose, and she knows it.

She overshot her importance when she bolstered herself with others. She won't make that mistake again, and I just sealed the fate of the rest of the ones here. I don't look at them. Their deaths may be on my conscience, but I wouldn't change anything if it means my life, and I don't need their faces haunting my days.

"You will go back to that shitshow and tell them whatever the fuck you have to, but I'm not going back. Don't *ever* fucking think that you can corral me and bring me down. The only reason you live is because I don't want to deal with the petty bullshit of turning down your job."

It's the same excuse I gave her before, and it was true. If you beat the Mother and killed them, by default, the title went to you, and the last thing I need is to be tied to that place.

The elevator pings and I shove her, blurring my way to Blaze. I beat Mother there by milliseconds, and my blades clang against hers, the reverb echoing through the hallway. Everyone here can hear the hard swallow behind me. I don't move a muscle, exerting the exact amount of pressure she is. I won't give more because I won't open myself and him up to a possible opening. She's close to me, and the stench of the Weaponry shoots up my nose. I narrow my eyes against the sick feeling in my stomach.

"Well, well. What do we have here? Arnica, tsk. Tsk. Just what are you doing with a Magical?"

She knows who he is. The sick sensation intensifies. She had to have followed me here. I brought the Mother and all the dark that follows to his doorstep. I refuse to allow my guilt to pervade my face and body right now. My eyebrow lifts and my mouth twists while I maintain the hold. Kick ass now, panic later.

"Mother, *dearest*. I had no idea you took such an interest in who I'm fucking."

Blaze jerks behind me, moving a step back, and I move with him to keep him safe. The Mother moves as well, and it's like a threesome box step.

Everyone in the Weaponry knows that sex is valued as a proper diversion. The more degrading and dark, the more it is used as a weapon, the better it's regarded.

Her face scrunches up in some kind of disgusting smile. I don't know why she even bothers. "You expect me to believe you're using a golden one as your sex toy?"

The vileness of the way they regard the bodies they use threads through me as I tap into memories of what I've witnessed. I use it to my advantage.

"You have no idea what exquisite pain fuels my orgasm when I have to restrain myself from stealing his soul through his dick." I shrug, careful to keep the line between carelessness and lewdness.

"Really. Then maybe you'll just have to share, and we'll all see for ourselves."

The way they've passed around a body for the enjoyment of many brings acid to my lips, and the vision of Blaze being tortured blinds me to everything but this moment. The heat of his anger emanates from him, hitting my back, but my own rage flows through me at the thought of her touching him—at the way they all would, given half a chance. He's going to be my husband, even if for a short period of time. Darkness rolls through me on the heels of madness, and for once, I'll make her proud.

"He's mine. If you want to keep the contents of your body inside you, you'll stay away from him. If you dare touch him, I'll keep you alive long enough to feed you your body parts after I roast them on an open fire. And then I'll spill your blood from you *by the pinprick* until you're begging me for mercy...and I will give you none."

The whispered words echo around the walls and the silence lays thick. She pales until a sick smile cracks open. "You've learned well, I see."

I tense as one of my Brothers moves up and murmurs in her ear, careful that I can't hear. Impressive...and I mark them as someone to watch out for.

She nods and steps back as if this had been a normal conversation and visit, and snapping her fingers, they all blur out of the building, taking the ones I incapacitated from the living room, and I wait long seconds, opening my hearing as high as it will go and searching for them. I don't lower my arm until they are far enough away, and even then, it's too close for comfort. Adrenaline burned through what calories I still had, and my hands shake as I sheath my blades. I turn to Blaze.

"You okay?"

I'm under no illusion Mother will accept my words and leave him alone. In fact, the faster I get him back to his people, or wherever he wants me to take him, the better. The low fire burns in his eyes, and for a second, I must've lost it. Because there's no way he's turned on by what just happened, but then I spot the bulge in his fancy-ass slacks and my eyebrows shoot up.

"You're scary when you say things like that. Like, really, really scary. But that has got to be the *hottest* thing I've ever heard anyone say."

I snort and move into his apartment. I need food, and he probably needs a reality check. I'm not as nice a person as he is. He has to start remembering it.

"I'm quite fucking capable of every word of it."

"Oh, I have no doubt of that. But the fact that you would defend me so quickly and easily, and clearly competently, well...*that* was hot."

He grins, and the smile pours something in me that I can't identify and probably shouldn't anyway. He brings me to a vulnerable place. Now, I have something to lose.

And the Mother knows it.

Chapter Twenty-Four

"I need to eat, and we have to move. Where can I take you where you will be safe?"

"Uh, what do you mean where you can take me?"

His face looks confused, and irritation shoots through me. Why doesn't he understand that he's in danger? Is this why all the golden ones can't keep their gold? Are they that oblivious?

I pause from making myself a chicken sandwich to stare at him. "You're kidding me, right? You think she's not going to come back here with a literal army of people to try to take me back? And you don't think that by threatening her and telling her you're mine that she won't do everything she can to use you to hurt me?"

Red tinges my vision and I grip the butter knife hard in my fist, wishing for one moment it was her neck. I should've killed her when I had the chance and fuck all the drama that would've come of it. At least she wouldn't have set her sights on him. Guilt blows through me. This is why I should be alone. Anyone I have an interest in will have a target on them. Why do I do this to people I care about?

Blaze steps forward, shoulders squared. "You do realize

that I'm a Magical. That I'm the son of the...previous Matriarch." He stumbles on the word before continuing. "That I'm not defenseless. Yes, the Nightmares I can't really defend myself against because I'm *sleeping*. And because I don't see my gold the way you say you do. But that doesn't mean I'm powerless."

His hands fist, and the muscles in his forearms bunch with the effort. Cute, but it's not enough. My eyes narrow. Who does he think he's fucking with? The big, bad wolf? His ignorance will cost him his life, and a sharp stabbing pain rips through my chest at the idea of them spilling his blood. It takes me a second to recognize the emotion that builds inside me, boiling over and forcing my next words. I haven't felt this scale of fear in at least a decade.

"You have no idea what you're talking about. Admittedly, I don't know much about Magicals and what you're capable of. But this is the *Mother of the Weaponry*." I enunciate the words carefully, in case he missed her title. "You know, the head trainer of the school that takes young kids and breaks them until they're capable of killing in the most grotesque ways, if needed. That are nourished on withstanding pain that would bring the most seasoned assassins and torturers to their knees, begging for mercy. They are *all* sick and twisted. And she's the worst of them. She makes your worst Nightmares look like a fucking fluffy baby bunny."

"Not all of them are sick and twisted." He looks me up and down, and this time I snort openly at his naivete. I will not be the cause of his death. Why can't he understand?

"You think because I have some semblance of compassion toward you that I'm not every bit the horror that they are? That emotion has been my downfall. And it has taught me to be even more lethal than them." I tilt my head a bit and study him. What he thinks of me is tinted by that gold oozing from his skin. He needs to know what I am.

What I'm capable of.

I step forward slowly, each movement dangerous and calculated, until his face pales and his lips look red. I fixate on them briefly before thrusting my lust aside. "I have not only brought down the Mother's vengeance and anger on my fellow warriors in my quest to be my own person, but I have willingly invoked it. I have *created* chaos and sown the seeds of terror in their eyes. I've been the instrument of their pain. I have beaten the Mother at her own game, both physically and mentally. And I did so easily. Because I am the strongest and worst of them all. Be grateful that I *do* have that compassion and that I have shown it to you. But don't for one second think that I'm the better option. That what they breed into those inside those walls comes out human."

He exhales shakily. Good, maybe now he'll understand that I'm not worthy of being his wife. Of being with anyone, let alone someone so pure in their deeds that gold melts out of them in a never-ending supply. That this has all been a mistake and he should agree to my previous requests and just get me the fucking potion and leave me alone. Before I get him into more trouble than I already have.

"So that's why you think you're broken. Arnica—"

He doesn't finish as I yank his arm, ignoring his gasp and the heat building in my body. I blur through the rooms and out onto the fire escape ladder before the bullet embeds in one of his walls. I drop his hand, only stopping long enough to spot some gold on his skin.

"MOVE!" I scream, running down the stairs and vaguely making sure his footsteps pound behind me.

I slide across the top of the hood of the Ferrari and jump in, pealing tires in reverse the second his door shuts. I floor it as another bullet flies through the air, missing the car. Whatever Sister or Brother is shooting at us better hope I never fucking find them. "Those cockroach motherfuckers. Fucking shady-ass seagulls. Rat shit eating fuckers. Spineless, Mother titty-sucking, fucking disgusting, lying bitches," I snarl, rage pouring words out of my mouth. And then I remember that Blaze doesn't like cursing and I turn to him, an apology on my tongue, only to see him staring at me with a grin.

"Creative. And I concur."

It doesn't make me feel better. In fact, it makes me feel shittier that I'm clearly a bad influence. Fuck.

We fly through the city until we get to a parking garage miles away. I park the car on the roof and sadly swipe my hand across her trunk as I pull on my bag, settling it cross body in front of me. She was gorgeous and I will miss her. I toss Blaze a bookbag full of extra water bottles and protein bars, and he wordlessly puts it on.

"From here we go on foot."

I move quickly to the steps and take them as fast as a human could possibly keep up, clearly not leaving room for chatting. He's out of breath as we round the corner out of the garage, and I walk at a fast clip up the sidewalk.

"Why can't we dri—" The small boom from the top of the parking garage stops the rest of his words, and I toss a key fob into a nearby trashcan.

"That's why."

I keep a quick pace, alternating between jogging and fast walking, and I'm only doing so as a courtesy. I'd be flat-out running, and I'm already not liking my chances of them finding us before we get to my safe house. I stop until Blaze catches up, and I grab the bookbag on his back, turning him around and rummaging about before removing some of the water and food. I zip it up and hand him one of each. I'm already cramming a bar into my mouth. I alter the tone of my voice in case anyone's listening.

"You good?"

He's just finishing guzzling down his water and a few

droplets of sweat slide down the side of his face. His button-down shirt, plastered to his chest, and the rolled-up sleeves that had been clearly yanked up to his biceps at some point seem damp. His breathing is already under control.

Clearly, he's able to keep up with the pace I'm setting, and I can't believe how incredibly attracted I am to him right now. Sweaty balls and all. He's going to have to lose the dress shoes and soon or it will leave nothing but blisters. If he's ever going to be hurting at my hands, it's gonna be because I tied him tightly to a headboard, not because we're running from a sadistic bitch. Fuck me. There's something more than a little wrong with me that I can think about sex right now.

"How're your feet?"

"Fine. I know they aren't sneakers, but they're custom made as I'm used to walking in them all day. I'll be fine."

"Good. Let's go." I'm antsy being out in the open, and we move quickly through the city again, crossing through blocks.

We finally hit the edge of the city and I risk siphoning his gold as I once again grab his hand and blur across the field. I quickly let go, and we move through trees until we get to stone rocks jutting out of from the woods. A waterfall pours in the background.

"I'm going to hold onto you one more time until we get inside because I need to move through rock, and it's going to be slow going. Is your gold okay with that? I don't know if you feel any pain or anything or..." I trail off because I don't have the words to describe what he feels.

"I'll be fine." He nods and holds out his hand, palm up. The tattoo seems to mock my own naked finger. I wish I were capable of blindly putting so much trust in someone. If it would be anyone, I'd pick him.

I take his hand and yank him through the trees, around the waterfall, and blur through the rock, pushing into the density until we pop into a cave I had carved out years before.

"Wow. That was...something."

I never thought to ask what it feels like. And honestly, I'd never blurred through anything with someone. We're all able to do it at the Weaponry. Thankfully, it had been a training lesson once. It hadn't ended well for the human who had volunteered. Not because they weren't capable of it, but because one of my Sisters had "forgotten him" and let go.

I stiffen as the shadows move behind him, coming out from the walls. Dozens of my former siblings from the Weaponry spill forth into the light, coming from an opening in the ceiling of the cave. It's not big, but big enough they must have found it. Dread fills my entire being, making sweat slide down my back. I can't even put Blaze behind me as they've surrounded us. Fuck. I would've had a better chance out in the open. I drop my bag and slide out my butterflies, the hiss of them coming out of the sheath echoing around the cavern. I only wish I really had as many as it sounds like I do.

Chapter Twenty-Five

"It's a shame, really. You were one of my best students."

The gloating voice of the Mother as she steps out from the rest grates on my nerves. Blaze turns around to face her, and I step forward quickly, closing the gap between us a bit. Not a lot, but enough to make me feel a little better. It's all I dare at one time.

I snort loudly. Fuck her. "I'm still the best, or did you forget the sensation of metal at your neck so quickly?"

"And yet here I am."

Her hands rise in question, but I'm already searching amongst the faces for the one that was smart enough to find my sanctuary. 'Cause it isn't her. The slim male that had whispered in her ear earlier stands three bodies away from her, and my eyes narrow.

He must be the one who found this location. He's a worthy opponent. He's also a dead man.

"Luck. That's all that was."

My body might be angled toward her, but I stare him down, making sure he knows I'm speaking to him. If he's smart, he'll run. My blood runs hot through me, and I can actually sense heat burning through my chest in an anger so fierce it's indescribable. Some people cry when they're angry, I fucking tear them apart.

But I can't focus on him right now, and I split my attention back to the Mother, slowly inching my way closer to Blaze, until the hairs on my forearm stand up, attuned to his body.

Her high-pitched laugh echoes around the cave, a vivid reminder that she might not be sane, and some of the seasoned warriors shift their weight. That's all that fear whipped through these people can do—bring more fear. They didn't have the advantages that I did. I had no longer felt fear at her hands, and *that* was what enabled me to beat her years ago. I had embraced the dark, welcomed it even. I had used it and twisted it to my purposes and spit it out, whimpering, back into its walls.

My body stiffens at the whisper of movement amid the crowd. They're antsy, and I can't blame them. The call of blood, of winning, hums through them. The dark that remains in me gives them an easy target. Too bad it's one they can't cage—my dark is soulless.

I thrust my arm out, blade and all, careful not to slice him, and hook Blaze at his belly and pull him, maneuvering with pressure until we're back-to-back. Adrenaline pours into me in anticipation, but it's coated with a sick feeling. I can't just attack and kick ass.

I have to watch over Blaze and make sure nothing happens to him. The feeling in my stomach intensifies at the thought that they'd hurt him. My brows scrunch together, my mind whipping through the calculations of running with him. There's no way I'd have time to reach for his hand, let alone blur out before they are all on top of us. They're too vigilant right now, ready and anticipating maneuvers.

There's movement to the left, and I turn my head slowly,

desperation churning in my belly as I watch as many of them as I can, but it's just not possible to see everyone. The silence lengthens and my muscles quiver from being held taut, but I won't move my hands or feet a millimeter. Let them make the first move.

The moment there's a ripple of muscle in Blaze's back, I shove my right blade into his hand without pausing to check he actually holds onto it, and I counter-attack, metal clanging against metal on my left, while I kick out with my right, catching someone hard enough to the groin he'll never regain the use of his balls. Fuck them for making the calculated choice to attack Blaze first.

The man drops, screaming and rolling at the same time another Brother rushes me. But he trips over the moving body, and I punch him in the ear, putting all my strength behind my fist, as he goes down and stays down.

Another warrior moves forward, but Blaze grunts, and I whip around, ducking and slicing until I'm almost at at his side. He's barely managing to not get his head chopped off, backed against a wall against two attackers, but it's a losing battle. Rage fuels my arms as I use both hands to cut through one body and into another. Blaze's gaze focuses on the man nearly severed in half and then back at me, his eyes firing a dark blue. When they cut to my right, I duck and slice through a pair of knees and pick up the other butterfly Blaze tosses at the ground. But now he's defenseless, and I've got to position myself in front of him. They'll kill me first before they get to him.

Rising, I scissor the swords and release, throwing my hands out and catching another three opponents in the neck. Blood splatters, hot and disgustingly wet, soaking my clothes, but I don't stop chopping through bodies.

We've got nowhere to go. My back's against Blaze, who's against a wall. They move swiftly, each dropping body replaced by another hellbent on taking me down, and I grit my teeth. They're purposely not giving me an opening to grab his arm and blur out.

Fuck.

The metallic zing of blood lays heavy enough that the air seems saturated with it, and each inhale chokes me with the taste.

But I keep going, because is there another choice? My arms move slower and there's darkness at the edge of my vision, and I know it's just a matter of time. I'm running on fumes.

"On the count of three, I need you to move to my side," Blaze whispers into my ear.

I shake my head. We'd both be literally against the wall, and he'd be closer to the army that is still fucking advancing. How many warriors did the Mother bring? All of them? The smugness I'd usually experience at the knowledge that that's how many she'd need is swallowed by the wish that this was the one time she'd underestimate me.

I've been afraid, angry, panicked since I started fighting. I don't know how much more I can take. How am I capable of *more* fear? Of guilt that I somehow brought him into this mess? That maybe, just maybe, I can't beat them all?

"I can create a diversion. Long enough for you to get us out of here."

I shake my head again, only to get clobbered in the side of it. The punch landed right above my jaw, and my mouth fills with my own blood. Each emotion fuels my actions for a moment, but it won't be enough. I know it. The Mother knows it. The smart man knows it. Fuck.

"You've got to trust me," he continues, but this isn't the time for conversation.

I spit a mouthful into the eyes of yet another attacker and attempt to pivot sideways but slide on the bodily fluids all over the floor. My ankle cracks alarmingly and gives out, and my knee rams into the rock floor, shooting pain from my ankle to my hip.

"Next time, wait till I count!" Blaze yells.

I raise my arm up, using my butterfly to shield my head from an oncoming hit, when there's a swirl of air behind me. The woman in front of me slows her movement, giving me the opening I need, and I plow my fist into her kneecap, forcing her leg to hyperextend back, and when it snaps, she lands on top of another body, screaming.

A stream of fire roars over my head and lands between me and the rest of the mob. Wave after fiery wave flies ahead, and I scoot over to Blaze and hop up on my right leg, keeping my left off the ground.

I grip his bicep, bunching and moving under my hand, and pull us back into the rock, melting as if we are one with it.

Each step I take shoots pain through me, but I use it to propel us through the rocky material. I have no idea how far back the mountain goes, and my energy is already depleted. If we don't make it through, we'll be forever trapped here, fossilized over time.

Chapter Twenty-Six

My feet feel like they're pumped full of lead, and I'm already dragging my left leg behind me. I no longer feel the razor-sharp stabbing through my ankle, and I know that's not a good thing. I've either severely injured it worse than I thought or I'm starting to lose consciousness.

Neither option is acceptable.

Blaze's hand squeezes mine, and I grip it harder than I should, but I don't think I'm holding on to him anymore. I think he's keeping a hold of me. My anchor in the rock.

My steps slow. We're molten lava already beginning to harden. That's what it feels like. Nothing I ever did prepared me for this moment.

And oddly, I'm not afraid of death. I'm not afraid of leaving this Earth. I'm tired of it. Of having to run and fight and never being able to do anything but breathe, and even that, never fully.

Regret weaves its way through me though, and I'm honestly shocked by it. I was content with my life. I'd found a balance of saving golden souls and kicking ass, two things that no one could beat me at. I thought I'd loved everything about my existence.

Until Blaze slept his way in. I want to snort at the thought so badly, but there's no breathing when you're in here. It's just as well. I'd fill my lungs with rock and die sooner.

But I do wish I had more time with him. Maybe actually married him and fulfilled that dream I'd had with kids and life —a real life.

I can't seem to move one foot in front of the other. Have my limbs solidified? My eyes squeeze shut, and I struggle to open them. To see Blaze perish. It should be my penance for all the things I've done wrong in my life. For all the dark within me. For the soulless, almost-Nightmare that I am.

To watch someone with so much gold become one with the brown rock. Everything good about him stripped down to the bare minimum and maybe no better than me.

That his body might resemble mine, that his soul loses that amazing color that shines bright and distinguishes itself from the dark fills me with rage, and I bend at the knee, forcing my leg to move with my thigh.

A tear drips down my face, but I keep moving forward, inching my way to the end. Fuck if I'm going to let him stay in here. But the anger fizzles out as quickly as it comes on, and I belatedly recognize my body's ability for one dying flash of energy. Unfortunately, it's the last one, and I come to a standstill, my muscles shaking with effort to keep going.

It's not enough. I should let go of his hand, slip my fingers out and end the torture it must be for him to not be able to breathe. It's selfish of me to want to hold onto him, to stroke my thumb against his skin. Another tear falls.

And I let my fingers slide slowly out. I should do it quick, mercifully, but his heat against my coolness is almost sensual.

Not sexual, but soft, like his sheets. It's like it brings every emotion I can possibly feel to the surface. As if his gold is slithering over me, and I desperately want to shiver at the deliciousness.

Blaze. I'm sorry you've ever met me. But I'm not sorry I met you.

Suddenly, there's pressure in my palm.

And then a tug.

Is he pulling me? I want to tell him that there's no way he can move us through the dirt and rock. That he can't just pick up where I left off. It's years of training, not to mention the ability. But I can't tell him that. That will end what little time I have left with him.

Blaze's hand once again tightens in mine, though he's finally stopped pulling at me. His arm goes around my waist. He's pulling me again, moving me against the rock, and I want to help him. I want to get out too, doesn't he know that? My thighs bunch and I lift my left leg, but when I place any weight on it, it cracks again and buckles, and I go down. The pain is excruciating, lancing its way up my leg until I think I'm going to have to open my mouth and scream after all. I just rebroke my foot that had been healing...the wrong way.

Blaze grabs my right forearm and releases my left hand, and it's as if the entire world went dark and my palm, my fingers, feel like they've lost a digit or something equally important. The loneliness washes over me, and I bow my head. I should beg the Fates to end this now.

And then his hand slides down my forearm and he twists, linking his left hand with my right, and the loneliness echoes louder, mocking me with what I can't have. This is my punishment.

His right arm slides under me, rolling me over and sliding behind my knees, and he's lifting me, of all things. What is wrong with this man? Does his gold think it can overcompensate reality? Warmth whips through me and we're moving faster and how the fuck is he moving through rock?

Maybe I'm dreaming.

And maybe I'm already dead.

Chapter Twenty-Seven

I gasp in precious air, and Blaze huffs right along with me. His hand, still linked in mine, feels natural, and for a second, I don't want to let go, but dammit, I can't just sit here and hold hands like a lovesick fool.

Pain sears across my shin and I wince. "How did you do that?"

"Where to now?" he asks at the same time. His voice sounds husky, gravelly, as if it's taken on some of the qualities of stone. "Safety first and then we'll talk. Where?"

"I don't know. I have to think. Just put me down already." I'm remembering how I'm supposed to be a badass Nightmare Killer, not some fucking helpless female.

But his grip on me tightens, even his fingers, and stupidly, my brain turns to mush. What was I thinking about? Fuck me. This is why we aren't supposed to fall in love.

OH FUCK. I'm in love? NO WAY! I'm in love with the idea of being in love. This is like a savior complex or some shit. I *can't* fall in love. Not only will that get into the way of every-fucking-thing, but I can't be with golden boy.

Wait.

My eyes widen and I turn to stare at him. He's still got gold oozing out of his skin, shimmering over and around me like...like a blanket, and shivers roll down my spine. Why haven't I taken it? What is it doing to me? Is it making me feel all this nonsense?

That must be it. Somehow, it's got me thinking about Blaze in weird and tender ways that are unnatural to me. Just like the gold pulsating on my arm where it's up against his chest.

"I'm not putting you down. They're probably right behind us?"

His guess is as good as mine. I have no idea why they didn't beat us here, actually. And the theorizing will have to wait because he's correct, we need to move while we still can.

"Anywhere I'd go I'm considering compromised. You have somewhere safe?"

"I have a friend who owns a cabin. Can you reach my phone? Luckily, it's in my back pocket. I'm going to start heading there, but I don't want to waste any more time. The name's Dex."

My hand stills. Small world.

"Could you, ah, get my phone? You're...distracting me."

The air moving through my hair had been gentler, but I hadn't noticed while I'd been contemplating the possible ramifications of Blaze knowing Dexter. My hand has stopped right on the side of his butt cheek, effectively cupping it. I give it a pat now and wink. To my delight, he blushes.

I reach in and remove the phone out of his pocket. It takes a little bit of maneuvering and sliding my hand in between us, and I can't help but focus on the hardness of his muscles or the fact that he's not even quivering with exertion.

It says more for his stamina than anything else had, and my heart races in anticipation of a possible wedding night.

Now that we've survived, I'm definitely considering a multi-night wedding night.

"Your passcode?"

"It's 1234. I know, I know. My mom used to tell me all the time that I shouldn't keep it like that. But honestly? Everyone's always told not to use that, so why not? And no one would expect me to actually have that simple of a code."

I glower at his explanation. "We definitely have to talk about this. There are too many bad people in the world. You do-gooders are always pushing the envelope. Never second-guessing yourselves, never searching for the things that can happen to you. I mean really, I have no idea how you have survived this long."

"Like I told you before, it's the potion."

"Clearly, taking it didn't do you any favors."

I scroll through contacts until I find Dex's name and raise my eyebrow at the EMERGENCY written under the company name. This probably qualifies, and I press the green button.

"This better be important." The growl accompanying the words makes me roll my eyes. The man makes that noise entirely too much.

"It's Arnica. Our mutual friend says you have a cabin...and we need it. You got a problem with that?"

"He's not supposed to be calling me, let alone giving that information out." He growls again, and there's a feminine giggle in the background.

"Listen. Put your sex games on hold. I'm injured and got nowhere to go. I need a safe space. You know, kinda like what I did for you. Or did you forget that?" I mean, he paid me, and he paid me well to get rid of the shadows hanging around his lover, but I don't usually hustle on the side. That shit was a favor.

The growl is low and long. Does he think he's a dog? Or

that I'd be scared? I'm tempted to growl back, but before I do, he responds. "Fine. See you soon."

"He's good with it."

The air becomes thick, and though I'm not moving myself, it looks like Blaze is struggling a bit, too. He bends at the waist, and I wonder if he's going to tip me out of his arms, but his eyebrows scrunch up, and then his eyes flame up, nearly white hot, and I stare at them. They're gorgeous in all their hues, but the white nearly takes my breath away.

He straightens, and suddenly we're moving much faster, before he slams to a stop and I'm staring at the most beautiful wooden building surrounded by forest trees. Cabin had been mildly deceiving. This was damn near a mansion, what with all the rooms and angles jutting out every which way. It looks like a hodge-podge hot mess, and I instantly love it.

"Well, that's good...since we're here."

I snort because it's a move I'd make. Except I wouldn't ask. Probably.

And then I snicker. Now I know the reason for Dex's growling and hesitancy. "No, let's give the man a minute. It's only decent."

"What?" Blaze frowns.

"Dex. He and Cassie are getting it on. And from the sound of it, they're close to cumming."

"Excuse me?" His cheeks pinken again, and I'm stunned at the idea that I might just do anything to keep causing that blush to rise.

"They're *fucking*."

"I got that. I just..." He trails off and clears his throat. There's a tremor in his arms, and I know he's got to be fatigued. "I didn't know you knew them."

Mm. Hm. "Put me down."

"No. You're hurt."

"I'll manage. I've dealt with stuff like this before. I'll be fine." I don't tell him that it's going to get worse before it gets better. My ankle is going to have to be re-broken. I've been healing as we've been running, and it's definitely not set properly.

He shakes his head, but then the front door opens.

"Fuck, you couldn't wait another couple of hours? I had plans." Dex stands on the threshold, green lounge pants hanging low on his hips, and I nearly whistle in admiration. Mm. I do like me some eye candy. Especially the rolled-out-of-bed kind.

Cassie appears at his side, the blond hair already in a pony-tail. Her stare bores into mine as she hands him a T-shirt, and I grin. She knows damn well what her lover looks like and she's territorial. Not that I have any intention of sampling. I've got my own man dish that I'd like to take a bite out of if he is down for it.

But I can respect her actions.

Chapter Twenty-Eight

"I'm sorry, you know I wouldn't bother you if it wasn't important."

Blaze walks up the stone sidewalk to the front door. The massive wood panels aren't as smooth as I thought they were from a distance. It's almost as if the builder decided they couldn't plane it. It's gnarled and twisted and hands down the most intriguing thing I've ever seen. Vines creep here and there, and there's some semblance of gardening along the walk. Some small bonsai trees, which definitely aren't native to here, and shrubs. It's strangely alluring.

"Yeah, yeah." Dex sighs when Cassie snakes her arm around his waist. "You're, of course, welcome. What happened?"

"I'd love to stand out here and chat...standing being the key word here. Can we get inside so he can finally put me down?"

Cassie's facial expression lightens, and from the slight smile I get, I imagine she understands what I'm talking about. Good. I'm a fan of women who like some independence. That means we'll get along just fine.

It changes the perception I've had of her. I've only met her twice, but both times she struck me as a scaredy cat—something I have zero tolerance for. The first time was that night at Ferraro's when I'd swallowed the souls of more than a few Nightmares that had attached themselves to her. It happens when they've been called upon, as is usually the case when humans dabble in the dark arts and have no idea what they're doing.

Dexter had assured me she hadn't intended that at all and that she'd been petrified. Earlier that day, I'd seen her during the meeting where that Destiny had warned me about moons. Cassie had seemed fearful of her, which meant her man had divulged that Delaney was a Destiny and what exactly she was capable of. All she'd done for me was piss me off, but Cassie had taken her differently.

"Come in, please," she says, her voice soft but firm. Not scared today, I see. Maybe I'd misjudged her.

They step aside, and Blaze walks in, arms still quivering. The movements are more violent, and I know he's got to put me down soon.

"This way." Dex moves ahead and we follow, but as I'm looking around, I catch the reflection of a kitchen in a massive floor-to-ceiling mirror. Like the house needs to look any bigger than it already is.

"Can we go to the kitchen first? I need food more than anything right now."

"Sure."

Blaze turns and deposits me gently onto a stool at a big-ass island as if I'm made from something breakable, and I don't know if I should be pissed-off or if I find it hot as fuck. He sways on his feet and finally let's go of my hand and I miss it as soon as he does. There's something about that skin-to-skin contact we had. The way that gold infused into me. Now, I'm cold and lonely, reminding me of too many years at the

Weaponry, and I grit my teeth. Oh yeah, it definitely pisses me off.

My head swims, and I prop it up with my hands, my elbows glued to the counter. I will not lay my head on the cool surface. I will not show any more weaknesses to these people I barely know.

A massive, oversized plate loaded with food appears in front of me, sliding in between my arms, and my stomach growls in anticipation.

A couple of steaks, medium rare, little golden potatoes piled high with pats of melting butter and herbs, a mound of some kind of chickpea salad with more green things, and baby carrots in some kind of glaze. Saliva pools in my mouth, and it takes everything I have not to pick it up with my hands and shove it into my mouth like some kind of stereotypical cave woman.

A fork, followed by a steak knife, slides across the counter, and I catch it, mumbling my thanks. I barely pay attention to Blaze sitting down next to me with his own plate, nor the iced mugs of something placed in my field of vision. I've got eyes for my meal and that's it. Hell, Terrors could swirl all around me right now and I would not give a fuck.

I slice and fork up mouthfuls of tender meat, popping baby potatoes in, followed by bites of the salad and carrots one after another. Cutting, chewing, swallowing, and repeating until my belly feels like it's going to burst. The food seems never ending, until suddenly it is, and I'm staring at the plate, kinda wishing for more, kinda wishing for a comfy spot to take a nap in.

I sip at the remains of spiced cold apple cider and savor the explosion of taste on my tongue. I finally glance up to see Cassie, Dex, and Blaze staring at me. I lean back into the chair and pat my stomach. "That was fucking amazing."

"I've never seen anyone consume so much food," Cassie

nearly whispers in awe, and I beam a smile at her. There's no condescension in her tone, and she's upping herself on my likeable scale.

"Now that you've eaten, what happened?" Dex leans against the opposite counter nonchalantly, but I know he's never not strung tight. Probably why he growls a lot. Cassie slips her arm through his, and he pulls her close. There's a twinge in my chest at the casualness of their touch.

Blaze shakes his head. "I think we need to take care of Arnica first. She's been hurt."

I wave him off. I have zero desire to rebreak bones right now, and I barely feel any pain. "I'm not exactly sure what's going on, but I seem to have irritated the wrong person and I was attacked."

"*We* were attacked," Blaze interrupts.

"No, I was attacked. If they wanted you dead, you would have been, no matter how good I am. There were too many of them and they're too trained. Too quick. And you're not that skilled with a sword. No offense."

Dex pulls off the counter and his stance becomes wider, more domineering. Anger rolls over his face, the jaw muscle clenching at the corner. "How many?"

I shrug, unperturbed by his attitude. I've been dealing with men pushing out their chests for too long for that shit to sway me.

"Easily a hundred."

Cassie gasps but straightens as well, and there's a glimmer of admiration for her, but I don't acknowledge it.

"I cut down half of that, at least. And for what it's worth, I don't think they're coming after me right now. They're gonna need a minute to regroup. Add to their numbers."

"Fucking hell."

"Exactly."

Chapter Twenty-Nine

"Why are they after you?"

Dexter's eyes stare into mine. If he thinks he's going to intimidate me, he's met his match. I shrug again.

"I have no idea."

His eyes narrow, but I don't move a muscle. He can think I'm lying all he wants, but he won't know for sure.

"What do you need then?"

"I just need to heal. It won't take me but a day or two. But I'm going to need your assistance."

This way, he can get some of his aggression out on me. He lifts his brow in question.

"I need you to break my ankle."

"What?" Blaze roars, nearly drowning out Dex's calm, "Now?"

Two different questions by two different men. Blaze obviously doesn't realize why I'd need to. But Dex does. I shift in my seat and look over, pausing briefly at the clenching of his fists. If that's jealousy, we're going to have a problem.

"I'm an extremely fast healer. It's already healed, broken

again, and re-healed. But it'll actually need to be cracked twice. Once where it's healed the wrong way and when I rebroke it. It's kinda triangle shaped in the way it busted."

Blaze nods. "I'll do it."

A strange sensation flutters through me and acid burns in my throat. "No."

"What do you mean, no? What difference does it make who breaks it? I'm a Healer and probably more qualified that anyone in this room to perform this kind of procedure." He motions toward Dex and Cassie, who looks horrified by the conversation. Both of them kind of murmur in agreement, but I don't care. This isn't a fucking democracy.

"I said no."

"Can we have a minute?"

When they both walk out of the kitchen, Blaze reaches over and swivels my chair, facing him, and places his palms on either side of my legs, gripping the seat. His eyes are flaming low, stormy and dark. If he thinks I'll be intimidated by him too, he can also go fuck himself. I cross my arms over my chest. This ought to be good.

"I'm actually a board-certified surgeon in the human's... world, for lack of a better term. I'm CEO of a hospital. Besides being a Healer with Magical abilities. I'm over-qualified and I would do a better job than Dexter, who'd just go brute strength and try to break your ankle."

"No."

His eyes flash gray. It's actually fascinating at how much they reflect a summer thunderstorm, all gray and blue and black, warring with each other, the flame of it almost smoldering against his obvious emotions. The muscles in his forearms bunch. He must be wishing the wood was my neck. I want to grin at the display of contained violence. I want to tell him I think it's adorable that he's willing to heal me. I do neither of these things.

"No."

"Arnica!"

"No."

"I don't understand. Explain to me why not. Do you not trust me after all?"

So he hadn't missed the fact that my ring finger is still bare. I've never explained myself to anyone, have never needed to. Have never had anyone want me to. Fuck.

I swallow hard and take a deep breath. My heart's pounding and a slickness spreads down my spine. Why is this so hard? I shake my head, and he jumps up and begins pacing the kitchen.

A glass of red wine pops up out of nowhere next to my hand, and it takes everything within me to not startle. "What the fuck?" I murmur, staring at the ruby-red liquid that flows all the way down the inside of the stem.

"Magic cabin," Blaze mumbles and continues to pace. His hands are linked behind his back, and he looks every inch like a rich, aristocratic board member. One born with a silver—no, golden—spoon in his mouth. A reminder that we aren't the same.

I guess the never-ending plate was more than seemingly attuned to how much I wanted to eat. I could get used to that.

I sip the alcohol and let it simmer in my stomach before the warmth disappears and sigh. I rarely wish I could change what my life is, but this aspect would be one of them. The alcohol metabolizes as quickly as I can drink it. No false relief here. Another reminder that we aren't the same. Speaking of which.

"You never told me how it was that you were able to take over and move through the rock, nor pick up speed to get us here so quickly."

Blaze pauses and his eyes roam over my face. "I'll tell you when you tell me why I can't work on your ankle."

My jaw drops open, but then I slam my mouth shut. Well, well. I hadn't anticipated this. Fine, I've got nothing to lose, and he's got secrets. Mine aren't nearly as interesting.

"You first."

"Uh, as much as I clearly"—he holds his left hand up—"trust you, I'm not that gullible. *You* first. I'll give you my word that I'll tell you after you tell me."

Low blow. My stomach rolls and clenches. His word last time meant a tear. No, no. He can't give me another tear. One of those things around my neck is more than enough. The thought of the sadness that would come over him crying it out makes me want to hurt someone.

"No need for that. I believe you." I inhale hard and let the words out in a whoosh. "If you hurt me, I'm going to hurt you." There. That wasn't so bad. I gulp the alcohol until it's gone and there's a pleasant buzz in my head for all of...thirty seconds.

He cocks his head and studies me again. "That's not all of it."

Fuck. Why does he need to be sexy *and* perceptive?

"All of it, or I'm not telling you."

That's blackmail. But maybe not really because I *hadn't* told him all of it.

"If I hurt you, I'll hate it." There. He can't ask for more.

"Why will you hate it?"

What is he a fucking therapist, too? I sigh. I didn't know I had a thing for tenacity, until it was too late. I hate that I find it attractive in him. I hate feelings.

"Besides my childhood, which was fine, I've not had a lot of normality. Nothing I ever did at the Weaponry was good enough... I was tortured okay? All I knew was pain and hurt, and I fucking despised them for it. I wanted to fucking kill them all, burn down the building and stomp on the ashes. But I knew that the building and the stones...that they would *want* me to feel all of that. And I would not give in and be like them.

It's the hardest thing I ever had to do. But I also swore that I wouldn't let anyone do that to me again. Hurt me ever again." I shrug and focus on my hands until my vision becomes less blurry. "Eye for an eye is my motto and I stand by that. I have no regrets about it. And that's because I knew that those that hurt me did it because they got off on it, because it rocked their fucking world. Because they hated me. I…"

I bow my head because the tears are stinging my eyeballs again, and damn if I'm gonna cry here. "I…don't want to be hurt by someone who doesn't hate me. By someone who is bonded to me for life. I don't want to be hated anymore. I don't want to hurt anymore."

Chapter Thirty

The air seems to have disappeared from my lungs, and my chest tightens till I wonder if I'm having a heart attack. Pain ricochets across my forehead, one massive headache.

Blaze moves forward till he's in front of me again and I swear his emotions roll off him and batter my skin.

The scent of something sweet and exotic, jasmine maybe, with a hint of warm chocolate chip cookies, flows around me. The air turns warm and seems to caress me, and I stiffen at the contact rolling through my clothes and onto bare skin. I lean away, panic warring with calmness, which only makes me panic more. I shake my head to clear the sensations seeping into my brain.

"What are you doing to me? Stop it." My voice sounds forced and unnatural.

"I'm not doing anything. Dex!" he shouts into the space behind me. My bones turn languid, the muscles relax, even as I'm trying desperately to keep my spine straight.

"Something's happening to her. Has someone penetrated

your defenses?" The fear in his voice makes me want to soothe him and tell him it's okay. That I'm not hurting. Far from it, in fact. It's almost as if I'm floating weightlessly off the ground. Why did I fight this? It's so...pleasant.

"It's the house. It's trying to help her."

The words penetrate the thickness surrounding me and I'm suddenly pissed. Why can't they all just leave me be? Let me be who I am? Why do they all think they have to fix me? Anger rolls harder through me and cancels out some of the lightheadedness.

"I don't need to be fixed like some broken household item!" I slam my fist onto the counter. "Stop trying to change who I am!"

The scent, along with the warm air and the strange sensations, recede, leaving behind just a shell of me, drained from the feelings flowing through me. Why can't I just be good enough? Everyone's standing around staring, *again*, and I want to scream that I'm not a fucking spectacle. This is what I get for talking about my thoughts. I glower.

"Dexter. Just break my *fucking* ankle already."

He glances at Blaze, and this time I do growl. I snap my fingers toward him. "Hey, boss of my own body here."

Cassie nudges him, and he moves forward, picking up my foot and looking it over for bruising patterns or something to distinguish the locations.

Blaze also comes closer, moving behind me, and the hairs on my neck stand up. He peers over my shoulder and points at two spots. "You'll need to break it here and here. But it's going to take effort. Simply breaking someone's bones with your bare hands is harder than it looks."

Dexter snorts, and using both hands. pulls in opposite directions. Pain shoots through my leg, but it's nothing compared to what it was, and he stops. He widens his stance and pushes and pulls harder, making my skin burn with the friction. Nothing. He grunts again, and I grit my teeth hard, because now it's not only hurting but seriously irritating me. My natural inclination is to kick him off, and I punch the counter hard.

I lift my arm to punch again when Blaze's hand shoots out and he grabs my forearm. Gold slithers over me, warming my skin. I wrench away from his grasp. Looks like he gets to get his cake and eat it, too. I cross my arms.

"Let Blaze do it." I can't help sounding petulant.

"I can fix your ankle without breaking it."

Even the cabin seems to have stilled. Tension rolls thickly around the air for several seconds.

"Excuse me?" The words sputter out of my mouth, wrapped in venom. I bared myself to him for *nothing*? Anger replaces irritation, and I barely notice Cassie pulling Dexter from the room. I guess that's why it's nice to have a woman friend. They know when shit is about to go down.

"I fucking told you things I've never told anyone else for *nothing*?" I nearly screech the words, but I pull myself together in time.

"It wasn't for nothing. I wanted to know, and I asked you."

"You made me think that you'd be breaking my bones and you used that to your advantage."

"Of course, I did! You don't exactly want to have conversations about anything, ever. You just state and demand and do whatever you want and expect me to roll along. Now, I don't mind, for the most part, but some things I do. That was the first time you've given me anything really about yourself. You're going to be my wife. I'm already bonded to you and am waiting for you to finally trust me. But you don't and I'm frustrated! And technically, we were trading information."

"Trust you? That's probably the easy thing to do. What's hard is having to trust myself not to take your soul, and I don't. So, no. I'm not going to even entertain the idea of trusting you. You're going to be waiting a long time.

"And, uh, side note: not being completely and transparently honest is going to help with not placing my trust in you. Never mind, don't take note. Just keeping doing that."

I don't want to be giving him tips on keeping me from him. I *should* want to be unbonded because he'd be safe. Instead, I want him to be persistent and stubborn. To fight for me. True to form, my needs and desires are horrible choices for the other person. It's never ended well.

When Angelica sneaks out through the window for a third time this week, an odd sensation slithers over me. Maybe this is intuition, maybe it's not, but something seems very wrong, and the longer I lay here, the more the feeling gnaws at me to get up, to follow.

Mom and Dad always act like she can't do anything wrong. Their little Angel. But they don't know the times that I've covered for her, telling them I forgot to tell her we had to be somewhere after school or that I'd swapped chores with her and then didn't remember to do the dishes. Everyone thinks I'm scatterbrained and clumsy, that I somehow lack common sense. But Angelica really is angelic. She never means any harm and she's serene and calm and all the things I wish I was. Instead, I'm passionate and outspoken, an advocate, sure, but also hotheaded and quick about making decisions. Act first and think later... something that really isn't prized anywhere—not at school and not at home.

I sigh and heed the need to save her from herself. I slip out through the window minutes after she does.

I shudder as the memory whips through me, and I force myself to stop thinking about the past. I've learned the lesson well; no need to rehash it. Wanting things doesn't mean I haven't figured out how to keep them suppressed.

Sliding off the chair, I land hard on my left leg, shifting all my weight, and drop into a pistol squat. The crack sounds like thunder in the quiet of the kitchen. I rise slowly without wincing or making a sound, staring deeply into Blaze's stormy eyes, welcoming the pain pouring into my ankle. It's a reminder that I don't rely on anyone, that I take care of myself. I don't need someone doing things for me, because then independence shifts and disappears.

I focus on the muscles around my ankle and continue to stand until the other newly healed break splits. The second crack isn't as loud, the bone not being healed as long, but it makes Blaze stiffen, lips compressed, fists tightened. His eyes darken till they're almost black, and he silently stalks past me.

I slump back into the chair and wait for Dex to come in with whatever medical supplies he's got. Super-hearing can be beneficial, and I know he won't take long knowing how fast I heal.

He's there in seconds and spikes the bandage roll at me. What's his problem?

"You're an idiot."

No, I'm not. But people always see what they want to see. I swallow the lump in my throat. It's better this way.

"Go fuck yourself."

He laughs and leaves. As I wrap my foot, I don't acknowledge the tear that rolls down my face until it drips off and disappears into my black leggings as if it had never been.

Blaze stalks back in and picks me up, cradling me like a baby. My heart flip-flops in my chest, and I ignore the joy that infuses me that he came back after my blatant fuck you. And while being angry with me—because I haven't missed the tension in the way he's holding me away from his chest. I barely touch him as he moves through the house.

"I'd have been fine in the kitchen. Or Dexter could've carried me."

He stops suddenly. "I want to take care of you."

I choke on the words, but he's got to quit while he's ahead. "I don't need you to."

He nods and keeps moving, starting up a set of stairs. "Fine. You're my responsibility, so you don't have a choice."

My mouth pops open. Does he not know who he's holding? "I'm not anyone's responsibility. I can take care of myself."

He snorts, and I almost scream at his audacity. I'm at a loss for something appropriately hostile when he says, "Need I point out that you can't walk without rebreaking your bones?"

He's got me there, but I still have choices. "You said I didn't have a choice, but I do. Dexter's here and quite capable of carrying me upstairs."

His jaw flexes, and the muscles in his arms bunch under me several times. He inhales hard and stops at a wooden door.

"Maybe you don't understand what bonded means. You're my wife, for all intents and purposes."

His voice has risen like he wants to tell someone who may have human hearing let alone someone with supernatural hearing. Did he just stake his claim, like I'm some sort of property?

I ignore the fact that it sounded sexy as fuck.

"Actually, you're bonded, I'm not." I raise my hand, in case he's got a thick skull.

He kicks the door open and shut before walking over to a four-poster bed piled high with pillows.

His head angles and dips down until his nose nearly touches mine. The flames in his eyes are translucent icicles.

"I don't think you understand. I will *fucking* kill anyone that tries to carry you into bed."

He places me gently down and kisses my tattoo-less ring finger and walks out without another word.

Nope. Not me wanting to call him back. Not me wanting to fuck his brains out at his possessiveness.

I had no idea I'd find his domination hot as hell.

Chapter Thirty-One

I don't have a chance to even lay back against the pillows when the door slams back open. Blaze walks in, and I can't help the quickening of my heart rate. Dammit. Why can't I keep my head on straight when he's near?

His posture, though stiff as ever, seems softer. He smiles sheepishly, one corner lifting higher than the other. "I never held up my end of the bargain."

Yes. I guess the least he can do is divulge some of his own secrets. I don't bother to hide my curiosity and sit up straighter, waving my hand toward the end of the bed. He walks to the other side and removes a pillow before coming back and sitting down. He slides his hand across the back of my calf and gently lifts my leg. He positions the pillow meticulously in the spot my foot had been and lowers it down. A small spark flits between us, and it takes everything I have not to jerk my foot out of his grasp.

"Can you please let go?" The way his shoulders round and the swiftness that his smile drops has me kicking myself. I didn't mean what he thought I did. "I have zero desire to suck your gold, okay?" I've made plenty of sexual innuendos, but this isn't one of them, and that it sounds like a lame attempt of one stretches the silence. There's a moment of more awkwardness and I rush to fill it. Change it. Fucking *something*.

"I don't want to take any more of the gold that lays on your skin. I know I already have, without even trying." The trip and his holding me notwithstanding. I have no idea why I haven't lost control yet, and I don't want to find what triggers me. Every time we touch is a risk to him.

His eyes blaze lightly before he clears his throat. "If you have, I haven't felt it. It's okay."

Does he not understand what happens when I take his gold? Does he not understand what that can mean for him? For the world? For me?

"No. No, it's not okay. It's never okay! Not only does it diminish the good that humanity needs from us as a whole in order to not dip into chaos, but it changes *you*. You're not going to be who you are anymore. I already see the difference." Even though the difference has been pretty hot.

He shakes his head, some blond strands flopping over his forehead before he brushes them back. "I haven't felt any change. I'm still exactly the same."

"Really? 'Cause not only did you used to frown at me saying fuck, now *you're* saying it."

His brow furrows and he seems honestly perplexed. I didn't know that the ones who lost their gold didn't remember who they were before, but that makes sense. Otherwise, maybe some of them could still do some of their do-gooding. But it's obvious he doesn't recall his previous aversion to the word.

"I'm not good for you. You can't be touching me constantly. Because I'm slowly siphoning off your goodness.

And I won't be a part of stripping you from your essence." And even without seeing it, it must be happening, control or no control. Because his attitude and the things he's been saying have been incrementally changing.

In general, I never want to take any gold, but in particular, I can't imagine that I'll like the Blaze he'd become without it. I've seen him grayed out and already feel enough guilt. I don't want any more.

"I don't have to touch you to heal you." His hand hovers over my ankle, and there's a warmth building inside me.

"Don't," I whisper.

I close my eyes when a cold settles over me at the disappearance of the heat. I need the pain to remember to keep my guard up with him. It won't take long anyway; the house seems to be speeding up my already swift healing process. The bones have knitted themselves together already, and if I concentrate enough, the cells within the bone marrow dance delicately, creating almost a ticklish, soft caress deep inside my limb.

When I first realized that I'm capable of sensing my own healing ability, I'd been fascinated enough that it pushed me to get hurt. I'd never hurt *myself* intentionally, but I trained harder than the others, took bigger risks and greater chances, which not only gave me the advantage of being the best trained Nightmare Killer that the Weaponry had ever turned loose, but also satisfied my dark curiosity.

I don't want to open my eyes, to see the disappointment in his, but he hasn't moved, and I'm almost positive he'll stay with me until I boot him out. I desperately focus on erasing any facial cues of my own disappointment, and I finally open my eyes only to see him leaned back against one corner post, his handsome face devoid of emotion, too. He's not mad?

"You're so sure you'd take my gold, as you call it?"

I nod. There's nothing else to say, but he clearly wants to keep beating this subject to death. It doesn't matter how often we talk about it or what things he comes up with as reasons to pursue touching me. I know what I'm capable of, even if he refuses to see it through that veil of color.

He gets up and opens a set of closet doors before opening one that reveals a decadently luxurious bathroom. He rummages about under the sink and finally asks the cabin for a handheld mirror before picking up the one that magically appears on the counter.

Blaze walks over, confidence warring with his shimmery gold. I frown. Just what is he up to?

He holds the mirror up, and I scrutinize my face. It's exactly like it always looks. Pale. Big, dark eyes, nearly black and almost too large for the whiteness of my skin. There are definite smudges under my eyes, and too many scrapes, bruises fading, and cuts along my hairline. They had to have been deep to begin with if they're still there. I also must have a pound of the rock cave we moved through on my face and neck and what I can see of my collarbone. The blood splatter makes me wince though. I look less like a badass Nightmare Killer and more like a pathetic zombie that just finished a meal —after crawling my way through the ground out of my grave. Bleh.

I push the mirror down. "I don't know what the point of that was."

"Do you have any gold?"

I stare for several seconds before a bark of laughter, laced with sarcasm, lets loose. "That is a poor attempt at making me feel bad about myself. I assure you that the Weaponry beat out any self-worth I thought I might have had."

I *am* surprised that he would try. This absolutely proves he needs to get away from me. Bonded or not. Soon he won't be the man I've grown rather fond of. Sadness and self-loathing twists inside of me at the mere idea.

"My point is you're not shimmering with gold. You haven't taken any of it or you'd be shimmering. At least, something."

My eyes narrow. I've never taken any gold but his, so I have no idea if I'd wear it like the golden ones do. The spark between us had been bright. When I'd unwittingly siphoned his gold during our kiss, I'd been euphoric. I don't know what happened to the feeling after I cut the connection. I...literally have no idea what actually happens to it. I've never wanted to find out, and I still don't.

"Dude. It's not that simple. I don't have a soul. You do. That's why your gold stays with you, unless someone takes it."

"I have part of a soul. As do you."

What the fuck is he talking about? I shake my head. Maybe the gold I took from him has addled his brains a bit. Something's a little loose in there now.

"You don't know what you're talking about. I can't have a soul. It's kinda what makes us Killers proficient at it. We take theirs."

"And have you taken any lately?"

His questions are getting ridiculous, and the itch of anger spreads across my chest.

"You know damn well I haven't. I've been here keeping *your* soul and *your* gold safely with you."

"You already have it."

Guilt nibbles away at my conscience. "I didn't mean to take your gold. That's why we can't touch, let alone kiss or anything else."

"Not that. You already have some of my soul."

"What the fuck are you talking about?"

He points to the tear around my neck, glistening against my blood-splattered T-shirt.

"I already gave you a piece of my soul. Maybe you don't trust me. But I trust you. With a piece of my soul."

The tear becomes hotter with the words, and I glance down, barely able to see the shimmer illuminating the pearl-like casing.

Chapter Thirty-Two

"How? What? I…"

I manage to stutter out and then trail off because I don't even know what I'm supposed to be asking. How I'm supposed to feel about all this. It seems like everything I've known has flown out the window since I met Blaze. I lift my fingers to the tear and roll it between them. It's not warmer than usual to the touch, but when I let go and it falls against my chest, it warms up again. Is this what his soul feels like? Hot? I almost snort at the double entendre. I'm wrapped up in the emotions that bombard me.

The sensuality and the intimacy of knowing I'm wearing his soul has the muscles in my body quivering. Like a tuning fork for water, my senses seem even more heightened. My body attuned to his. My skin tingling.

He kneels down in front of me and takes my hands in his. The gold color weaves between us, the spark tingling when it touches me briefly. It retreats and comes forward again, shimmery waves riding the air current.

Our linked fingers look so strange together. My slim ones

within his bigger hands. I didn't notice just how competent they seem.

I'm not used to touching people, though the Fates know I've wanted it more and more as time has gone on. Even with us touching more than I have touched anyone since I lived at home with my real family, it feels weird. Not so much strange as forbidden. Beyond our branches combining, I've been told for so long how detrimental it would be that it might just be ingrained. I might never get used to it.

And I don't want to.

The slide of his hand against mine, the calluses that stand out on my palms from years of gripping my butterflies catching on his skin. The texture, the sound of skin rubbing, overwhelms me, and I think my chest might burst from the intensity.

Is this always what it's like to simply *revel* in the sensations? I want to feel it forever.

His thumb slides across my knuckles, and I almost sigh in contentment. This is what it's like to not have to worry about control, worry about taking a soul, worry about getting my rocks off; just orgasm and roll. Gah, but I could probably drown myself in touch all damn day long. My eyes widen. We've been fine. We could. Maybe I could be in bed touching him ALL. DAY. LONG.

Fuck, I'm gonna die. And I'll die happy.

"As a Magical, I'm capable of learning certain abilities rather quickly. As your bonded partner, I'm capable of tuning into your particular abilities, even within a different branch of the Infinites. And as long as you've got a piece of my soul, you're my soulmate, and I can clone your abilities nearly perfectly."

"What the...?" I'm scrambling to change gears. He's probably not feeling the same things I am.

I had no idea about any of this. Did any of the Dreamers

know? We could have a formidable team of Nightmare Killers. Shit, there's one thing that he's forgetting. The biggest difference between us.

"Not everything. You have a soul. No killing Nightmares for you." I shudder at the thought of a Terror slipping into him. Of the insidious dark sensations that come with them. Of the shards of black embedding into him. It makes me want to vomit. He's too pure for that. But I'm not.

"Is that why I can't hear them anymore? Because I wear your soul?"

It takes me a couple of seconds to fully comprehend what I'm saying. Oh shit. My own truth slams into me and my stomach clenches, sweat breaking out on my neck. I can't hunt them anymore. Dread skewers my other emotions, and it's not because I make a damn difference to the world.

"I don't know, honestly."

The wonder at our touch, only moments ago, dissipates as if it never existed. I barely hear him over the sound of blood rushing through my ears.

When I arrive at the corner of two well-known streets, I hesitate. Which way did she go? Angelica's voice carries from the right, and I hurry toward her. I don't know what she said but she sounds scared.

I skid to a stop, my sneakers sliding on the wet pavement. Angelica is with some guy, who's definitely not our age—maybe seventeen based on the thin, scruffy beard he's trying to grow. His limbs, however, move with the precision of a trained man, slicing and swiping two blades through a shadowy...thing. When it disappears into the boy, I yell for Angelica to run, but she doesn't move. It's then that I realize there's another one of the beings and it's...sucking?...something out of another girl I recognize as Angelica's best friend before turning toward her.

"NO!" The thing grows an extra set of limbs that stretch out, elongating toward me, and I duck and turn to hide behind

something, anything. But there's nothing there. Suddenly, the boy-man is in front of me, metal whistling. Angelica runs up just as the boy's blades run through the dark mass and it disappears. But the swords had found a different target. She's staring down at her stomach, and I'm screaming for someone to help. To do something. The boy reaches out and touches her....and chokes on words I can't make out.

Angelica's body stiffens, and I sink to the ground, watching the boy mimicking the very movements the shadow had done. Her body collapses, and the screams coming from her mouth seem deafening on the night air.

The boy turns toward me, his eyes now an eerie blood-red color, and he steps forward. The pointy end of a blade pulsates out from his chest, and he halts, gripping the silver. It disappears back into his body, and he falls awkwardly to the ground.

"Are you okay?" The words ring in the air, but I can't answer them. I can only focus on Angelica's screams fading. Tears burn my eyes, and a woman moves toward Angelica's friend.

Suddenly, the words the boy had said register. "Save your soul."

And I don't know how, but I know that's what the darkness took from my sister. And I know that no one can live without a soul. And that my parents can't live without their Angel.

And I can't live without hunting Nightmares.

"You have to take this thing off me." I grip the pseudo necklace, yanking and tugging, but it doesn't break. All it does is burn into the back of my neck at the pressure.

"What?"

"Take this off of me! Now!" My voice breaks on the words and my body shakes with adrenaline at the realization that I can't hear people screaming from Nightmares. That it's tied to his soul hanging around my head. With it, I'm no longer soulless.

My eyes fill with tears and a sick feeling in my stomach churns round and round. My knees don't seem like they'd be capable of supporting me if I stood. Fuck, even my limbs seem boneless, and I slump against the pillows. The helplessness, the sorrow, years of pain and torture. All of it for nothing? Rage fills my body, pushing my blood in my veins. My heart pounds faster and faster and I can't gasp in enough air. No. I *need* to be able to kill Nightmares.

I *have* to be able to kill them.

They *have* to pay for what they've done. For what they *are* —monsters hiding in the dark.

And for what they made me do.

Chapter Thirty-Three

I crawl to Angelica and reach for her hand, making hushing sounds that I know she can't hear. I can't hear them above the shrill, horrified screams still coming from her. Our skin touches, hers cold and clammy, mine hot. Too hot. I don't know how to give her my soul, but I know that the ache in my chest, the tears in my eyes, the full-blown panic rolling through me has to be enough.

"Take my soul. You need it more than I. You're the Angel, the one that Mom and Dad have so much hope for. Take it." Nothing happens, but suddenly her howls halt and she looks so peaceful, but she's still breathing. Is that warmth in her hand? A gold spark shoots between us. Does she still have her soul? Is she taking mine? My tears come faster, but they are happy tears. I did it! I saved her! Or she hadn't lost her soul. It doesn't matter —she's safe!

I laugh at the joy spilling into me and breathe in a deep breath. That was close.

Darkness looms over us and I scream to the woman, to anyone, to come help. But it's too late. The same motions occur *like the replay of a movie clip and horror roars through me. It can't have her! I have to do something!*

There! The blade by the boy's side. I roll to it and grab the handle, standing quickly, dashing toward the monster sucking on my sister's soul.

It's heavy and I'm not trained. Anyone can use it though. You take the pointy side and stab through whatever you're trying to kill. I raise my arms high, the weight making my arms tremble.

I ram down and into the dark and it's weirdly easy, sliding in like softened butter until it meets resistance. NO! This thing is going to die, and I'm going to make sure it never terrorizes anything again. I push down, both hands on the handle, and brace my legs, using every ounce of energy I have to shove the sword down to the hilt. Until my hands are in it. Until other-worldly screams erupt. There's a dark satisfaction rolling through me. Triumphant.

And then the dark shadow backs up, my arms swallowing into the thing, still coming back until it disappears into me.

My hands are still fisted around the hilt. The sword standing up, straight through my sister's heart. A scream builds in me as the guilt, the horror of what I've done takes root inside me.

Gold whips in the air between us like a vortex, faster and faster. How is it still here?

The dark infiltrates my body, and my own mouth opens, no matter how hard I try to keep it shut. The shimmer funnels toward me and is met by its counterpart. A black funnel shoots out of my throat, and the two souls merge and twist around each other like ice cream swirls.

I'm drowning in joy and sorrow. Swimming in pain and pleasure. First hot and then cold and back to hot again. My arms flail out, the souls dip into me and out again, battling each other for dominance.

A blade comes out of nowhere and slams through the swirling souls. The shadow slips out of me, howling. But I'm louder. The screams pound through me, cresting, until they pour out of me. I'm spewing pain, but it doesn't help. I drop slowly to my knees, my hands sliding down the blade buried in Angelica, until my blood runs down and pools on her shirt before soaking in. My head drops onto her silent chest. No!

What must be tears of metal stream from my eyes, burning and scraping the delicate sockets. My body catches fire and ices over, robbed of breath. And oxygen plunges back in, long enough for me to inhale and shriek out my grief and pain.

Words whisper through my head, but the only ones I focus on are, "Would you like it to stop?"

My nod seems to take years, and suddenly every sensation is gone, until I'm an empty shell of a body.

I'm rocking through the memories, struggling to keep myself from screaming at reliving the horror of that night.

Blaze's body seems like a reminder of the heat I'd experienced. Somehow, he moved from the floor to sitting next to me, facing me. His arms, tight around my stiffened torso, an inferno firing around me. The gold shimmering between us is like a twisted version of long ago.

That night had been the catalyst of my life, the no turning back complete pivot. One day, I had been a carefree girl, living life blissfully unaware of things that go bump in the night. I'd been like some other Dreamers, those of us born without obvious abilities, just waiting for destiny to step in and point me in the right direction.

Instead, I had taken my fate into my own hands and made the decision that would bring me to the Weaponry.

I push back, forcing him and his gold to pull back. My voice comes out even and normal. He won't be able to catch the undertone of fear, layered by guilt. No one knows what happened, and as far as my parents were concerned, they lost two daughters that night.

"I can't wear your soul and be a Nightmare Killer. Please remove it."

He shakes his head, but before I can say anything he blurts out, "You weren't hearing the Nightmares before I gave it to you. Remember, you came to my house and accused me of doing something to you? I hadn't given it to you yet."

Incompetence weaves through me, frustrating me. Fuck. I hadn't thought about that. Panic at the idea that I couldn't continue to atone for my deeds, couldn't continue killing Nightmares had me rashly reacting. I frown. Everything had started changing at the same time—it's hard to keep track and consider rationally. My hand drops from the necklace. Maybe it's my desire to keep touching him. Maybe it's my need to be normal, or maybe it's my dark, soulless self, behaving like all the rest of its selfish brethren, but I nod. Even though I shouldn't. Even though, somehow, I think he's wrong, I don't want him to be.

"Okay."

His sigh doesn't go unnoticed, but I can't think about why right now. I need to figure out what's changed. Something I was intent on doing but keep getting derailed from. When he reaches out again and gently rubs my ankle and the gold shimmers in the sliver of space, I consider Angelica. Maybe it's time I do something that might have helped her and would help others with pure auras.

Maybe it's time I let someone into my life. Especially if that someone has access to potions that could hide all the gold from the dark. Starve them out permanently.

And maybe that someone could help me figure it out.

Maybe it's time to embrace the gold instead of running from it.

Chapter Thirty-Four

"I 'm sorry. It's...my instinct to protect...me. Maybe that's selfish, but the only person who looks out for me is me." I lift my hands, palms up, and motion toward the length of my body. "This is all I know."

"I despise that, more than you know. Not that you have to protect yourself. But that no one looked out for you, protected you. Don't ever apologize for it. You've got me now, and I'll always be here." His hand moves over my ankle again. "Your bone is almost healed. If you stay off of it, at this rate, you should be ready to go by tomorrow."

He continues talking, not realizing that my heart just shattered at his simple words. Everyone says a broken heart means you've got sorrow and pain—that you've been hurt. But that's not true. I had pain and sorrow—more than my fair share— and my heart had been in one piece because I'd poured superglue over it. No penetration, no breakage. Without heart, I could live the way I always have.

And he'd offered himself to me with a single promise. He'd trusted me with a single tear. And my heart broke for him.

The pieces feel like love and heat, life and sustenance. Solid and dense. No whimsical, fleeting tendrils of puppy love, but the hard and fast torching of everything I've known to be important before. In its place is the realization that everything I have is right here. If I could trust him with his own soul, the giving of it to me, I'd have the entire world at my fingertips. But I don't know how. And I don't know that I'm capable of expressing any of this, communicating anything without seeming stupid, and so I sit and watch his fascination with his aura, not saying anything.

Blaze observes the golden swirls and tries to touch them with his finger. They move back and forth with him much like a normal shadow would.

"I've never seen the gold you always spoke about. Does it always look like this?"

"For the most part, yes. Each person's gold has a slight difference to it, unique to the owner. Some seem, I don't know...denser? Some have a slight hue. Most people, even if they could see it, wouldn't be able to distinguish the difference. I can, only because of my enhanced vision."

"It's pretty."

I tilt my head, watching it, and then nod. I guess it is. I've never looked at it as anything other than something that needed protecting. I never bothered to learn about it, or at least, I always assumed that the Weaponry and the Mother had taught me everything I needed to know. *Why* I thought that is beyond my scope of understanding. I've never trusted anything they'd done to me. I'd seen the entire operation as something to run from, and I can't believe I blindly followed orders and never questioned the knowledge given to me.

I was a soldier just like the rest of my Killer family. Just as mindless. Well, fuck them. That's about to change.

"We need to have a meeting of the minds. I don't know how much you know about Dex and what he's trying to accomplish, but we need to bring you up to speed. First though, I desperately need a shower."

Blaze moves off the bed, and I quickly swing my legs over but don't get a chance to stand before he's scooping me back up into his arms. I really want to say something snarky. How I'm a fucking badass and how I've managed to move around my entire life without him swooping in. Except it gives me butterflies in my belly when he does it. And not in a scary I-need-to-fight way, but in a this-is-really-fucking-nice way. And dammit, no matter what, he always smells good. I always smell like Nightmare. Or blood. Or icky...whatever they spill out.

He carries me to the bathroom, and I resist the over-whelming urge to snuggle into his chest. Fuck me.

"House, I need a shower that will accommodate Arnica not putting weight on her foot."

I twist my neck to watch the shower widen and elongate, the lip of it rising high enough to keep water in. In the middle, a curvy chaise-like structure begins to form, and I'd bet anything that's it's going to be made to fit my body. Multiple showerheads pop out of the three walls on various levels, and little nozzles shimmer into existence on the chaise a couple inches off the edge, all the way around the seating. If I hadn't watched the whole thing happen, I wouldn't have believed it.

Warm-colored wood planks line the walls of the room, a gorgeous complement to the light-gray stones that make up the shower. When it had changed width and depth, the stones became irregular, and in lots of places some sort of greenery grows out of the cracks—vines and plants alike—several of them flowering. It's like I have my own private chaise in a hide-away amazon. The counter, made up of alternating slabs of wood and...maybe slate—I don't know much about bathroom materials—blends into the walls without any seam, and I wouldn't be surprised if there wasn't one.

The sink and mirror are stunning pieces of art, made of

some kind of metal, but instead of looking industrial and out of place, it appears just as natural as the wood and stone. Fluffy rugs scatter the wooden floor, and there's a linen screen on wooden posts and framework which I imagine hides the toilet.

It's a fucking bathroom, but it may as well be home, as comfortable as it makes me feel. Blaze doesn't comment on it, and I wonder what kind of lifestyle he's used to that this doesn't seem to faze him. He steps over the shower edge and gently places me on the chaise, which I expect to be hard and rock-like. Instead, it's maybe composed of lichen or fungus, as squishy as it is. I don't sink into it, which is more than absurd. My senses are overloaded with textures that should be here and aren't and vice versa.

A bamboo basket appears next to me, free swinging on a stand, filled with bottles and lotions and washcloths. Everything I could need to shower, even a razor.

"Thank you," I murmur quietly, weirdly embarrassed to be speaking to a house.

"You're welcome," Blaze responds, and I don't correct him. "Call out if you need help."

"Are you offering to scrub my back?" I can't help the response. I still remember my desire to spend all day in bed touching him.

"If that's what you need, I'll happily assist."

And then he winks. My jaw drops open, and he laughs, shutting the door, but not before I spot the slight blush on his cheek.

And not before my heart flip-flops once in my chest.

I could get used to a Blaze with a little less gold. Just enough to expose a hidden, spicy side.

Chapter Thirty-Five

I t doesn't take me long to become clean, and I lay for several minutes reveling in the warm water, spraying my body. It's nice to not have to run constantly. The cabin thought of everything. Items were within reach, and the water's controlled by voice commands, which I happily find includes speakers and music. The chaise, soft and inviting, the soothing sounds and scents, combine with the heat of the water, and I doze off long enough to become pruny. As much as I'd love to stay here, it's probably high time we discuss the Mother and her crew.

I ask the cabin for towels and a set of clothing, and they pop up next to me in the suddenly dry shower.

My shoulders droop a bit and I frown. The clothes are exact replicas of what I always wear, down to the black combat boots, and I wish I could want something different. One of the candles flickers and goes out, the wisp turning into the shape of a question. Fuck. It can read minds? The smoke dissipates, and I wait for an answer in the shape of any type of sign, but there's nothing. I guess even houses like to have their secrets. That's fair.

I think of something to wear, vaguely, but nothing materializes. Either it's playing dumb or it's just really good at reading body language. "House? I don't actually know what to ask for. All I know is black and efficient and good at keeping me out of harm's reach. I'll leave it up to you. I just want to be comfortable."

I'm not sure what emotion currently rocks through me. I don't feel stupid or embarrassed, but definitely on edge. What if I don't like what it picks out? Is this...anxiety?

A folded pile of clothes appears, and I reach for them. The matching bra and underwear are white and made of cotton, but so soft it's almost like silk. I put them on, squirming onto one butt cheek and then the other. I briefly wonder if the house is watching, and I bite my lip hard to keep from smirking. If it is, it's probably seen its fair share of Dex and Cassie and has either learned to look away or taken pleasure from it. Either way, it's probably best not to go down that path of thinking.

The dark-blue leggings are soft as well, and while not as skintight as I usually wear, they still manage to cling a bit. I easily put them on while hopping on one foot. A dark-gray button-down shirt completes the outfit. It's unlike anything I've ever worn before. I'm stunned when I pull at a button. It's only decorative, and I quickly yank the material over my head.

Besides being a hindrance, these things tend to open up at the breasts, which while it may seem cute—there were plenty of men and women I'd fucked who loved me ripping their shirts and popping their buttons—I despised it on myself for that very reason. The last thing I want is to give a Nightmare a peep show while it's dying. And the sleeves aren't tight in the shoulders, which is usually the main discomfort I've heard people complain about. It's long enough it covers my ass, all billowy and airy without being too loose. And it has pockets. I love absolutely every article of clothing. There's no holster for my butterflies, so I leave them resting against the chaise. On one hand, it feels strange to leave them off. On the other, extremely liberating, and I'm not sure why.

"Thank you."

Another candle flickers but stays lit, and I figure that's all I'm gonna get. "Blaze!"

There's a knock on the door and I roll my eyes. Why would I call for him if I didn't want him in? "Come in!"

He enters the bathroom in jeans and a T-shirt, his own hair still wet. "How was your...Wow."

"You mean my shower? It was wonderful. Warm and comfortable and...I took a nap." I smile, still in awe that I can do things, like sleeping and taking long showers.

"I mean you look..." He swallows hard enough for me to hear it, even with my hearing turned down low. I have zero desire to listen to the couple coupling again.

"Isn't it great? The buttons aren't real!" Blaze swallows hard again and I pause. I must not be making any sense. "I mean, they're real, they're just not functional. There's no seam in the front of the shirt." A blush blooms on his face. "What the fuck is wrong with you?"

"You look like you're wearing a man's shirt."

I look down. Really? It doesn't look like it to me, but I don't know anything about clothing let alone fashion. I shrug. He steps into the shower, and I have to lean back as he places his hands on either side of me and leans in close.

"Like you're wearing my shirt because I destroyed yours."

The flames in his eyes simmer, and I lean forward, millimeters from his face. "I want to see you try."

The blue blazes higher and his hands slide under my ass and cup me before hoisting me up and into his arms. I wrap my legs around his waist and my hands around his neck. We're nearly nose to nose, and he stands still. The flames in his eyes speckle with sparks. His heart pounds in his chest, and I don't know if he's waiting for me to give him a sign or if he's waiting to see if the gold stops pulsating so fast between us.

"Are you okay? Your ankle doesn't hurt?" His voice sounds gruff, and he clears his throat.

"I'm fine, and nope, doesn't hurt." I know the sexual tension between us has been building. Shit, anyone with any kind of sex drive could probably see the tension. What is he doing?

I move closer and angle my head, his cheek next to mine. I flick the lower part of his earlobe with my tongue, quick and light, but he inhales hard, and his heart picks up speed. The scent of sex leaks into the air. So...not lack of interest, for sure. I lean in closer and whisper loud enough for him to hear, but soft enough no one else should.

"I want to taste the droplet of pre-cum that just leaked out of you."

His golden shimmer nearly solidifies before swirling again.

"Fuck." His arms tremble and my own heart rate accelerates at the word.

Uh, yes that's what I've been thinking. Let's do it.

"As much as I want you, they're downstairs waiting for us."

I lean back. "Dex can wait." I lean forward again, staring at his lips. I can't wait to feel them on my body.

"There's a couple others here too."

I jerk back and open my hearing. Dammit, the Destiny and her Protector are here, too.

"Fine. But if I don't get a taste of you soon, I'm gonna start getting pissy."

"You're not the only one." He breathes out the words and carries me to a chair in the bedroom. "I don't think you want me to carry you down in this position." And he sets me down carefully.

"I like the position just fine, but you keep telling me I have to wait." I stand, putting all my weight on my left leg.

"I promise the wait will be worth it." And he taps my nose.

I scowl. Do I look like someone who gets their nose flicked? I cross my arms over my chest because my initial reaction is to punch him in return.

He chuckles and swiftly scoops me up, cradling me. I sigh because his muscles feel damn good, and his heart is pounding and he smells like delicate cedarwood and lemon. And because I'm a fucking Nightmare Killer who secretly likes being treated like I'm fragile. Fuck.

"Less than a day, and I won't carry you anymore. You can go back to being independent."

I sigh harder. That's what I'm afraid of. I'm sure there's a way I can make him carry me again. At least, every once in a while. When no one else can see.

Blaze takes me into the living room where a large L-shaped couch and leather armchairs are placed invitingly around a massive fireplace with an equally large fire merrily burning away. When you've got a magic cabin, I guess you don't have to worry about it burning itself down, but now I'm rethinking the house watching people in their privacy.

Clearly, it's got some masochistic tendencies.

Chapter Thirty-Six

D elaney and Drew are on one end of the couch and
Cassie and Dex on another. The Destiny, obviously
at home in any situation, in anyone's home, sits
curled into her Protector's side, his arm draped around her
shoulder. It looks homey—until I look closer. The muscles
move minutely under his skin in the forearm and bicep, and
the set of his jaw dares anyone to come and touch her. As if she
wasn't capable of burning everything down around us—magic
cabin or no.

Cassie seems ill at ease more than anyone, but I know she's
new to our side of the world. Dexter tugs gently on her
shoulder and her back touches the couch. She relaxes further
when his hand gently rubs circles into her thigh, and I clear
my throat as it moves slowly closer to her crotch. I'm not here
to watch live porn, and I'm already uncomfortably aroused.
They need to stop that shit.

Dex grins and moves his hand back to his lap, but Cassie
grabs it and threads her fingers through his. My heart lurches
at the sight. I...think I want that. Both of the couples—tough
as hell in their own rights. Both men, killers in a variety of

ways, and their equally strong and trained women could decimate an army. And yet they're leaning on each other in ways I don't understand. Comfortable touching, and if not showing emotion, definitely projecting some degree of being lovestruck. And it looks...nice.

Delaney moves her head in my direction and her eyes narrow the barest amount, and I narrow mine back. Does she think she's going to be the one to intimidate me? I don't give a shit that she's a Destiny; she can fuck off right along with everyone else. Drew stiffens, and I flick my eyes toward his face and nearly laugh out loud. If looks could kill, I'd already be dead. I lift my middle finger and then use it to point to a seat for Blaze to put me in. He does and opts to stand behind me, and the fact that it doesn't bother me, instead giving me a sense of relief, isn't lost on me. I don't know if it's because I'm getting used to standing in front of him to protect him or if I'm getting used to him being at my back, and suddenly, it doesn't matter to me which it is.

The silence drags on. Cassie seems lost in thought, staring at the blazing fire, and Drew and I seem to be holding a staring contest.

"This is fucking dumb. Are we all going to erupt into a fight? Because I'll gladly whip some ass. Let's go then," I finally say, fisting my hands and pulling them up in front of me, a mockery of my words.

Drew leans forward until Delaney puts a hand on his chest. "There will be no fighting," she says. "Can we all agree that each of the men has the same size penis, and we all have the same size breasts?" I almost roll my eyes. She's such a spoilsport.

"My left is slightly larger," Cassie says quietly, and I snort, which quickly turns into a laugh, and Cassie grins. Maybe she's hiding some big balls, too.

Everyone joins in, and just like that, the tension cuts

mostly in half. Still there, and really, those of us that are part of the Infinites will never *not* project our strength. Egos are one thing, survival is another. The last time the people in this room met, I learned that Guardian children weren't even taught we still existed and how that is even happening still amazes me. It's not as if we aren't here.

Instead of Magicals and Dreamers coming together to overthrow whatever the fuck is going on with the Guardians, we'd collectively distrusted everyone, and there's a massive fucking division amongst the three parts of the Guardianship. And now we all think we're superior to the other.

Blaze steps forward and lays a hand on my shoulder. His gold slithers over my back and to the other shoulder before receding into his hand. My skin tingles underneath my shirt.

"Arnica and I are bound together."

For fuck's sake, why is he telling them that? Cassie's left breast admission isn't a lets-tell-everyone-everything game.

Delaney sits up straight, her feet hitting the floor, and she raises an eyebrow. Blaze clears his throat.

"Or at least, I'm bound to her." His body temperature rises, and for the first time, I'm embarrassed. Not on his behalf, but mine. I wish he hadn't needed to amend that statement, and I jump in to defend his poor judgment in partners.

"It's a me problem that it's not reciprocated. And not by choice."

He squeezes my shoulder, but it doesn't make me feel any better. If only he wouldn't have said anything at all, I wouldn't have to apologize for myself.

"That's wonderful news." Delaney claps her hands like she's a child, and my gaze narrows. Why the fuck does she care?

Son of a bitch.

"Did you..."

She shakes her head before I'm even done forming the

words and talks over me. "I had nothing to do with it. It's just a path I saw."

I clench my fists but keep my mouth shut. She and I are going to have words, but not now when everyone seems vastly interested in our conversation. Her denial seems overly fake, considering she warned me about the moon and all. I growl softly and stiffen when Dex grins. He fucking better not be laughing at me.

I force down a retort because it's not productive. Efficiency-is-fucking-me.

"We need to discuss the Weaponry and the fact that the Mother is bringing her people after me. I don't know why. I've not done anything to them that warrants such an attack." Which is true. No book is worth them risking the death of their people at my hands.

"And the fact that you possibly brought this to my doorstep by coming here," Dex says drily.

He can kiss my ass then. I don't need him or anyone. I stand up, pushing past Blaze's slight downward pressure—I want to fuck him, not allow him to manhandle me. I'm not going to sit back down, dammit.

"Fine. We'll leave. I wouldn't want to inconvenience you," I snarl. This is what happens when you lean on friends. Even if they aren't mine. They can't be depended on.

Dex also rises. "*It is* fucking inconvenient when you're bringing warriors to *my* place of sanctuary when my *soulmate* is here."

Drew also stands, followed the barest quarter second by Delaney, who claps her hand over his mouth. "I came because I need to be here," she interjects and turns and addresses Dex. "We all need to be here. We've talked about this before. We need more concrete plans about the cracks in the Guardianship. This is a part of it."

I loosen some of my muscles from their fight response. I was right, there was more at play here than a mere theft.

Delaney points to me. "Your actions aren't off the hook here either." I know she knows about the book, but she doesn't say anything. Interesting. Maybe I need to take a closer look.

Dex smirks, probably because he has no idea that the Destiny isn't talking about me coming to the cabin, until Cassie stands up and places her hand on his bicep and leans toward him. I'm not sure if she doesn't realize most of us can hear her or if she wants to give him seeming privacy, but she whispers, "And your soulmate can take care of herself."

Good for her. He growls softly, and this time I don't bother to hide my eyeroll.

Chapter Thirty-Seven

After several seconds of no one talking and all of us pretending we hadn't heard Cassie, Drew sits back down, his ass on the edge of the couch, hands clasped loosely and elbows on his knees. It's an incredibly nonchalant posture and one we all can appreciate. It takes extra seconds to separate your fingers and come to attention, and it does more for the tone of the room than anything else had done. We all follow suit, sitting in various casual poses. Blaze drags another chair next to me before sitting down.

"The most important thing I can't stress enough is that not all Guardians are blindly following orders," Drew says, Dex nodding at the words. "And while there is only a small handful of us that know the other branches still exist, we've been trying to figure out a way how to talk to other Guardians without letting the wrong Guardians know we know."

"And without knowing who the wrong Guardians might be," Dex adds.

"Yeah. So, if any one of you has any brilliant idea on that, please share."

Obviously, they mean Blaze and me, since I'm sure they've

talked this all over with their soulmates already. I may have attended a meeting a while ago, but I have no idea what they've been up to in the meantime. And Blaze knows Dex, so what does he actually know about the Guardianship problem?

"So that everyone is on the same page, let's drop some info right now. It's safe to do so, I assume?" Dex nods, and I continue. "The Guardianship is falling apart and has been for at least what, the last eleven hundred years?" My parents had never really talked about the Guardianship, which means it had to be their generation—and their parents, too, had to be oblivious. Maybe that's not far enough back.

Cassie jumps in. "Shorter than that. I've been doing some research, and from what I've found, it looks like maybe seventy years. Maybe a little less."

"That's...a short-ass time. It's not even about the fact that the Guardianship maybe brainwashed people into believing two whole branches didn't exist...but that no one has ever questioned, or I don't know, ran into someone from another branch at some point in time is...incredible. And others had to remember a time we existed. It's unbelievable that not one person ran into, say, a Magical, and was like, hey, you're not a Guardian. Or what happened to Mary the Dreamer? How the fuck does this happen?"

And it's so obvious, it takes me more time to think about the ramifications than the answer.

"It's not just the Guardians in on it," I say pointlessly to the room. They either knew it or thought it before I did. Well fuck me sideways. I guess not being involved with people does have its drawbacks. I hate being the last to know.

Dex nods. "Yeah, Magicals and Dreamers, too. We have no idea how far this goes. Or any idea on how to tell.

"The Mother has to be in on it. She knew I was with Blaze...and that things changed for me." I ignore Delaney's obvious interest as she perks up. "Which stands to reason that anyone seen interacting with another branch might know what's up. And that they would attempt to eradicate the entire scenario." The likelihood that the Mother wouldn't allow Blaze to survive if caught is increasing by each word uttered, and fear weaves it's tendrils through me. I won't let anything happen to him.

"There might be something to that," Cassie says. She angles her body to Dex. "What if we set up meets?"

Drew shakes his head. "We can't risk the lives of people we expose. And asking them negates the secrecy we need to keep."

Dex's thumb rubs across Cassie's fingers. "Actually, we could use the club for that."

"Can you tell enough by their body language?" Her hand tightens around his fingers in response.

"Drew, Arnica, and I could." I jerk at Dex's response. I'm going to be helping them? Warmth blooms in my chest. No one has wanted me to be on their team in...years.

"Uh, first we may have to take care of the army coming for me." They're definitely the first threat. I won't rest until Blaze is safe.

"I'm not worried about them. Let them come." Drew scoffs, and Delaney punches him in the arm.

"The fuck is wrong with you?" Dex jumps up, violence emanating from the tension pulling his muscles taut. "This is my house."

"Exactly. And it's a fucking magical one. The defenses could be on par, with a little work around."

The fire erupts, flames shooting upward and out, sparks flying toward Drew.

Blaze throws his hands out, and blue flames stand firm against the orange-red ones, until they recede into the stone fireplace. "I don't think the house likes that," he says unnecessarily.

Even the cabin has a penis it wants to flaunt. Or at least an ego. Cassie sits wide-eyed. I lean toward her and whisper loudly, "Welcome to the Guardianship. Where everyone thinks they're stronger than anyone else."

"This is ridiculous," she says. "We're not going to accomplish anything by fighting."

"No, we're not." There's no way any of us are going to just sit around calmly and take insults either. "Let's go get some drinks or something."

I narrow my eyes at both Cassie and Delaney and jerk my head toward the kitchen. This is going to be done properly, by the smartest and strongest of the group—the women.

The three of us stand up, Blaze jumping to his feet to help me. "I'm fine. I'll limp along carefully. The three of you guys... just sit here. And for fuck's sake, don't kill each other."

When the house pops up three mugs piled high with whipped cream on the counter, I raise an eyebrow. That's a whole lot of yumminess.

"The cabin has my mom's special hot chocolate recipe. I promise you it's wonderful." Cassie slides spoons toward Delaney and me.

Dipping the spoon down and cutting through whipped cream to the hot chocolate and getting a little bit of both, I bring it to my lips and slurp it in. The explosion of melted chocolate and cream on my taste buds is like heaven.

"This is damn near orgasmic," Delaney says, humming appreciatively. I concur.

"I know, right?" Cassie smiles. "I figured we needed it after that display of...manliness?"

"Testosterone?" Delaney supplies.

"Idiocy?" I offer. There's a growl from the living room, and both of them laugh. I grin. I haven't had female companionship that wasn't sexual since...before the Nightmares entered my life. Too long—something else to rectify.

I lower my voice, even knowing two of the three men can

hear and are probably straining their senses to ensure they do so.

"Whatever happens...we can't let Blaze get captured by anyone from the Weaponry. They'll...torture him. And he won't survive. Please." I let the desperation and ache of worry lace my words—without it, they may not realize how important it is to me.

Delaney reaches out and covers my hand. Years of training keep my breathing even and my hand from twitching out from under her palm. I may not be intimidated by her, but I sure as shit wouldn't ever invite a Destiny's touch.

"I've heard the rumors. I'm so sorry." Her voice, velvety and soft, filled with genuine emotion, brings prickles to my eyes, and I blink rapidly and shrug.

"I wouldn't be who I am without it."

It's true. But her gaze bores into mine anyway, and the sensation that she knows every secret, every guilt, every thought pours into my body. My hand trembles slightly under hers. I want to yank it back, turn from her gaze, but sheer willpower keeps me in place.

"You are an extraordinarily strong person, and were, even before your time in the Weaponry. If only you could see what I do."

This time I do shudder at the words. No, thank you. You couldn't pay me to deal with Destiny-type shit. "I'll pass, thanks."

Delaney smiles, but it doesn't quite reach anywhere except her lips, and it occurs to me that we're alike in a lot of ways. "I can't say much, but I will say this. When you finally see yourself for who you are, you'll be unstoppable."

She sounds like Blaze. I should be relieved when she finally pulls her hand back, but instead there's a strange yearning in the pit of my stomach. Maybe it's like a phantom ache where my soul should be. I want to believe her, but everyone knows that your destiny isn't etched in stone.

And still, I'm willing to wager on her for Blaze's sake.

"Promise me you won't let him get caught."

Her eyes cloud over, and I know she's not seeing me. Is she having a vision? Looking into the future? My fists clench and I swallow the bile that sits in the base of my throat. *Please, please let him not get caught.* Asking the Fates is just extra support for what she finds.

Her eyes readjust and she picks up her hot chocolate. "I promise he won't get caught."

I blow out a deep breath and my entire body relaxes. Cassie looks like she's not sure if she should run or stay, and I pick up my own mug and toast her. "This really is amazing. Thank you."

I limp back to the guys. I'm itchy to get back to Blaze, just in case Drew and Dex decide to take advantage of his lack of enhanced hearing abilities.

He sits in the chair, the least relaxed in the room, the other two giving me glares. Whatever. They should know by now that eavesdroppers never hear good of themselves, and I smile widely toward them before I stand in front of Blaze.

"Would you mind taking me up? I think I've overdone it." It's not exactly truth in what he's thinking, but it'll work in getting us out of here.

He rises up a bit stiffly but bends down and easily swings me into his arms. I glower at the other two. I hadn't listened in to their conversation because I was intent on the women, but obviously, they had said something to him. I'll fucking kick their ass if they messed with him. He's too good and won't see them for what they are.

Plus, I've been good too. And I don't want to be anymore.

I think it's time I show the gold my dark side.

Chapter Thirty-Eight

He carries me up the stairs without saying anything to me. What the fuck did those two say to him? I'm going to march myself right back down there after he goes to bed and give them a piece of my mind and maybe a piece of my fist.

He sets me down on the bed. Did he put me down a little harder than before? I narrow my eyes. Maybe I'll give them my entire fist.

"Good night, Arnica."

Wait. What? I watch, dumbfounded, as he turns and leaves, closing the door gently behind him.

"Damn. Nothing like being let down. I guess I should be used to self-service by now," I mutter, not even caring if Dex and Drew hear me. Tomorrow, I'm challenging both of them to a round on the mat. It's high time someone took them down a notch.

The door slams back open and Blaze comes in shutting the door. The muscle at his jaw jumps, and he walks slowly toward me, removing his shirt. The chiseled abs I've admired since that first day ripple with movement. His shoulders and biceps seem more pronounced. Flames simmer in his eyes, and he slowly unbuttons his jeans but leaves them on. Did I realize he was barefoot earlier? Or had he already taken off his shoes? Doesn't matter. There's a hot, apparently angry, Blaze stalking me. Oh, hell yes.

My heart rate increases, but I don't move an inch. What is my do-gooder going to do? Me. For fuck's sake, please, let it be me.

He reaches for the lamp and turns it down. The low fire crackling merrily in the fireplace sends dancing shadows onto the walls and sharpens his cheekbones. His eyes glow blue without so much artificial light hiding them.

Like earlier, he slides his hands under my ass and lifts me up, my legs automatically wrapping around him. When he walks to one of the wingback chairs and settles me in, I can't help but be disappointed. He slides the ottoman closer but doesn't use it. Instead, he kneels to the side of me, and his hands frame my face. "You shouldn't be used to anything, let alone self-service."

He heard me?

"I'm able to clone your abilities remember?"

His warm fingers caress my face, my jaw, around my neck and ears, his golden shimmer gliding silkily along my neck to my collarbone. I'm going to end up one of those women that has to remember to breathe because I'm so focused on the sensations. I want to close my eyes and float on them.

Wait. "Why were you mad then? I thought the guys said something to you."

"Because you made Delaney promise you I wouldn't get caught by the Weaponry. I'm not some lost boy incapable of defending myself, and it's a little...frustrating that you keep thinking so. I don't need a protector."

I raise my eyebrow. I distinctly remember him asking for

protection. He shakes his head. "I couldn't see the Nightmares attacking me while I was sleeping. That's different."

"Fine, what about at the cave?" It wasn't as if he wasn't just standing there flailing one of my blades around.

"They had some kind of block on the cavern, because there was very little I could do. I did get us a way out. And I got us *through* the rock."

I run my tongue across my teeth. Fine. "Okay, maybe you're not completely incompetent, but I can still run circles around you, and that's a fact."

He lets go of my face and drops his head, his shoulders shaking lightly. Oh fuck. No. I made him cry? How did I do that? I didn't mean it, and I reach out to pat him on the arm or something. Do I hug him?

The shaking becomes more violent and panic races through me. I scoot to the edge and try to pull his arm, but he's not budging. Suddenly, there's a rough sound coming from his chest. A slow rumble that becomes louder, until he lifts his head up and back and wraps his arms around his waist. The gruff laugh has my nipples tingling in response. Some people think a man growling is hot, but Blaze's laugh—the rough timbre of it—strokes my sexual ego in a way I didn't think possible. I should be mad he's laughing at me, but instead I want to make him do it more. I smack his arm.

"I thought you were crying!"

He laughs harder, until there're tears leaking out the corner of his eyes. "I am now!"

I punch him.

"Ow!" He rubs at the spot, but the rumbles quiet down. "Sometimes...the way you say things." He smiles, and it's like the sun has come out. It's so fucking cliché, but it's literally what I'm feeling. How did I not know loving someone could be like this?

"You're right, you can run circles around me, and that's

one of the most amazing things about you. You fascinate me. Your complete disregard for rules and norms. You say whatever you're thinking. And you're strong. Not just physically, but mentally. I'm constantly stunned by your ability to parse through a situation and execute whatever you think is best. And I don't want you to ever change that."

I snort. "I'm not capable of changing those parts of myself."

His smile loses some of its light charm and becomes something a little darker. The shimmer of his golden aura snakes back into him just the tiniest bit. The hunger in his expression becomes more...feral, and my heart leaps in anticipation.

His hand slides up my leg slowly, stopping to squeeze lightly at my knee before moving up my thigh. His fingers flutter gently near my hip, and I lean back, slanted in the chair. Fuck me, but I'm pulsating and instantly wet. I had hoped he was going to finger his way to my core, but he continues walking them up, trailing higher on my waist, pausing a split second at the side of my breast before continuing up and lifting my arm.

The sensation of his skin through the lightweight material on the sensitive parts under my bicep and around my elbow sears through until I can only focus on the heat. But my eyes don't leave his, and the flames smoldering in them burn whiter.

He's at my wrist and he wraps his palm around it, cuffing it to the top of the wingback with his grasp. He might as well have a choke hold on my neck with that lockdown move—I'm sure I'm holding my breath, but I don't think I need air.

He leans forward, his eyes dropping to my lips, and I part them, wanting—needing—the kiss. My heart continues to pound in my chest, and if he doesn't move any faster, I swear to the Fates I'm going to die from desire.

But he moves past them until his cheek is against mine,

that blonde stubble hard against me, until cedarwood and eucalyptus fills my nostrils. My body trembles, and I'm not ashamed to squirm in the seat, my thighs clenching together. His tongue licks my earlobe, and his voice drops lower.

"You can tell me what to do all the time and I'll mostly follow your demands. But sometimes, I'm not going to listen. Sometimes, you'll *beg* me to follow—and I'm still not going to listen. Sometimes, I'll tell *you* what to do...and if *you* don't follow, you won't get what you want."

Fuck. My underwear is soaked through, clinging to my skin, and when I clench and unclench my thighs, it sticks harder and slowly moves off, and I imagine his tongue lapping gently. I raise my hand to my own breast and squeeze gently, trying to ease the heaviness.

He gently kisses my ear but doesn't move away. I'm going to orgasm from his words alone if he keeps talking. His other hand covers mine and pulls it away. I arch my back, desperate to touch myself, but his stomach and chest have me pinned to the chair.

"Remember what I told you in my kitchen? I said I didn't want to fuck you. I wanted to suck and taste until you saw yourself the way I see you, but I was so much nicer then."

He brings my hand up to the other and grabs my other wrist so he's got both pinned. I can't see where his hand drops, and I squirm in the chair again, wanting him to touch me, afraid he won't.

"Please." The word sounds loud in my head, but I know it's not. "Please," I say louder. He wants me to beg? I'll beg all day long.

His hand finally grazes my collarbone and a finger dips under the shirt, stroking the upper swell of my breast and so fucking far away from my taut nipple that too late I realize I really do want buttons that will pop. I gently gauge the pressure holding my wrists down, but he doesn't budge, and I try to lift them harder. He quickly moves his fingers out from my shirt.

"I guess you don't want me to give you what you want."

The fuck I don't. I still immediately, and his voice drops even lower if that's possible, and the rough tone isn't lost on me. Looks like I find a growl pretty fucking sexy too.

"Now, with a piece of my soul gone, I find I'm not so nice. I still want to suck and taste, but now I want to fuck you too. I want to lick every droplet until you see yourself, and I want to fuck you until you see me. Until you're screaming my name. Until you're damn sure I'm not incompetent."

He kisses the corner of my jaw, then slowly kisses his way to my lips, and my eyes flutter shut. I turn my head because I need him *now*. He presses a kiss softly to my open lips and licks the corner, my own tongue darting over to touch his. He releases my wrists and slides back down again, and my arms quickly snake against his neck and pull him in harder. His tongue plunges into my mouth, and the kiss turns urgent and rough.

He pulls away, the flames in his eyes brighter than anything I've seen yet, and the most adorable pink blush stains his cheeks. He hasn't lost his gold any. In fact, its tone is shades different, like a rose gold, and I wonder if the blush extends to his goodness. Fuck, but his face makes me want to cum.

"But no matter what, if you want to stop, say the words. I won't ever hurt you."

I lean forward until my forehead rests on his, and the angle has him staring straight at my breasts.

"I swear to Karma herself, if you don't fucking *start*, I'm going to hurt *you*."

Chapter Thirty-Nine

"Yes, ma'am," Blaze says, playfully, but there's nothing humorous in his gaze or in the quick intake of breath.

He cups my jaw and gently nibbles on my mouth. And right when I think I'm going to expire from unsated desire, his hands drop to my waist. His fingers dig in under the band and he grips it tight enough to pull the leggings down without me even getting off my butt.

His mouth never stops, his tongue never quits seeking mine. My own hands have lifted without conscious thought until I'm stroking his jaw, my fingers tracing the high cheekbones, sliding back to his ears, and finally gripping his hair at the base of his head.

I can't get into his mouth anymore, my breath feels hot, consuming the gold that shimmers around us. Sparks whip around my neck and his, like figure eights. I can't get enough of him.

When he pulls away long enough to pull my pants off, taking extra care of my previously injured ankle, it takes every ounce of self-control not to whimper. I've had a taste of him now and I don't want to let go.

I raise myself up on one leg long enough to yank my underwear down. If I have to wait for him, he's liable to torture me. And while that may be the kind I could live through, I don't think I have the patience.

I plop quickly down and yank my shirt over my head. I don't have a chance to reach around to my bra when he grabs one hand and kisses it. "There's no hurry."

"The fuck there isn't. If I don't get you inside me, I'm going to rage. You haven't seen me fangry."

"What?" He stills, and I want to smack him. We do not have time for lessons.

"Fangry. It's fuck hangry instead of food hangry."

And I yank my hand out of his and finally release my breasts from the tight cups of my bra. They feel ten times bigger, small as they are, and they need to be in his hands, dammit. Or mine. I'm not picky at this moment.

His rumble of laughter dies off the second I reach down and squeeze my nipple. The flames shoot up in his eyes, and he reaches for my waist and pulls me to the edge of the seat again. "May I taste you?"

"Fuck. Yes, yes. Stop asking me questions."

Blaze places a hand on each knee and spreads my legs slowly open, stopping to pick up my left and place it carefully on the ottoman. "Consent is important."

"If I didn't consent, you wouldn't own your limbs anymore."

He nods. "That's fair, but I'm still going to ask you."

Why me? The one man in the world who I want to take me fast and hard, no questions asked, and maybe even hold his own in roughness wants to kill me with kindness. Fucking do-gooders. I sigh gently. But he also wouldn't be the man I've given my heart to.

"Yes."

"Yes, what?"

"Yes, you may taste me."

The words don't want to come out, semi-stuck in my throat. I'm probably soaking the chair right now. Who the fuck knew consent could build me up on the way to orgasm?

"Thank you."

He's really going to kill me. He places small kisses on the inside of my thigh, his stubble scraping my skin, and it's like he knows, and he backtracks to gently lick away the slight burn. I reach for his head, intent on pulling him up so he can finally taste me, but he doesn't let me hurry him. My eyes narrow. He doesn't want me to *have* to self-service. Clearly, he's got a thing for wanting to do it for me. I grin. I just figured out a way to get what I want.

I slide my finger into my mouth, wetting it, still letting my other hand curve into his curls. I slowly slide my hand down my stomach, and while he's still kissing my other thigh, I insert it quickly into the wet heat between my legs, a gasp flying out of my mouth. Fuck, but I'm drenched and fucking sensitive.

He growls and I grin again, but quickly lose it when he pulls my finger out and sucks it slowly into his mouth instead. He slides it out. "That was supposed to be mine."

He bends his head and immediately laves my clit, alternating gently sucking and licking until an orgasm rips from me. I pull his head in harder, bucking against him as the second one builds almost instantly. And when his finger replaces his tongue, swirling around the nub and dipping into me, I climax again.

"Fuck, please, I need you to fuck me."

He stands, and my hands are on his chest, down his abs, yanking at the loosened jeans. I leave them pooled around his ankles and yank down his fucking all-cotton boxers and let his dick out...right into my mouth. Gripping his ass, I slowly back out, and he pulls me up by my armpits as if I weigh nothing. He rests his head on mine. "Fuck, if I can control myself right now. One more suck from you and I wouldn't be fucking you."

His breath comes in gasps, and I don't think mine is much better. He opens the condom he'd been pulling out of his jeans when I took them off him and rips it open.

He rolls it down and picks me up, before sitting down on the ottoman himself. His hands still cup my ass, and he positions me carefully before letting my weight down the length of his shaft.

I try to lift up, but he shakes his head. "No, let me do the brunt of the work. I don't want you to hurt your foot again."

And he uses his arms to lift me up and down slowly till I think I might go crazy at the slow pace. His mouth sucks on a nipple and I'm drowning in the sensations building in me again.

"Fuck. Fuck." He's not worried about my foot; he's trying to torture me.

The minutes seem like eternity as the intensity builds slowly and I use my hands to push off his shoulders, frantic to move faster to let the orgasm crest, but he's gripping my hips and ass, setting the rhythm. And fuck, maybe I like giving him the power.

"May I rub my clit?" I whisper in his ear. He lets go of my nipple, and after flicking it with his tongue one more time, says, "Yes."

"Yes, what?"

"Yes you may rub your clit."

And when I do, the slow build leaps and rises, and he lifts me higher, thrusting up into me, sliding me down faster, then slower, alternating the speed until I scream his name.

"Blaze!"

"Fuck, Arnica. Fuuuck."

And he shudders right after I do, and I collapse over his shoulders, holding his head to my chest and gasping in air.

Fuck me. And he'd done just that better than I had hoped and dreamed.

Chapter Forty

Once we gather ourselves, Blaze getting rid of the condom and properly getting dressed in a pair of gray sweatpants and T-shirt, he orders "room service," the house popping in a plate full of meats and cheeses, grapes and strawberries, yogurt and nuts in a rather massive wooden charcuterie tray. It's almost too pretty to eat.

"You know, I think the house might be a bit of a voyeur." I pop a grape into my mouth, the juice exploding on my tongue.

"It might very well be, but I put a veil over the room until I ordered food and then turned it back on."

"A veil?"

"Kind of like a screen...it's also soundproof. I didn't think you'd want them to hear us."

That was thoughtful of him and something that hadn't even occurred to me while in the heat of the moment. It's a good thing he's so good.

Now, we lay together on the bed, our fingers loosely linked, staring at each other, and I can't help but wonder if this could be the rest of my life. And if I'd be happy with it. I've been go, go, go for so long that this seems amazing...but the antsy hum in my body is more than from orgasmic oblivion. It's a need to move. And I just can't figure out how I can have both.

The first step will probably be to bond with him. Unfortunately, allowing myself to let go and trust myself to not consume his soul during sex had not been enough, and my finger remains tattoo-less. Blaze doesn't comment on it, but I wonder if it inadvertently hurts his feelings, and *that* makes me angry.

I'd been the cause of my parent's pain, taking the life of their angel, and then further buried the knife with their loss of me. I knew they'd loved me, even though they didn't love me as much as her, and I had made my peace with that when she'd still been a toddler. No one could resist Angelica. And I'd been aptly named, too. But Nightmare Killers weren't allowed to be around family or anyone they cared about unless they wanted to take their soul. Untrained Killers were uncontrollable.

He's bound to me and one day I hope to be bound to him too. I don't want to be the cause of his pain. Ever.

"I...haven't been quite honest with you." I hesitate, not wanting to disturb the tranquility but also suddenly compelled to tell him. Maybe that's *why* I haven't bonded with him. I need to trust him with the truth.

"I stole a book from the Weaponry."

"Oh?" He doesn't seem too worried, still languid and relaxed.

"I think that's why they're coming after me."

His body loses its nonchalance, and he props his head up in his hand. "What kind of a book? If you think they're after you, it must be important?"

"That's the thing. I have no idea. But you might know. It's a Magical book."

He lets go of my hand and sits up. "Do you have it here? Can I look at it?"

I nod and point to the bookbag he'd been carrying when we left the Ferrari. When we'd stopped for water, I had removed it from my bag and slipped it into his, in case the Mother somehow had managed to capture me. It was the only reason I'd let my bag stay behind when we left the cave. There had been nothing in it of true importance, and I knew they'd search for it hoping it was there.

He rummages in and withdraws the book, carefully putting the bag down. He walks slowly back to the bed, his hand caressing the outside cover. Blowing softy on it makes the black float away like dust, leaving behind an extremely shiny golden book. Blaze's eyes flame, and for once it holds steady, obscuring the pupil completely like the first time I saw it.

The reverence and stunned awe across his face obviously means he knows what it is.

"I'm guessing it *is* important."

He lays it carefully on the bed between us, and I sit up fully, the both of us looking at it. The delicate scrollwork on the front seems etched in black.

"Magical Myths, Memories, and More," he whispers.

I bite my tongue so I don't say something along the lines of him being able to read and wait patiently for more information.

"This has been lost for a long time, centuries, maybe."

"That still doesn't tell me what it is. Or how it came to be in the Weaponry."

"I don't know either, but the stories were murky. Everything, from it had been stolen, to someone in the Magicals had run off with it, to it burned up in a self-fire. It's literally all the recipes to all the potions."

He can't possibly sound any more stunned. His hushed tone speaks volumes.

My heart drops. He won't need to marry me anymore for

them then. I wonder if he'll be mad that he's now bound to me. Maybe that's why I hadn't bonded to him. Destiny or Fate knew we'd be here, in this situation. I was simply the catalyst in bringing back the Magicals their rightful property. Weariness weighs on me. I'm tired of not being important. Of always being used. My stomach churns until acid burns the back of my throat and I swallow hard, reaching for some water. I take a sip and put it back carefully, making sure my face doesn't show any emotion.

"That's good then, right?"

He nods slowly, but he hasn't opened it or touched it in any way.

"I couldn't read it, as it seems to be written in another language, and there's large sections missing. But I'm glad you have it back."

And I am happy for him, for his people. He'll be able to experiment with whatever potions he wants to without needing anyone's approval. And without marriage as a prerequisite. I imagine it'll change the scope of power for Matriarchs and their sons.

"You wouldn't have been able to read it, as a non-Magical. The language changes are a protective measurement."

It's my turn to nod. It makes sense. But I don't want to be stoic. I don't want to take this news calmly. I want to scream when is it my turn to be happy? When do I get to keep what I love?

Tears burn in my eyes, and I pretend to fuss with the sheets, desperate to get a hold of myself before I outright lie to him. "My ankle is really starting to bother me. I think I must've over done it. And I'm tired. I think it's time for me to turn in. I'll see you in the morning."

As expected, Blaze immediately jumps up and places the book on the nightstand, carefully covering me up. I yawn and worry it might be a bit overdramatic, but his eyes keep straying to the thing as he straightens the sheets. He leans down to kiss me, and I close my eyes, turning my head. His lips land on my cheek and his hand strokes my head. When he turns the light off, I slit my eyes open to see him snatch the book up and hold it to his chest like it's something precious, and I can't blame him for it. It's everything that's good in his world...and I'm not.

The tears silently drip out of my eyes, rolling off the side of my nose, and soak into the pillow before he even shuts the bedroom door behind him.

Chapter Forty-One

I didn't sleep well at all, lost in dreams of Blaze driving away to wherever his home is and leaving me to Dex and Drew, who keep laughing and telling me I should go back to doing what I do best—being alone.

When the sun's rays peek over the horizon and shoot in through the windows, I finally roll out of bed and ask the house for my typical clothing, down to the black combat boots. I strap on a back holster and slide in my butterflies, grateful at least for the comfort of metal. Out of habit, I ask for thigh holsters and knives and strap down.

A hike in the forest will clear my head, let me focus on arranging my thoughts so that when he breaks the news to me, I don't break. Or at least not in front of him. The ripped pieces of my heart had shattered into more pieces last night, and now I know why singers croon about broken hearts and dreams. Both of mine were crushed by an object, and I really wish I hadn't taken that moment to tell him about it.

Of course, it doesn't matter. Obviously, I'm not meant to be his. Probably because I'm not good enough. And I'll never *be* good enough. The soulless Nightmare Killer will never be good enough for a gold-shimmering, do-gooding, Magical Healer. In what world did I think it would work? That we could be together.

No wonder bonding didn't happen. It doesn't matter what information or action I trust him with. We aren't meant to be. Destiny or Fate had seen to that. No wonder Delaney had been interested in our relationship. She probably knew and was like what the fuck? As usual though, whatever she says usually goes.

I kick some rocks, wishing it was her face. I'm so tired of not being deserving of nice things. The morning air mocks me with the scent of many cedarwoods. It's like my own brand of torture. Why the fuck did I come here? I don't pay attention to the pushback of the magical boundary. And I don't notice the eerie quiet until it's too late.

The net springs up out of the forest floor like in some fucking movie the minute I step on it. It shimmers, not quite gold but some kind of iridescence, all the same proving something or someone Magical is involved.

Whatever it's made of is immune to my strength and my various blades. I stomp my foot, pissed that I never considered a trap. Knowing the house was protected made me lower my guard, and it hadn't crossed my mind that they'd find the place and wait me out.

My new personal nemesis, the Mother's prized possession, steps out from behind the trees. "I'd love to say I'm surprised, but since I set and predicted this trap...I'm not."

The man's slim and young. But the hardness in his face—his eyes—tells me more than anything else could. Nothing puts that look there except for years of pain, years of figuring out how to beat the system and then annihilating it. There's a certain tenacity, a will to live, to hand out a fuck you—I'm capable, just fucking watch me—that I recognize. I'd seen it in my own face more times than I cared to count.

Except instead of leaving, he obviously revels in the power since he's still there. There's a fine line between learning and mimicking every torturous move—executing them—in order to win, ruthless decisions and deaths at your hands, that you put down as necessary steps in order to escape and *liking* it, *choosing* it. And when you cross that line, the difference between doing what you must in order to survive and enjoying it, it makes you no better than the horrors you're fighting.

And that makes him my number-one priority to put down. Fuck the personal reasons. This is for the good of the world. The Mother of the Weaponry, vicious and heartless and tenacious, had been bad enough. But even I can see she's... tired. Losing her edge. Still more than formidable, and until me, unbeatable. And yet I can sense this is just the first step in her downward slide toward defeat. Someone, somewhere, will be able to take her down like I did. And for whatever reason, this man has not.

And when he does, because it's a matter of when not if, he's going to put everything she's done to shame. I will not allow it.

I snort. "The problem with cockiness is blindness. Watch your vision, kid."

There's a miniscule movement in the shoulders betraying him. *Not expecting that, were you, you little shit.*

"Don't pretend that you wanted to get caught in order to save face," he scoffs.

I raise my eyebrow, making every muscle in my body relax. "You're kidding me, right? I'm fucking Arnica. Maybe you need to run back and find out who you're actually talking to."

I motion with my fingers for him to run along and bite the inside of my cheek when he jerks himself taller. He still has a lot to learn, but maybe he's just a good strategist and not as much of a threat as I thought he was.

"If you think you see a weak boy, maybe it's your vision

that needs checking," he snarls, his lips twisting into nothing resembling a smile. The adrenaline shoots through me. He's right, I almost made the same mistake I accused him of.

He stalks forward. Can I yank him to the net, make him talk? He's close enough for me to see a few wisps of man-child beard that he'd missed shaving off, and my fingers itch to curl into his shirt and beat my release out of him.

"I bet you're wondering if you can make me let you out. That you're seeing my young face and thinking maybe I've got the brains but not much more from a warrior of the Weaponry. It would be the last mistake you'd make while I'm holding your still-beating heart in my hands."

It's my turn to make sure not a single twitch betrays me, and I stare, unblinking, into his eyes. I move close enough that there's no question of what I think of him. My first instinct had been right, and I should've stuck with it. I won't ignore it again.

"If you think you can intimidate me, you can fuck right off. And as a courtesy due to your obvious youth, I'll tell you this. You better fucking run. Because I have every intention of putting you down like the disgusting pile of skin you are."

He tilts his head, the unwavering gaze dark. Black thoughts and emotions batter me. Fuck, but he's let the Weaponry infuse his body. It's enough to make nausea roll through my stomach, but I'm made of stronger stuff, and I swallow it down.

"I have no doubt you'll try. I wonder...will that be before or after I cut your lover to pieces?"

Rage thunders into me and my vision tunnels until all I see is the smooth face of the threat in front of me. I don't bother with coming up with anything suitably impressive because he's clearly getting off on the exchange.

I shrug and my hand rises, but instead of ramming my fist

through the net and into his fucking teeth, I slowly lift my middle finger and grin, my own pearly whites flashing.

He inhales hard, again not expecting my response. That's all he'll get from me, and I sit down cross-legged on the floor to wait out whatever or whoever my transport will be.

Chapter Forty-Two

There's probably fifty or sixty of them, and I'm simultaneously pissy that they thought that would be enough and pleased that that's all they think they'll need. Either they're dumb or dumber, and I'm okay with either option.

The formations around me are intricate enough that my estimation of the man-child's brain rises. Rings of alternating numbers of warriors fan out. There are ten next to me from what I can tell, armed with a variety of blades strapped every-fucking-where. Then five in the next ring with tasers, twelve or so with no weapons, seven with. And so on. There are point guards forming diamonds in between each ring.

I don't think I can escape the magical netting though, which has been placed onto a slab of rock that floats a few inches off the ground, since they let me keep every one of my weapons. Or they don't want to risk opening my shimmery prison to take them. I'm not sure what the formations are actually for in either case.

Contrary to what he might think, I'm going to allow them to take me back. The disappointment in his face when we round the corner to the Weaponry and with it, the last chance at attempting escape is perfection.

The Mother greets the party at the door, a huge smile on her face, and the urge to tell her she's counting chickens before they hatch is strong, but I keep my mouth shut.

The perversion of the stones, the despair and fear, simmers in the air, and I hold my breath as much as possible. I can't fucking stand it and have no idea how I lived in this place for so long.

They bring me right to her, and she doesn't waste any time. "Where's the book?"

"What book?"

Her hand snakes out, backhanding my cheek hard enough my neck bones crack. Fuck, but I forgot how hard she can hit. I swipe a hand across my face, flicking off the blow. The man-child steps forward, his face calm and devoid of any emotion. I thought for sure he'd be gleeful. "Allow me, Mother."

"No, she'll be remembering her place soon enough, Kit."

I laugh, a short, humorless sound. "Kit? As in a *baby* fox?"

I can't help needling him, knowing I'm going to annoy the fuck out of him. He steps closer again, anger rushing across his face, flaring his nostrils. His hands fist and he shakes his head. "Your mouth should be shut. Shall I make that permanent?"

I angle my chin upward in a bro-type nod, as if we're just hanging around. "Whose gonna do that for you?"

"Kit. Enough." The Mother backs up and points down the nearest stone stairwell. "Take her to the dungeons."

"Goody. It's always fun down there. Come get me, Kit. I'll be waiting."

Maybe he'll be stupid enough to actually follow through. It doesn't matter how good he is—I'm better. And it'll make the perfect statement.

Any one of them want to fuck around with me, they'll find out exactly what I'm capable of.

Unfortunately, Kit doesn't follow us down, and the warriors still left with me don't talk or make eye contact. They're too scared of the Mother and her swift punishments. And I don't blame them, but I will judge them. Spineless cowards.

The stones are slick, and one of them slips off the edge and tumbles to his death, too many feet below for anyone to see. They just keep moving without even shifting in their stance, and anger burns through me. If I could, I'd set fire to this place countless times till even the rock melts.

After they bring me into the cell, a woman appears at the bars, and suddenly the net lets me out. As it floats to her and through the bars, along with my weapons, my eyes narrow. Fucking Olivia from Crofton Hospital.

"You know, I don't know what they do to Magical traitors, but whatever it is, it won't be enough."

She sniffs and flicks her blond hair over her shoulder as if she's better than me. "Who says I'm a traitor? I'm just helping out my fellow Guardianship members."

"You can't be that dense. Which means you either don't care or there's something in it for you."

A peculiar hiss cracks on the air, and the accompanying scream echoes down the hall, setting off a cacophony of moans and shouts. I'd turn down my hearing, but those types of abilities can be blocked, and mine had the moment I crossed the threshold. No acute hearing or vision. No speed.

"Looks like there's a whipping taking place. You should go see what they do here, what you're supporting with your non-traitor actions."

Fear flits across her face and she looks around before turning to me. "I'm sure they deserve it."

Which effectively removes the 'she doesn't care' part. "I don't know what they promised you, but I assure you, you're not going to get it."

Olivia glowers. "You're going to say anything to try to get me to help you. They told me what you were like. And I was already on my way to getting what I wanted before you stepped in."

"What the fuck are you talking about?"

She blushes and the similarity triggers my original thought about her calling him.

"Blaze. You think you're getting Blaze." I shake my head at the ease with which they've used her naivete. "He's not an object they can hand over to you."

The blush becomes redder with her anger and her neck becomes blotchy. "The book you stole will take care of that."

Fuck me. "I guess you're the Magical that's going to decipher it for them."

She's going to be collateral, and she doesn't even know it. And if she gives them recipes and potions, who the fuck knows what she'll unleash in the world. I have no idea what's in it, but Blaze's reaction had been potent. It was important, and that means falling into the wrong hands is not an option.

She's a Magical that worked at the hospital with Blaze. She must have had a golden soul at one point. Not anymore, obviously, but maybe I can appeal to the goodness she thinks she still has.

"They're sick, Olivia. They torture people. They have no soul. Do you think they won't hesitate to lie to you?"

She shakes her head.

"They won't let you live. They'll get what they want from you. You'll give them access that no Non-Magical should have, and they *will* kill you."

She backs away slowly. "I'm not listening to you anymore."

My chances of talking her to my side were slim at best, but I had to try. I guess everyone has to learn the hard way.

"Blaze will never marry you. He's bonded to me." There's

no way she can see in here without spectacular vision, and even then, probably not well. The fear and emotions move sinuously around the walls.

Her gasp rings in the cell and she materializes in with me. That was too easy. No wonder they targeted her.

"Let me see your hand."

"No, I'm not letting you touch me. How stupid do you think I am?"

I move backward, drawing her into the stones. Their permeance wafts from them, moving toward her, feeding off her anger, hate, terror. I won't let them torture her, but I also won't let her simply hand over centuries-old recipes to anyone at the Weaponry. When she's close enough that self-preservation takes over and her body stills, doe-eyes trained on the stones, fear oozing out from her pores enough that even with the loss of my supernatural ability to smell it assaults me, I pounce on her.

My arms wrap around her neck and head. "I'm sorry, but I can't allow you to follow through with this."

And I twist quickly and viciously, snapping her neck in one swift movement, and thrust her body toward the stones. I throw myself backward to give myself enough distance. Her soul wisps out and is swallowed by the rocks.

I didn't want them to have her soul either, but the alternative was to take it myself and fuck that—I'll pass.

Chapter Forty-Three

Word spreads fast, probably among the stones, the greedy fuckers, and warriors come in with 'messages' from the Mother. They arrive in pairs, six at a time, and inflict whatever pain she's demanded. I curl up on the floor and protect the sensitive parts of me to the best of my ability. There's no stopping them, and they won't kill me. She's never been known for mercy or gentleness.

They kick me, combat boots digging into ribs. They whip me with belts and ropes. They punch me, standing me up and letting me drop to the floor after each round of hits. I don't give them the satisfaction of so much as a grunt. I've endured far worse. They break several bones, and I lose track of time. But I've been here before and I've survived. I'll survive again.

When the sword master comes, he knicks various parts of my skin, steering clear of any arteries or anything I might actually bleed out from.

And then she comes.

"I see you haven't lost your defiant spirit. They say you haven't made a sound."

Of course, that's what she wants—if only so she can

punish me for being weak. My years out of here may have been long, but my memory's longer. I'd bite off my tongue before giving in.

I stare at her quietly, swaying gently on my feet. No matter how hard I tell my body to stop moving, it refuses to cooperate. Blood coats the floor beneath my bare toes. There's not much left of my clothing, and between the cold and the blood loss, my body simply refuses to listen to me.

"I'm disappointed in you, Arnica. You killed the girl that was going to decipher the book you stole from me." That tone, like a true mother berating her child over bad grades, singes the air with its false innocence.

"We checked your apartment. Blaze's apartment. The cave. Everywhere you've been. Which means you still have it. Where is the book?"

I don't answer and she can't make me talk. She waves her hands slowly about. "Your lover has to leave that house at some point. And when he does, we'll be waiting for him, I promise you."

Fear whips through me and forces my body to attention in a way I hadn't been able to make it do. I grin through bloody lips. "And don't forget my promise to you if he' s hurt."

She laughs, a grating sound that vibrates my eardrums with its pitch. "I want to see you try. Honestly, I don't think you can get out of here in your condition, let alone beat my warriors. And then, you'd have to beat Kit too. He's my pride and joy, better than even you." She leans forward. "He's actually so good that he's beaten me many times. But unlike you, he has big goals and dreams. He knows no one in the Weaponry will take him seriously at his age and so he hones his craft, slowly becoming more cruel, surprising even me with his ability to think up suitable punishments."

The reverence makes me want to vomit all over her. I fucking hate this place and what it stands for. I hate her and what she turned me into, and the first chance I get, I'm changing her life status.

She's going to fucking die at my hands if it's the last thing I do.

"I know what you're thinking. That you want to kill me." Her face, serene and dangerous in its stillness, takes on a sheen. Her excitement causes dread to sit heavy on my chest. "But honestly, I'm not sure you have it in you."

Her head tilts, her beady eyes looking distinctly birdlike. "You see, though you may be strong, deadly even, you don't have what it takes to kill me. You know I saved you. When you couldn't do anything but scream and wail pathetically that you were missing your soul. And why was that? Oh, because you killed your sister. After saving her and giving her yours, you killed her. Was that your cruelty, Arnica? Did it make you feel powerful to give her life and then give her death? Did you like the way it tastes?"

Her hushed voice takes on a dreamlike quality, and my body sways again. I close my eyes against her assault. I know she's wrong. It was a mistake. I didn't do it on purpose. But the memory seems fuzzy.

"I think you liked it. But you had no idea that you'd killed your own soul. And that doesn't feel real good, does it?"

The phantom pain of my soul ripping away, my body convulsing without it, makes me shudder.

"You're just not good, Arnica. You're never going to be good. You're never going to be anything but what you are. A soulless killer, mindlessly inflicting pain."

The warmth burns against my chest. No matter how many times they'd tried, they couldn't remove my necklace. It's resting in a groove in my skin, in the back of my neck where it had literally been pulled into me by the warriors. No matter how it had hurt, I gained strength from it. They couldn't take it away from me.

The warmth becomes warmer. A reminder that I'm not soulless. I may be a killer, but I'm never going to be her.

I pop my eyes open, my hands fisting. "I am good. Better than you'll ever be. Maybe I'm not all gold and shimmer, but I'm not as dark as you. And he'll come save me because I'm worth something to him."

"Oh, I hope he does. I've got plans for him."

Fury covers me with strength, and I step forward. "Don't forget my promise."

Pain shoots through my head as images I don't understand swirl unseen. I don't look down, but the sting of a tattoo forming on my finger spreads joy through me until all the anger and pain evaporates and I want to dance around. Blaze's trust in me and my trust in Blaze has bound us to each other. And when he comes here or when I get myself out, I'm not going to let him back out of the marriage. He's everything I want, and I'm going to fight for him, dammit.

I grin, and Kit chooses that moment to enter the cell. Great. How many more want a piece of me? Because I've replenished my energy and look forward to the fight. I raise my fists and adopt a fighting stance.

He halts suddenly, and there's a glimmer of...something in his eyes. Was that regret? Empathy? No fucking way. I must be projecting my faith in myself. He sighs quietly.

"I thought we were going to wait on the torture. The Magical might not cooperate if we can't give him proof of her safety."

"She's safe. She's still alive. He can't expect much more. This is war." She shrugs and pulls out *my* fucking blades. "I actually don't think we need her anymore. He'll come because he'll think with his dick, and then he won't have a choice. He'll buckle under my plans for him."

I hiss. Maybe I won't have a chance to tell Blaze that I love him and that he's stuck with me for the rest of our lives. I barely can beat the Mother when she's got swords in her hands and I'm in top shape. But beaten and bleeding out, let alone two on one with the probably formidable Kit is a losing battle. I'll give it my all, but at least Blaze will see my tattoo when he gets here and know that in the end, I trusted him to come for me. That I trusted him with everything I have.

My body, my heart, and his soul.

Chapter Forty-Four

"I don't think—"

"I didn't ask you!" the Mother snarls, my butter-flies whipping faster and faster in the air. She's always been incredible with the blades, and I had learned every maneuver from her, studying her practices and fluid movements for years. I take a step backward. Unless Kit wants to get sliced, he better move back too.

The first blade whistles past my ear, a warning, no doubt, and I duck, rolling on the floor to the side, barely escaping each slice into the earth as she attempts to hack my body into bits.

I reach a wall and stand up, vaulting over her, and the blade knicks me at my collarbone, an inch away from my carotid artery. Fuck, but that was close. My eye catches sight of a knife on the ground by the door. Had Olivia dropped one of mine? It doesn't matter. I dash over to it and pick it up, parrying the longer butterfly blade with my much shorter one.

Confidence soars into me once I have a weapon in my hand. Before, I could only dodge. Now, I can inflict. The years of torture and torment, the physical and emotional

LIV MACY

battering I'd endured at this woman's hands fuels my arm. I switch from hand to hand, allowing the other to rest a bit as we swirl around the room in a dizzying circle. I manage to break through her arcs, thrusting the knife in several areas, each time barely missing critical body parts. All I need is to stab through a kidney or preferably her heart and I'll win.

I have no idea what Kit's doing, and I can't check even if I need to. The Mother takes every bit of my attention if I don't want to die. She catches me in the bicep deep enough that it renders my left arm useless in the fighting. She kicks out my right knee and I crumble to the ground. That is a definitive break. Fuck. I'm on my left knee and she's coming at me, bringing both blades down. This is it. I gave it a valiant attempt. And I do the only thing left.

I give her the middle finger.

Suddenly, instead of metal slicing through my head, there's a loud clang, and the echo reverberates around the walls. I whip my head up and stare in silence.

I'm not the only one. There's a beat and then two before the Mother screeches.

"Get out of the way!"

"No." Kit stands in front of me, his own butterflies crossing hers. While he appears nonchalant, barely any tension in the muscles of his arms, hers are vibrating with effort and a slick sheen of sweat covers her forearms. Silence again, and I watch, shocked, as a bead of sweat drips down her arms and onto the handle. Her muscles bunch and move, but she's not gained even a millimeter. And Kit looks for all the world like he's simply standing there.

Finally, she shoves backward and huffs, catching her breath. He sheathes his swords and crosses his arms behind his back, like he's holding his hands. My jaw nearly drops at the knives in them that he's motioning to me.

What the fuck is going on? I don't move because I'll draw

296

the Mother's attention to myself. I watch the motion become more agitated. I snort lightly, knowing he can hear me. Does he think I can't fucking see them? I can't just grab them though. He stills in acknowledgement. I'm not sure this isn't a trap of some kind. My mind races, attempting to come up with any scenario other than the one where he's helping me.

"If you don't move, I'll take it as a direct challenge. Just because you've beaten me a few times doesn't mean you'll win every time."

He shrugs. "It's your death." It's the same irritating tone he used with me, and I'm not sure if I want to laugh or scream.

"Boy, don't make me take your soul."

Uh, what? She's done lost it. She really has gone insane. All of us are soulless.

"You can try," comes the deadpan response.

I can't stand not knowing what the fuck is going on anymore, and I shift to one side. My jaw drops open. Have I somehow been transported into a hallucination? I snap my mouth shut and shift back, focusing on the metal in Kit's hand. I know why he's giving me the blades.

I reach around and gently disengage the strand of hair from around my neck, removing the tear, and I roll it as gently as I can behind me, hopefully hard enough that it won't get stepped on and broken. I know the casing will protect it, but without it, I have no idea—and I don't want the Weaponry to slurp it up. Blaze said I could take it off when I wasn't angry. He trusted me with a piece of his soul that I could simply take off at any time. He was true to his word. Thank the Fates. I needed to be able to remove it in order to do my job.

Because shuddering and shifting out of the Mother's body is an extremely large Terror forming from her. The thud of a body hitting the ground startles my brain into overdrive. Is she dead? Was it possessing her? Is she alive?

If she isn't quite as crazy as I thought, and Kit really has a soul, there's no one left to take the Nightmare's soul but me. And I'm not sure what I'm up against anymore.

Kit's calf muscle flexes, and I shoot up, grabbing the knives out of his hand, forcing my useless one to grip it tightly.

He pivots, his own blades back out and screaming through the air. He clashes with the Terror's own shadowy blades. The thing is smart enough to keep its weapons solid and its body mass a shapeless mass indestructible by any means. And it can fucking move. The two of them pirouette in some kind of macabre dance, and it hits me that Kit's attempting to draw the Terror away from me so that I can slip into it.

I'm momentarily paralyzed. That thing has been inside the Mother for who knows how long. That last time I entered a Nightmare, I had been nearly consumed by its thoughts and feelings. How will I be able to deal with the inevitable bombardment? And she knew things about me, my past. Would I make it out alive? Would I be able to lock down on its soul? Kit growls as the Terror connects with his skin, and I stiffen. My fists clench around the blades, and I stalk as quietly as possible forward. The fuck if I can't.

I'm fucking Arnica, dammit.

I blur into the Nightmare and nearly gasp at the assault. Memories of me, seen through the Mother's eyes, pour into me. Like a rewound movie, I can't do anything but watch myself slam a sword into Angelica. Tears run down my eyes when I observe my body brace itself and shove the blades in harder. I hadn't been able to see through the Nightmare nor was I able to kill it when it wasn't solid. The scream rips out of my throat at the sight of my sister taking her last breath.

Memories of my torture parade through my mind, and my knees buckle, hitting the ground. I'm barely hanging on inside the Nightmare. And then the movie stops. It's dark and I can't see anything. It's not so bad here. Not being able to see isn't the worst thing. Without sight and sound and smell, there's no pain. No dark to fight or gold to protect. There's a shimmer in my peripheral. I turn my head but there's nothing there. Again, it's just out of sight, but gold nonetheless. Had Blaze come?

Blaze!

He'd seen me for who I was. I stand slowly. For who I am. He believed in me enough to give me a piece of his soul before he was bound to me. I straighten and push through the Terror until I'm in the middle and I open my internal cage. The soul swirls in and the cage clangs shut and I blur out, landing on a pool of my blood soaking into the cavern floor. I slide on my knees, bits of rock digging in and cutting more of my skin open, and I thrust my blades up and into the Terror rising over me.

It disappears, and I drop the knives, my arms full of the ick of Nightmare, and collapse onto my ass, my legs at an odd angle.

Kit nods once and leaves, leaving the cell door wide open. But I can't seem to stand anymore. My eyes can't stay open anymore, my head lolls back and I barely feel it hit the ground.

Chapter Forty-Five

Lemon wafts into my nose. Cedarwood. Eucalyptus. Heat builds in my chest. I try to force my eyes open, but they're swollen shut. I groan and make my body obey. When I win, there's only a sliver of a room. I know Blaze is here, I can smell him. I turn my head, searching for the only sight I want to see.

He's next to me, a hand on my bicep. The gentle slide of his golden aura shimmers over me, and I panic. He can't be here showing off his gold. They'll take it. His hand settles on my shoulder. "Sh. Arnica, sh. You're safe. I've got you, you're safe."

The dark pulls me under, but I need to tell him one thing. I whisper, "I've bonded with you."

I'm not sure if he really replies with, "I know," before I close my eyes.

When my eyes open a second time, they open all the way. I'm back in my room at the magic cabin. I turn my head, expecting pain, and aching at the very least, but there is none. Blaze, snores softly next to me, dark circles under his eyes. A bottle of water pops up next to me on the side table and I shift carefully. I guzzle the entire thing and devour the high-protein bar that appears next. The wrapper disappears and an electrolyte drink plops into my hand and I down that, too.

"Thanks," I whisper and pad softly to the bathroom. I stare at the reflection in the mirror. There isn't a single sign that my body had been through anything. Either I'd dreamed it all or Blaze is capable of some extremely potent healing magic.

My hand reaches up to where the tear had always lain. It hadn't been a dream after all.

"You okay?" Blaze walks up next to me but doesn't touch me. I remember telling him I was bound to him, and I look down at my ring finger. The tattoo is stunning, a delicate scrollwork of black and gold intertwined.

We never got a chance to talk about the book, about us. Does he still want to be with me? Can he leave now that I'm bound to him? I have no idea how any of this works.

I nod then turn to face him fully. I'm not one to back down from anything, even if it means getting my ass kicked. Or in this case, my heart.

"Give it to me straight. Are you okay being bonded to me? Did you want me to release you or however this works? I can divorce you, right?"

His eyes flame up and then smolder down before they disappear completely. His aura recedes into his skin and the room seems to dim like a stormy day. It's like that day he gave me his tear. Is he sad now?

The room brightens and his gold shimmers again, but much closer to his body. "Did you want a divorce?"

"Fuck no. I bonded to you, in case you didn't hear me." I step forward and hit him on the chest, and he backs up a step.

"That means I trust you." I step forward and hit him again. He backs up. "And you're stuck with me." I step and hit. He moves. "Unless you don't want me." I step and hit, and he steps back. "Actually, fuck that. I want you. I love you, and you're going to have to learn to like it." I fist my hands on my hips. "Don't you have anything to say?"

"Are you done hitting me?"

I growl and spin around, only to be spun back around by my elbow as he pulls me into his arms.

"You never let me finish." He kisses my forehead. "Yes, I'm more than okay being bonded to you." He kisses my nose. "No, I don't want you to release me." He kisses my left cheek. "No, you can't divorce me." He kisses my right cheek. "And yes, I want you. Always." He kisses my mouth, and the shimmer rolls onto my face and swirls round and round.

Our tongues touch gently, exploring each other's mouth as if we've never felt it before. And maybe we haven't—not from this side of love. The kind that's committed and spoken. Affirmed. Wait. I pull back, my eyes narrowed.

"I told you I loved you and you didn't say it back." I lift up my fist and he grabs it, kissing my fingers.

"I still wasn't done. I love you. I think I loved you the day you exploded in my room, staring down the barrel of a gun. You should've been intimidated. You should've been scared." I snort, but he keeps talking. "Instead, you harassed me and made fun of me. I knew then that here was a woman I could admire, that would do whatever she needed to do and fuck the world."

"You said, fuck."

"Mm, hm."

"But I don't have your piece of your soul. Does that mean I lost it in the Weaponry? I'm sorry."

"No, it's right here." He moves toward the nightstand and opens the drawer, taking out the strand. "When I saw you had removed it, I thought maybe you didn't want it anymore. I hadn't seen your tattoo at that point."

I snatch it from his hand and spin around. "Please put it back on."

I sigh when he does so, the familiar warmth against my chest soothing me in ways I would never have predicted wanting. I lean back, and he's there, his chest against me, and he wraps his arms around me. My head falls back into the crook of his shoulder, and I close my eyes, breathing in his scent. "I love you."

"I love you, too."

My heart gallops in my chest at the words. I'll never stop wanting to hear it. And I'll never stop wanting to be held by him.

"I want to stay here, in bed and in this room, with you for a very long time, but I'm sure the house has notified Dex that you're awake. We've all been waiting for you to wake up to tell us what happened."

"Fine. I don't want to leave here either, and really, I kinda would like to fuck your brains out right about now, but I get it. Nosy fuckers."

That sexy rumble of laughter vibrates through my back, and I wonder what they'd do if we stayed up here? If they could hear us having sex, they wouldn't come in. Maybe. Fuck.

I turn in his arms, kissing his mouth for several seconds. Blaze pulls away, leans his forehead against mine, and brings my hands up to his chest. "I can't tell you how frantic I was when you left. I thought you left because of me. Because of the book. And for a while, I couldn't locate you."

He tightens his fingers into mine. "And when I realized you were at the Weaponry and when I started imagining what they could be doing to you...I may have gone a little berserk."

The butterflies in my stomach wing about and my heart

gallops. I don't know why the thought of violence from Blaze gets me going, but man he revs my engine when he does so.

"What did you do?"

"I may have gotten into a fist fight with Drew and Dex because they wouldn't let me leave without prepping properly." He sighs, sounding exasperated, and I pull away from him.

"You took both of them on? What is wrong with you?"

"Nothing a few healing touches didn't fix." He smiles slightly, and my heart pulls back into larger pieces.

"I should kick your ass for that, but they ought to know better than to engage. I'll kill them."

He kisses my fingers. "No, you won't, they were right. Let's go so you can fill us in."

Chapter Forty-Seven

W alking down the stairs, Blaze laces his fingers with mine, and fuck if my heart doesn't skip a beat.

Delaney, Drew, Dex, and Cassie are sitting around a new room that's been added onto the cabin. If it isn't an exact replica of one of the conference rooms from Ferraro's Club, it's pretty damn close. Except this one has wooden walls and green plants hanging around from wall sconces and in the corners of the room from the ceiling. There's even ferns hanging down the length of the table the way hanging lights would be positioned. But the furniture is the same, and it's jarring with its sleek, sophisticated, modern edge pieces set inside the coziness of the house.

But I guess no one wants to be cozy when conducting meetings.

Someone else sits at the table, farther than most. Only Dex sits near the dangerously rugged blond man. The tinge of gold in his pale skin isn't an aura, it's a part of him, and I wonder why everyone accepts it without questioning why the head investigator of the Guardianship doesn't look like other Guardians. Especially since he hunts Magicals and Dreamers.

Tension radiates from Blaze, and I squeeze his hand to let him know nothing will happen to him, and he squeezes back.

Dex stands. "This is Bishop Savage. Bishop, Blaze and Arnica."

I nod in response to Bishop's nod, and Blaze doesn't acknowledge him at all. Instead, he says, "Why the fuck are you allowing this asshole in here? Have you lost your mind?"

Bishop's thick blond eyebrows rise. "Well, well. If it isn't the Healer son."

Blaze's eyes flame bright, and he pivots on his heel. "I'm leaving. You can tell me what happened, later."

"Oh, grow a fucking brain...and maybe some balls," Bishop retorts.

I've never seen anyone actually look like their blood was boiling, but if I need to, I know all I need to do is make Blaze furious. Maybe it's his skin that allows those blushes to show, but his beet-red face looks like he'll explode.

"Hold up. You are *not* going to talk about him that way." I point my finger at Bishop, in case he doesn't know who I'm talking to. "You guys want to fix this, get on a mat. Otherwise, be fucking grownups and act civil." I move my finger toward Dex. "And you, you shouldn't allow this in your meeting room." My hand waves around. "You like to portray elegance and refinement, then fucking refine the environment." He throws his hands up, like what can I do, and I grit my teeth in frustration. It's like a bunch of fucking kids.

I turn to Blaze. "What's the problem?"

"He killed my mother."

There's a stunned moment of silence, and I turn around slowly. "I'll kill you for making his heart ache with loss."

To his credit, Bishop doesn't flinch, but he does incline his head. "And I'd allow it if it were true."

I throw my hands up, too. No wonder Dex doesn't want to get involved. I want to sigh, loudly, but I don't because I'm sure this is part of being in a relationship, and if I had any clue of what I'm supposed to do, I'd gladly follow it right now.

"Clearly, there seems to be some kind of misunderstanding. Bishop, do you swear on your soulmate you didn't kill his mother?"

"I don't have a soulmate. My soul will have to do. I did NOT kill his mother."

"But you probably will. You're a damn Guardian. And your soul is looking kinda tarnished. But I'll take your word."

I turn to Blaze. "If he swears he didn't do it, and he's here —in a magic cabin—surrounded by other branches of the Infinites, I think we may be all right believing him."

I'll leave it up to him and support him with whatever he decides. He doesn't know, and I can't tell him right now, that Bishop was the one who called and warned me about the army coming for me. And I know I'm not the first one he's done that for. I don't know what his deal is or what fucking games Bishop's playing, but I can't alter what I know.

"Fine. I'll be civil."

I turn to Bishop and stare him down until he agrees.

"Seriously? Fine. I'll be on my best behavior, Mom."

I give him my cherished middle finger and pull Blaze over to sit as far away as possible.

I quickly tell the group what happened at the Weaponry, including Kit helping me, which everyone seems in disbelief about. "I know. Me too. He's got some kind of agenda, and I have no idea what it could be. I'm guessing he stepped into the Mother's shoes and will be running the place now. We'll have to do something about that."

A shiver rolls up my spine knowing his cruelty seems to have no boundaries. That type of leader running an army designed to kill is asking for more problems than I even know how to deal with—besides killing him—and I'm not sure that will be an option.

"I'll look into it. See what I can dig up."

And this is what I was hoping for. No matter what may have happened with him and Blaze's mother, there's no one better at ferreting out information than Bishop. He's not head of Investigations for nothing.

"Thank you." It's not often I say those words and he'll know that it's double edged. He dips his head slightly.

"And now, duty calls."

Blaze grumbles but doesn't say anything as Bishop leaves.

"So, tell me what happened after I was taken." I've been dying to know how Blaze located me.

Drew clears his throat. "The cabin sounded the alarm."

Blaze picks up where he stops, his voice softer than usual, and I know he's fighting his emotions. "But there was some kind of magic being used and we were unprepared. There was no way to get around it."

"Delaney tried a vision, but nothing was coming to her," Drew says.

"You hadn't made any decisions, and there were too many possibilities. I am sorry for what you endured," she says.

I try not to shrug, as is my usual habit. I want to start working on those aspects of myself. I don't deserve all the bad things. I may live through them, I may survive, but I don't want them anymore. And they aren't okay. The visions that the Mother's Nightmare showed me brought me to tears with years of anguish and pain rolled up in it.

But it also did something for me that nothing else would have done. It showed me that what happened had been an accident. A very bad one with repercussions that reverberated through the years, but an accident, nonetheless. I didn't have to be punished for it. It wasn't my fault.

"I know. And I appreciate it."

I also kinda signed up for it, knowing what would happen. Knowing it *needed* to. There will always be things I have to do, that I have to endure for the sake of humanity. That's my job, my life...as soon as I figure out a way to do that again. Having Blaze next to me will make those things so much easier.

Blaze reaches over and grabs my hand. "I was frantic because I couldn't find you. The only reason I did so was because there was a potion in the book. And the cabin has a plethora of plants growing here that I needed for it. I was able to locate you, kinda beam myself there, gather you up, and beam us back."

What now we're part of an outer space team? But I'm grateful for it. Maybe that's why he's tired. All these potions, plus healing me, must have taken a toll on his body.

Drew and Dex simultaneously growl, and Dex reaches across the table, pointing his finger at my face. "You lied to me and brought one of the most powerful books into this house knowing they'd be coming after it. Couldn't you fucking warn me at least?"

"First, the growling is ...not as fucking macho as you think it is," I snap. He's right though, I should've told him. I sigh. "Second, I'm not good at leaning on people. And that includes trust. I'm working on that."

Delaney leans forward, propping her elbows on the table and her face on her hands. "Trust is a high commodity. Something all of us here have learned to deal with and embrace. We're going to need it more than ever. Bishop will do what he does best: gathering information and passing it on to us. We'll have to teach others they have to trust us and not whoever is behind the Guardianship division. It's going to be a long road, but there's a feeling of urgency in me. I've had no visions; I've had no signs. But even Drew is on edge, his Protector instincts waving big red flags. Because I'm so closely involved, I may never see anything."

Cassie speaks up for the first time. "Whatever comes, we'll handle it. I've never been around so much competency—"

"You mean testosterone," I interject, which has Dex and Drew glowering.

Cassie smiles but doesn't acknowledge my sarcasm. "And all of us will find them and make them pay. Because we're really fucking good at doling out justice. Each of us has our own brand of right and wrong, our own code of honor. And that's why we'll fucking win."

I clap because it seems appropriate, and everyone else joins in. "Fuck yeah, we will!"

A fireplace pops in at the end of the room and a fire roars loudly before simmering down. I grin widely, joy filling me. These people have never been my family and some of them might not ever be. But maybe we can be friends, something I've never wanted before and find I desperately do now. I kinda like them in an odd way. They irritate the fuck out of me on various levels, but who wants nice, normal people in their lives? How boring would that be?

We all get up and leave the room, Dex and Cassie making their way upstairs—fuck, they're gonna fuck again? Damn.—and Drew and Delaney to one of the, weirdly, many workout rooms. I head to the kitchen because I'm fucking starving again.

After downing several rashers of bacon and half a dozen eggs filled with all sorts of chopped vegetables, I take a newly filled coffee cup and toast the cabin. "Thank you for everything." The fire in the living room roars to life and dies off.

"The house has an obsession with fire, have you noticed that?"

Blaze smirks. "Maybe it's got the hots for you."

"For fuck's sake. No. That's the worst cheesy line you could've come up with."

"It's got a thing for pain, maybe."

And that rings true for me. Fuck, but that sucks. The house is incredibly beautiful and unique, even without its magical properties. All the light and air, the greenery and nature. Trying to reach for its own joy? I let my hand drag along the counter, and I pat it in not so much a caress but a here-for-you gesture. I don't get a response, but I'm not expecting one.

Chapter Forty-Eight

I shut the door to my bedroom, leaning against it and observing Blaze. He's taking his shirt off and removing his shoes and socks, his watch.

"Are you going to watch me the whole time I'm undressing and showering?" That cute-ass blush hits his cheeks, and I smile widely. I'm going to enjoy making that color rise for many, many years.

"Maybe I will. Maybe I'll join you and make sure you're all clean." I wink and the blush deepens. Fuck, but I love this man.

"You can join me. I'll wash your back."

Oh, will he? I saunter over and hook a finger in his pants, pulling him to me. He's pulsating against me, already hard. And isn't that just what I wanted?

His gold oozes over my wrist and the heat of it warms me like nothing else. I'm not sure how I can continue to be a Nightmare Killer with it, but I refuse to give his soul up.

I move backward, pulling him into the bathroom. The chaise has disappeared since I was last in the shower, which is kind of a bummer. I was looking forward to seeing how springy it could be.

He watches me, his eyes flaming white as I slowly slip my clothes off. I channel my inner molasses because his dick twitching in the air like it can't wait for me is a sight for sore eyes. Those eyes, those abs, those muscles veeing into the ultimate reward for my desire. Fuck. I raise my hands to my breasts, but don't do much else, like I'm offering them on a platter for him.

"What do you want?" he asks, each word dropping in timbre.

"I want you to make me ache more than I ever have."

"You want pain?" He growls low, and fuuuuck. I was wrong. A growl does sound macho. And sexy and...Fuck me, but I'm already wet.

"Yes, but only if it involves you fucking me so hard I can't help but beg you to make me cum."

He moves forward and pulls my hand away from my breast, tugging me into the shower. He lathers the bar of soap and swirls it around my nipples.

"Are you aching here?"

They stand so hard at attention that they can't get any more taut. "Yes, they fucking ache."

He swirls it again, grazing each nipple with the soap and then his thumb. The slower he goes, the more an ache builds between my legs.

He moves the soap over my shoulders and down my arms, up them and down the sides of my torso. The ache grows.

He moves down my leg, and I inhale hard as he makes his way up my inner thigh. He pauses at the apex, moving his sudsy fingers over every inch of me. I swallow hard, panting soft breaths. How the fuck am I ever supposed to wash myself again and not think of this moment?

He continues down to the other leg, and I attempt to fix

my breathing pattern. "You can rinse. It's my turn now."

Oh yeah. My turn to make him squirm. I shove my hand out, palm up, for the bar.

"Oh no, I'm doing the washing. You...just stand there."

He...no. He's going to fucking touch himself and have me watch? The ache between my legs, in my breasts, even in my chest expands. What breathing pattern? I don't need air.

And he slowly washes his entire body, bar swirling around his nipples, and I nearly swallow my tongue as I watch him stroke his hands across the length of himself, down to his balls and back, so slowly I think I might scream. His head, thrown back, reveals his muscular neck and shoulders, and I want to take a nip there right in the hollow. And there's that fucking growl again, rumbling up his throat.

I can't take it anymore. I step forward, my hand encircling his shaft, nudging him away, rinsing off the soap.

"If you don't fuck me right now, take me hard and fast, I'm going to explode."

He shakes his head, droplets flying everywhere. "What if I don't follow your instructions?"

A feral smile is all I can manage. "You can go fuck off, while I fuck myself. Or you can watch." I purposely shrug and step back, moving one hand over my stomach and lower, one finger poised above my clit and one hand gently rubbing over my nipple. I step back again, toward the corner of the shower where there's a built-in bench, and I prop my leg on it. My finger dips down and slides right into my pussy as a moan erupts from my mouth.

I know he hates it when I touch myself; he'd rather it was all for him.

He doesn't bother saying anything, but the flames in his eyes flash and he stalks toward me, yanking my hand up.

"Mine." His tongue strokes my finger, and I shudder, legs already quivering.

He spins me around and pushes lightly on my back, and I bend over, my hands slapping the bench and I spread my legs wide.

He grasps my hips and thrusts deep, a growl coming from my own throat. Fuck, but he feels good.

His hips slam against my ass cheeks over and over and he reaches around, rubbing his finger over my clit, building the ache higher and higher. Each drive into my pussy forces another moan from my mouth. I want tell him I love him, but I can't catch my breath.

His golden shimmer caresses me every time he's near, like silk stroking me.

The orgasm hits hard, and I shudder through it, a never-ending sensation that keeps climbing. He slams into me three, four times more, and I cum again, this time both of us together.

He pulls me up and spins me around. "I fucking love you."

"I fucking love you too." I smile against his chest. The rest of my life, right here, is exactly what I want.

We dry off and get dressed, my lips still curved up in a smile.

"You don't look so badass when you smile so much."

I flip him the finger. "I won't kick your ass, only because I love you."

My skin prickles and I dive for the knife laying on my nightstand and throw it before I even see what's there. It flies through the Nightmare and embeds in the wall, quivering. I'm already in front of Blaze, my hand out—keeping him behind me. Fuck, but I miss my butterflies.

I grit my teeth as the Nightmare drops down like it's a human on feet and solidifies, turning a pale skin color. The body shudders and shapes until it's formed.

Kit.

Chapter Forty-Nine

"**S**orry to interrupt. We need to talk."

"Excuse me? If you want to keep breathing, you'll get the fuck out."

My fists clench because the only weapon I had is in the wall behind him. He may have saved me, but he's the new Mother of the Weaponry, and by default, kindness isn't in him.

"We can stay here all day, me telling you, 'you don't stand a chance without a weapon,' and you telling me you are a weapon and blah, blah, blah. Or we can just fucking talk for a minute." He puts his hands up in the air and twirls around. "Look, no weapons. A sliver of trust."

I frown. Fuck if we didn't just have a conversation about trust. Was he listening the whole time? Dex better make sure his magical house is a little bit more protected.

"Fine. Talk."

"I saved you."

"You kidnapped me."

"You were supposed to get away."

I throw my hands onto my hips. "And how the fuck was I

supposed to do that?" I might be fucking a Magical, but I'm not one.

"You're supposed to be 'fucking Arnica.' I thought you'd figure it out." He shrugs, and I want to strangle him. Obviously, our talk isn't going to be without insults.

"What. Do. You. Want?"

"I want to give you a piece of my soul."

I choke on my own spit, and Blaze helpfully pounds me on the back. "Run that by me again?"

"Actually, it's a piece of our soul, if you want to get technical."

He's going to piss me off. "Talk faster, what the fuck are you spewing out of your mouth?"

"You and I. Remember? Your sister's death? The Weaponry warrior that was there trying to protect her?"

Stunned, I look over his face. Maybe? I don't know that I actually really got a good look at him that night.

"You're still alive? Wait. How? What?"

"The great Arnica is speechless."

I flick him the middle finger as my brain tries to make sense of what he's telling me, but I'm not sure I can. I'm missing too many pieces. He continues.

"The Nightmare took over my body."

I jerk at his words. We've always been put down when that happens.

He nods, guessing what I'm thinking. "I started to take your sister's soul..." He rolls his eyes. "Again, I guess... technically. But it was your soul. And she must've died before she actually got your whole soul. And the Nightmare...er, me... trying to take your gold—"

My heart stutters in my chest. My gold? "I had a golden shimmer?"

"Yeah, anyway—"

I thrust my hand up and cut him off. "Hold up, she was already dead?"

"Pay the fuck attention. Yes, she was already dead. So, your gold soul was just hanging out in the wind for anyone to take."

I sit down on the bed, my knees suddenly weak, and try hard to focus on what he's saying.

"And my soul...me, the Nightmare, is trying to take your soul instead, because you know the gold is more powerful." What? I shake my head. "And well, then the Mother tried to cut me down. Or my soul. I don't really fucking know what she was trying to do."

I remember the gold and dark swirling around me. Of course, I had no idea what I was seeing. The sword jutting out of his chest. He died. I narrow my eyes.

"You're fucking with me. You had a sword through you. I watched you die."

He tilts his head, those dark eyes, so dark they're almost eerie...as if any of that bothers me.

"Did you really? 'Cause all I remember is you fucking screaming all over your dead sister and the Mother trying to convert you to the team, since she lost a body."

Every time he casually dismisses Angelica's death, it's like a knife twists inside me. I'm simultaneously flooded with relief that I hadn't killed her, not even by accident, anger that for years I punished myself with guilt, and sick at the simplicity in which he talks about her dying.

I put my head in my hands and Blaze rubs my back. He doesn't say anything, because like me he's probably in shock about what the fuck is going on.

"So, you didn't die. And you're a Nightmare? That can change into human." The tale is bizarre. He yanks up his shirt, body still youthful, still muscled like a man. A scar runs from about two inches from the center of his body.

"It's dead on. How did you survive that?"

"I think it's because the Nightmare had taken over me already and I wasn't completely solid anymore. I can shift in and out of both forms easily." And he does so, popping back and forth between Nightmare and Dreamer.

"What about your soul though?"

"Remember when I said my...Nightmare...soul was out of my body trying to take yours on? Well, when she cleaved her sword through, it did...chop up the soul. Except there was still some of both in me and some of both in you."

I stand upright so quickly I nearly trip over Blaze's outstretched foot. "I have pieces of mine and your soul in me?"

"That's what I said. The thing is, they mostly cancel each other out. You *seem* as if you have no soul. The darkness covering the light. Especially, we as Nightmare Killers, take dark souls in and they're kinda always masking the light.

"That piece of soul there around your neck is changing the balance. You can't hear screams anymore, you can't be a Nightmare Killer if you're not soulless...for all intent and purposes." He waves his hand around, in case I can't follow along.

"I'm...taking too many souls in and the Nightmare is getting stronger. Obviously, I don't want that to happen. Which leads me to why I'm here. I want to give you a piece of my soul. You need it to even you out, and I need to get rid of some."

I stare at him dumbfounded. He's got to be kidding me. I look at Blaze, only to see the same reaction on his face. He's going to be no help.

"I'm not..."

"It's not weird. It's really like we're sisters."

"We are not fucking sisters." He's insane. His Nightmare self and Dreamer self probably can't coexist and he's insane. That's got to be it.

"Technically, the Nightmare took your sister's soul. You

gave her some of your soul and I have both. We're either soul sisters...or the same soul-person, which is probably closer to soulmates. Take your pick."

"I. No." I sit down hard on the bed. I don't...I can't... contemplate any of what he's saying.

Blaze finally clears his throat. "If Nightmare Killing is important to you, it sounds like this might be your solution. Unless you want to give me my piece back."

My hand reaches up to the tear and I grip it within my palm. "No, I don't want to give it back. And I do want to still have my job."

"I'm not taking your piece in me, and it has to stay on a strand like this," I say to Kit.

"That's fine." He turns into a Nightmare and plunges an arm into himself, and twisting a few times like he's ripping a grape off a vine, he pulls his hand back out, rolling his fingers like Blaze had done.

"You probably ought to contain it though," he says to Blaze, who stands up and mouths a few words, then blows on it. The shimmery coating looks like the one his own soul has. I remove the strand and hand it to Blaze, who reconfigures the way it looks. Now it's like a cowboy string tie with what looks like a shiny white pearl on one end and a shiny black pearl on the other. He places it around the back of my neck and fashions a knot in the front, so that one hangs lower than the other.

He taps his, which is longer. "So it's closer to your heart."

Can I love this man any more? He leans down and kisses me, and Kit clears his throat.

"I'm going to go now."

"Wait, just like that? Aren't you going to tell me anything? What are your plans?"

Is he going to continue the work the Mother did? Was he going to be cruel? Did the soul leaving him make him nicer?

"Why would I tell you? So you can tell me how superior you think you are to me? No thanks."

That answers that question, I guess. "Thank you... for helping me at the Weaponry."

He nods, for once not saying anything and, turning into a Nightmare, slips through the walls.

"Remind me to tell Dex to protect his house better."

"I thought the same thing."

My fingers touch each ball gently. I don't feel any different. The darker one seems colder than even me, and that kinda makes sense.

"I was going to give these to you as a wedding present, but it looks like you're going to need it if you're going back to work." He walks over to the closet and comes back out with a beautifully wrapped golden box.

"What is it?"

"Open it."

I undo the wrapping, ripping into it, and his rumble of laughter fills me with happiness. "I like to do it fast."

"I know." I jerk my head up in time to see the slight blush. Before I can make a sexual comment back, I peel back the tissue paper and gasp.

"You like them?"

"I fucking love them! They're beautiful."

I take the set of butterfly blades out of the box and test them in my hands. Perfectly weighted. The handle has a stunning and intricate design in black and gold and I glance down at my ring finger. The pattern matches.

"Thank you."

I ask the cabin for a back holster and put it on, sliding them in. Framing my hands around his face, I whisper, "I love you, golden boy."

"I love you too, fucking Arnica."

I inhale his scent and push him onto the bed, prepared to

show him how much fucking I can actually do, when my body stiffens. The scream rips through my head, and I grin. Bending down, I place a quick kiss on his lips. "I'll take a rain check. Work's calling."

And I blur out of the cabin on my way to kill some fucking Nightmare whose misfortune it is to fight me tonight.

The End

Coming Soon

Continue with Raine's story in
Tempting Curses
The fourth installment in the Infinites Universe.

SPRING 2024

Watch for updates on my website
www.LivMacy.com
or sign up for my newsletter.

∼

Read Cassie's story in **Becoming Justice**
Check out Delaney's story in **Resetting Destiny**

Acknowledgments

To my Readers and Infinites Universe fans: I don't even know where to start. This year has brought so many of you to my tables at book signings, to my social medias, to my website. You floor me with your love of my books, generosity in giving reviews, and your willingness to post and spread the word about my stories. I've taken pictures with you, signed copies of my books, and chatted with you like old friends at events. I'll never, ever forget the way you make me feel, the knowledge that I am where I am because you believe in me and because you adore my characters. I'm grateful for every one of you. Thank you for bringing my stories into your lives and onto your bookshelves—real or virtual.

To my Fabulous Dev Editor: You're so much more than an editor. You're my support, my encouragement, my pick-me-up-per. You're the voice of reason in an endless pool of sound, and I literally would not be here, in the publishing and business-of-writing place I am today, without you. I can't thank you enough times for this. Like, ever.

To my Amazing Husband: Soulmates exist because we cannot live without the other, because we need what the other has. This is us. I need you and love you always. Thank you for loving me, for supporting me, for helping me. Thank you for all your hard work, for making me laugh. I love you.

To my Wonderful Kids: You're my world. Thank you for everything you do to help me, from stuffing bags for events to helping me pack, to reaffirming that readers and fans love my books:) I love you more than you can even imagine. Infinity-Infinities!

To my #PitSquirrels: You're always going to be here, in this space. What would I do without you? (What would you do without me? LOL.) Saying thanks will never be enough for all the support, help, laughs. Every day, every book we're going to crush it. Because we're squirrels! (I was gonna add *fuckin'* in that sentence...but you know, it didn't read right. LOL)

To my Copy Editor: As usual, I CANNOT seem to stick to a nice, normal deadline! Thank you for your amazing ability to hit that GPS goal, for your willingness to bend time to complete my copy edits. You're a badass and I'm truly fortunate to have you by my side.

To my Work Soulmate: Damn, I don't even know what the fuck to say here. Like, legit you're the bee's knees. Without you, I'd still be figuring out my website, I'd have a nonexistent newsletter and probably *never* have trailers for my books. (Not to mention the fifty million other things you do.) Thank you for your investment in me and my words—for your enthusiasm and hard work every week, every day, every hour. I'll never forget this either. You're so fucking kickass and don't even know it—it's ok, I'll tell you all the time!

To my Friends and Family: Thanks for always checking in on me. (Wondering when the next book will be out because you can't wait! LOL) Thanks for the words of encouragement, the texts and calls full of great comments when you're reading my work. Love you all!

To Everyone Part of Team Liv: Ferraro's Favorites in particular, but *everyone* on my team—my cover designer and liaison, my beta readers, my ARC readers, my PR Manager. You are all incredibly appreciated and loved. More than you know. I can't imagine you not working with me, and I never want to!

And last but not least, to ME: Taking a page from the

super talented Snoop...I want to thank me. For all my hours, my dedication to the characters in the Infinites Universe. For the tears I've shed of frustration and fear. For the joy and laughter I've felt at each win. For the long days, the short sprints. For the words running through my head. For every bit of grit and determination and sheer stubbornness and willpower to meet deadlines and makes storylines work. Thank you, me, for never giving up on my dream.

About the Author

Liv Macy is an author in the adult paranormal romance genre. Becoming Justice is the first novel in the Infinites Universe.

A mother, chef, taxi driver, maid, referee, teacher, shopper, wife, and advice-giver by trade, Liv spends her free moments dreaming of characters that refuse to keep their story to themselves.

With a lifetime passion for reading and writing that infused every spare moment, it was only natural that Liv took her love of words to the next level. When there are leftover moments, she loves to cook and hang out with her family and friends—and if there's time remaining after THAT...well, Liv likes to sit in a cozy chair with a blanket and a cup of coffee and contemplate life.

Learn more about Liv Macy by visiting her website and sign up for her newsletter.

www.LivMacy.com

facebook.com/LivMacyAuthor
instagram.com/livmacyauthor
tiktok.com/@livmacyauthor
bookbub.com/authors/liv-macy
x.com/LivMacyAuthor

Made in the USA
Middletown, DE
29 October 2023